EVERYTHING YOU'VE EVER KNOWN

A STORY ABOUT FRIENDSHIPS, EMPTY NESTS, AND DISCOVERING WHO YOU ARE IN YOUR SECOND ACT

CLEARWATER DREAMS
BOOK 1

JESS AMES

CONTENTS

Book cover and illustrations by Ashley Santoro

* PLAYLIST AVAILABLE *
To access the Everything You've Ever Known playlist, scan the image below
with your phone's camera app, click the link, and select "Playlist: Everything
You've Ever Known".

Sign up for Jess Ames' newsletter and get updates when new books and
exclusive bonus chapters are released at JessicaAmes.com!

To the strong women who've shaped me, the strong women I'm raising, and the pathologically supportive men who keep showing up to cheer me on.

You're my everything.

1

"TO BUILD A HOME"

THE CINEMATIC ORCHESTRA

The blink of my cursor mocked me, the pages of my 'Great American Novel' as empty as my house since everyone but me grew up and left. I stared out the window of my second floor home office, admiring the vibrant green of the summer foliage and all the *life* that was happening on the other side of the glass. Some neighborhood kids were riding bikes in a figure eight around two bright orange buckets in the cul de sac. The muted sound of their laughter that had at first distracted me took me straight back to Saturdays past when I'd put away my little boy's laundry in that very same room.

Back then, I'd been in a hurry to finish so the four of us could all go outside, but there was nothing and no one to hurry for anymore. I looked up to the ceiling, the edges blurring on my imagined future—a gray, slushy expanse of another winter in Madison. Alone.

Well, not *alone* alone, but no one but the dog to keep me from fully disappearing within the four walls.

My eyes slid to the puddle of fur at my feet. I wondered how long I'd been sitting there and whether Roxy needed to go outside. As if hearing her name in my thoughts, Roxy turned her head, her floppy strawberry-blonde ears sliding across the wood floor, and looked up at me expectantly from where she lay sprawled on her back under my desk. I sighed, placed my hands across the top of the screen, and slowly closed my laptop. No writing would get done.

Again.

I stood up and stretched, prompting Roxy to scramble to her feet.

"I spent a lot of time accomplishing exactly nothing today, Rox," I said as I bent forward to scratch behind her velvety ears. I didn't really expect a response, and I wasn't disappointed by her silence, but I knew it was time I spoke to someone with better communication skills. With that thought, I grabbed my phone off the top of the drafting table that had at one point been my son's desk, checked the time, and slipped it into my back pocket. Kari would be calling soon.

When my oldest, Jason, had left nearly six years before with his visions of the skyscrapers he'd yet to build poured deftly around the jars of peanut butter and packs of Ramen he was taking to college, I'd pictured him returning to his room four years later. I'd assumed I would help him draft his first resume, practice his first interview, and pack his lunch for his first day of work as I had done every day through twelve years of school. Life had other plans, because during his senior year of college, Jason earned an internship with the largest architecture firm in Boston. They ended up hiring him directly after graduation, and the abandoned drafting table became mine. If I hadn't been so damn proud of him, I might have called the table my consolation prize.

Possession being nine-tenths of the law and all, I took it over when it became obvious he wouldn't need it. And the room—in which I had at one point endlessly rocked and nursed a colicky baby boy—became my 'den of creativity.'

Around that time, my daughter, Anna, left for college and my husband had already put us in the rearview, so it seemed as if it were my time to shine—on my own. I had big dreams of turning the experience I'd gained working from home as a marketing content specialist into a career as a novelist, so I moved my laptop into my 'new' office and assumed it would be a simple transition from copywriter to published author. Over the next two slow, increasingly painful years, that had proven not to be the case. I had excelled in my role in writing marketing copy... and had failed spectacularly at writing anything else.

A quick trip down the stairs with Roxy at my heels and I was standing in the kitchen. I crossed the room, let a very antsy golden retriever out the back door, and headed for the junk drawer to begin my nightly ritual of rifling through the takeout menus. Spreading them across the counter, my mind wandered again to the past, to the days before the takeout menus had replaced defrosting meat and pages upon pages of homework strewn haphazardly across every surface. Looking up, my eyes landed on the dusty Vitamix. I had always wanted one, but could never justify the expense. As soon as it was only me I had to justify anything to, I bought the damn thing, but once it was in my kitchen and out of the box, I could never figure out what to do with it. Much like the free time that stretched out in front of me like the dark and endless highway miles on an overnight road trip.

Insert the off-key crooning of a tiny violin.

I shook my head to sweep away some of the malaise, and took a good look around the kitchen. During 'better days' my ex-husband, Mark, and I had gutted the whole kitchen and fully renovated it to reflect the visions of stainless steel and slate blues and sleek grays in my head. For the next five (mostly) glowing years, the four of us had gathered around the expansive pewter-streaked granite countertop as we all talked over each other, sharing the most important bits of our day while I put the finishing touches on dinner. Jason habitually spun in circles on the center barstool at the counter as he recounted the points he'd made at soccer (or basketball, or baseball, or football) practice that day. In her younger years, Anna had floated by in a brightly colored tutu, waving her magic wand to transform each of us into 'fairy princes and princesses.' As she got older, she sat beside her brother and engaged in a bit of sibling competition over the records she'd broken at the track meet, the spike that had won the volleyball match, the ground ball that had slipped past the pitcher *and* the shortstop at softball practice.

But without a warning, the last of those busy, loud, magical days of parenthood had slipped through to the bottom of the hourglass. The barstools sat idle. The magic wands, spent. I looked around me and marveled at how, without me noticing, the glow had worn off in their absence. The room was tired, and I had absorbed its colors.

Two short years after Jason left for college, Mark got the twenty-seven-year itch and was the next to leave. He simply came home from work one day and told me he wasn't in love with me anymore, packed a bag, and left. Anna and I sat there stunned as he walked out the door, and it was months before I finally understood why. I bumped into him in the produce department looking quite cozy with the personal trainer he insisted he needed when he turned fifty. He didn't even have the decency to find somewhere else to buy his kale. Like perhaps Mars.

I wondered sometimes if my need to sleep with the window open was the straw that broke commitment's back. Menopause was a bitch. Maybe sometimes I was, too. I didn't think so, but I'd never be a hundred percent sure. What I was sure of was the fact that as hard as I had tried to be the best wife I could possibly be, I had failed at marriage twice—the first being a hormone-fueled twenty-year-old-girl's attempt at proving her independence—and I had no desire to 'try again.' None.

Mark had been gone for four years, and one by one the kids had grown and flown from the nest, and there I was. Three half-finished books under my belt and a growing angst heavy enough to sink a ship.

I knew I should have been in therapy. It was no secret that I had some adult-onset abandonment issues I needed to work through, but I had spent the last thirty-six months trying to convince myself that finishing a book would be the cure for my persistent melancholy. It was the *finishing* part that had proven itself to be the biggest challenge.

Roxy scratched at the door and barked at the same moment my back pocket began singing about milkshakes and boys in my yard, a practical joke courtesy of Anna, the night before she left for Washington State two years later. Empathetic, silly, and thoughtful to her core, she'd secretly changed my ringtone while I cooked our last dinner together before the big world swallowed her up. When it began ringing as we loaded the dishwasher together that last night, she'd laughed like a hyena.

"Every time your phone rings, you're gonna die of embarrassment, then laugh. You better laugh," she'd said.

I couldn't bring myself to tell her I wasn't sure how much laughing I was going to be doing once I dropped her and her luggage off at the airport the next day. But I had humored her because, as parents, that's what we do, and the ringtone had stayed the same for almost three years.

That night, it had been my parents on the phone, calling to check on us (probably mostly me) and they sounded delighted to hear laughter in the background.

"Paige. It sounds like things are going well over there." my mom exclaimed. *"Is Anna all packed up and ready for tomorrow?"*

"Oh, yes. There's a stack of suitcases as tall as me by the front

door." I had played along, not wanting to tip her off to my wilting spirit.

"*So.... two? Is that going to be enough?*"

Mom's one joke of the year and it had been at my expense. I wasn't sure if I should be offended or honored. I may not have grown past 5'1", but I made up for it in spades with my wit and determination, or I did at one point, anyway. After talking to Anna for a few minutes, my mom had passed the phone to my dad so he could wish our girl a safe trip and crack a total Dad joke before we hung up.

The next time the phone 'sang' that night, it was Kari, my ride or die since we'd met at sleepover camp when we were ten and found we were practically neighbors back home. We had been inseparable ever since. She had called that night to check on us (me)... and continued to call at five o'clock every night after.

My trip down memory lane was cut short as the milkshakes brought me back from my reverie. The clock on the wall gave me a pretty good idea of who was on the phone before I even had it out of my pocket. It was a little after five o'clock. Kari was calling, but for the first time ever, she was late.

"What did they do today?" I asked, turning back to the door to let the dog in. Kari's twin boys, Matt and Alex, were always up to something, and I was looking forward to a little comic relief courtesy of my godsons.

"These freaking knuckleheads are going to be the death of me. You are *not* going to believe this. After almost eighteen years, you'd think I'd learn to expect the unexpected from them, but this takes the cake. Are you free? You need to see this for yourself."

"I'm on my way."

2

"YOU MAKE IT FEEL LIKE CHRISTMAS"

GWEN STEFANI, BLAKE SHELTON

I headed out the front door (ignoring my overgrown eyesore of a yard), and walked two doors down to Kari's house. She met me on her front porch with her hands on her hips and murder in her eyes.

I had a tendency to trip going *up* stairs, so I watched as my foot landed on the bottom step, but the sound of her even, measured tone caused me to pause and look up.

"You know how the boys have been watching *The Office?*"

Eeeeeeek.

It was her "shit's about to go down" tone, and while I was grateful it wasn't directed at me, I knew the twins were in for it.

"Oh God. Oh no. What did they hide in Jell-O? Or did they send you faxes from the future?" I'd discovered long ago that her anger was best diffused with humor, but I had also discovered (around the same time, unfortunately) that I had to be subtle and ease my way into *certain situations*. It was clearly one of *those*.

"Well, you're close. Just come in, but brace yourself."

She held the storm door open for me as I continued up the stairs and walked into her foyer. I stopped to pet her short-haired mixed-breed dog, Charlie. He was always excited to see me, but today he was in rare form, spinning in circles every time I reached to scratch his ears.

"He's out of his gourd today, but he's the least of my problems. Follow me."

We walked down the hallway toward her family room in the back of the house, and as soon as a corner of the room came into view, I knew exactly what I was there to see.

The entire room was covered in wrapping paper. Not just a few things, or the table, or the remotes for the TV. The entire room.

"These boys went through all the wrapping paper I bought after Christmas, and they wrapped every. Single. Thing. Look at the television. How on earth? *It's attached to the wall.*" Her pitch continued to rise, and by the end of the last word, she was almost shrieking.

I was trying to hold it together because I could tell from her voice and flushed complexion she was ready to snap.

I followed her pointed finger to the TV which was mounted above the fireplace. It was covered in what I could only imagine was the result of two seventeen-year-old boys with too much time, wrapping paper, and tape at their disposal. I didn't know how much wrapping paper she'd bought at the end of the last Christmas season, but from the looks of her family room, no two rolls were the same pattern. The television was covered in bright red paper with four-inch Santas, the table below it, white with red and green diagonal stripes. The walls (the *walls!*) were a hodgepodge of festive designs—floor-to-ceiling stripes of green with white trees, white with red sleighs, and gold with pink ornaments—neatly held together with what had to be three miles of Scotch tape.

A giggle bubbled up, but I was able to stifle it quickly. Not quick enough.

"Oh, you think that's funny? You haven't even seen half of it."

Her fury was radiating *into* my pores and knew I needed to play it cool for just a little longer.

I didn't know where to look next; the entire room looked like the floor of a Macy's gift-wrapping room on December twenty-third. The couch (the *couch!*) was sporting at least four different patterns, none of which had been repeated from the walls. Multi-colored "JOY" on white for the seat cushions while the back cushions were a combination of snowmen on red and reindeer on green. The armrests and base of the couch were silver snowflakes on hot pink, as were the multitude of throw pillows across the back. It was... shocking.

At that point, I began to emit a high-pitched noise, not too unlike a tea kettle trying to get your attention. I glanced in her direction to see if I needed to make a run for it, and while her face had darkened to a shade of purple I'd never seen before, her posture was starting to loosen up.

"Do *not* laugh. These are your godsons and you are partially responsible for this behavior with all your ridiculous pranks."

For years in her thirties, Kari had struggled to carry a baby past a few weeks gestation and finally found a doctor who could tell her why—a medication she'd taken as a child was the culprit. It had irreversibly damaged her eggs, and she was devastated to learn she'd never be able to have a baby the "traditional" way. A few months after that appointment, Kari came to me with a huge favor to ask, and I agreed without hesitation. What were a few eggs I wasn't using anyway? I'd had a boy and a girl—a matching set—and the rest of the eggs that had been with me nearly since conception were fated to grow old along with me. Kari had always been like a sister to me, and having the ability to potentially give her the one thing she wanted most in the world was a heady feeling.

A few months of hormone injections after I'd weaned

Anna, a quick egg retrieval procedure, whatever Nick had to do for his part in the process, a bit of turkey baster action, and presto-chango, nine months later—twins. They were fifty percent Nick Peterson: deep voices, an acumen for math, and linebacker physiques; and fifty percent Aunt Paige: thick, brown, curly hair, blue eyes, nonstop tomfoolery, and a missing 'off' switch. I would never apologize for that, but I did feel bad that my no-nonsense best friend was surrounded by knuckle-heads, thanks to me.

I was thinking at that moment she might regret that deci-sion, and the next words out of her mouth almost confirmed my suspicions.

"You're a terrible influence." Her voice broke at the end and I turned my head fast enough to see she was starting to find a tiny bit of humor in the situation. But as quickly as it had turned up, the corner of her mouth rejoined the thin straight line formed by lips that were undoubtedly holding back count-less expletives.

"Are you ready for the cherry on top?"

I wasn't sure if I was. A full belly laugh was looming heavy in my chest and I knew better than to let it out just yet, so I clamped my lips together tight and nodded. "Mm-hm."

"So, you know how I've been asking Nick to break down those boxes since we replaced the appliances two months ago?"

Oh God. I can't do this anymore! Do not laugh. Whatever it is. Do not *laugh.*

"Yeeeees?"

"Well, I walked through the door after teaching yoga in a ninety-degree studio all day, and by the time I had hung my keys on the hook, I already knew something was up. This trai-torous dog was dancing in circles at the edge of the family room, and there was no sign of the boys who are usually tack-ling me at the front door to see if I picked up anything at a drive-thru on the way home. If I hadn't already invested so much time and money into these two, I would drop them off at the fire station. Anyway, I practically ran down the hallway, and as soon as I passed the corner at the end, I could see why Charlie was spinning in circles and chasing his tail. This..."

She swept one arm Vanna-White-style across the scene in front of us.

"...greeted me. They had to have used every single roll of *expensive* double-sided Hallmark wrapping paper I bought last December. Where did they find all this tape? Did they have it hoarded in their rooms? Because I know when *I'm* looking for a single roll of tape, it's nowhere to be found."

She was really getting wound up again. I was desperate for a deep breath, but opted for tiny sips of air out of fear that a giggle would find its way up and out and jeopardize my very life.

I'd at least like to finish writing one single bleeping book before my last day on earth.

"Did you happen to notice the two rather large gift-wrapped cubes in the middle of the room?"

I hadn't, but as soon as my eyes landed on them and saw the holes torn through the double-sided multi-colored polka dot and striped paper, I knew exactly what had come next. Those boys were nothing if not inventive. And entertaining (to me, anyway).

"As soon as I saw the rest of the room, I gasped, obviously, which was their cue for phase two of their nonsense plan. Two knuckleheads came tearing through the tops of the boxes, screaming, 'IT'S CHRISTMAS IN JULY!' I tell you, Paige, if I didn't teach yoga four days a week, I'd be on the floor right now. My heart can't handle this shit. I'm getting too old for this."

That was it. That was all it took. The mental image of two enormous nearly eighteen-year-old men popping out of gift-wrapped boxes in the middle of a gift-wrapped family room was more than I could take. I *was* only human, after all.

I was doubled over at that point, unable to catch my breath or wrench my eyes open. After what was probably a full minute of my neglected laughter finally set free, I was able to stop long enough to open my eyes. I immediately wished I hadn't. Hands on her hips, she was looking down at me as if *I* were the one who had handed them each strip of paper to hang.

I took a deep breath through pursed lips and let it out slowly, hoping no new giggles would escape. "Please don't give me your 'mom' look. It's terrifying, and you know I'm not good in these situations. I could barely hold it together when Jason and Anna pulled stunts like this."

"Uh-huh. So are you going to help them take it all down since 'Aunt Paige' is genetically responsible for all of this tomfoolery?"

"Where are the boys, anyway?" I looked around behind me. "Do I need to do a wellness check?"

The corners of her mouth started to quake and I knew I almost had her.

"About five seconds after they both tore through the tops of their jackass-in-the box, they realized the error of their ways. They're lucky their father is traveling this week, but I yelled enough for the both of us. I sent them to their rooms so I could calm down. Hence why I called you right away. I knew you would laugh and I needed to not be so mad."

I started to feel a little less guilty about my utter lack of self control. At least she knew what she was getting herself into when she called me—and it wasn't a lecture on responsible wrapping paper storage.

Another thought flashed into my mind, however. One more terrifying than the stare down from moments before.

"Do you—? Should I—? Am I supposed to help them clean this up?"

I could feel Kari finally relax a bit. Heard a quick chuckle.

"No, this one is all on them to clean, but I wanted you to see it before they started. And I needed some comic relief."

"Well...," I looked around the room once more, then punched her lightly on the shoulder. "I hope I delivered."

"That you did." She cleared her throat and put her hand on my forearm. "While you're here..." She looked at me earnestly and squeezed my arm. "Do you have time to sit outside and talk for a few minutes? I had a great idea during one of my classes today."

Oh, hell *no.*

Kari didn't ask if I had time to talk unless I was about to get a "friendly" lecture, and nobody's got time for one of *those* on such a beautiful Saturday evening.

"I actually have a lot of work to catch up on, and there's laundry all over my bed that's waiting to be folded—"

"That laundry has been there for a month. And it's Saturday. What work do you have to catch up on?"

"It's a new project. I haven't told you about it yet. And this morning I was buried under the laundry avalanche and could have died. I really must be going. Kiss the boys for me. Good luck." I continued deflecting with increasingly lame excuses as I backed down the hall and out the door. Her look of loving disappointment was the last thing I saw through the glass of her storm door before I turned and fled down the porch stairs and back to the relative safety of my self-made prison.

Ten seconds after plopping myself down onto the tropical-print cushions of my porch swing, I heard a bing as a text came in. I knew who it was from before I even unlocked my screen.

Kari Kari Bo Berry: Coward.

Guilty as charged. People might think you're all peaceful and shit because you're a yogi, but it's a fool who thinks that. You're scary. I'll stay here with my fluffy dog and my unfulfilled dreams.

Kari Kari Bo Berry: Which is what I wanted to talk to you about. I had some ideas. Good ones.

Just don't. Please. Don't you have a room to unwrap?

Kari Kari Bo Berry: I know you're sick of hearing it from me, but we've been friends, practically sisters, for almost half a century, and it's hard to see you stuck—

—You're cranky.

Kari Kari Bo Berry: And you're avoiding. I love you. I have to supervise Wrapfest 2023 because I'm willing to bet they won't have nearly as much enthusiasm for the cleanup as they did the mischief that got us into this position in the first place.

That's what she said.

Kari Kari Bo Berry: Exactly. Exhibit A, ladies and gentlemen. Goodbye.

I was reading over our exchange and enjoying the ability to finally let my laughter free (because the whole thing deserved to be laughed at) when another text came in, and my phone auto-scrolled me to it.

Kari Kari Bo Berry: Think about what you won't
let me say because you know it's true. You
need to shake things up. You need to get out
of that house—as much as it kills me to say—
and you need to get out of your comfort zone
and start searching for the beautiful adventure
that's waiting for you on the other side of
everything you've ever known. It's going to be
hard. I know you're scared, but I believe in
you, and I'll be there to cheer you on every
step of the way, I promise. I've got you.

Not wanting to read whatever was being furiously typed at that very moment, I dropped my phone facedown on the table next to the swing, pushed off the ground with my foot, and forward through the air I sailed.

I was painfully aware that something in my life needed to drastically change, but I didn't know what—or how. I wished sometimes there were blinking arrows pointing us through life.

At that moment, the only blinking arrow was coming from my stomach. As I rose from the swing, I took one last lingering look at the buzz of activity on the sidewalk in front of my house, picked up my phone, and went inside to order my dinner.

THE NEXT MORNING, I was awakened by the sound of the doorbell, which might be the worst way to start the day. No leisurely cup of coffee. No lazing around in bed, scrolling through my various social feeds (because who doesn't love a bit of digital eavesdropping on all the best parts of someone else's life?). No avoiding the world on the other side of my bedroom door. I considered lying there for a few minutes in the hopes that whoever they were would just fluff off somewhere else. I rolled over to face the window instead of the pile of unfolded laundry that greeted me when I opened my eyes, tucked my pillow between my knees, and pulled the duvet over my head.

"Ding-dong." the insistent bell called again, announcing that whoever couldn't take a hint was still on the other side of the door. Roxy's ears were slightly less floppy as she listened to see if there might be imminent danger, probably so she knew whether she needed to hide.

"It's Sunday, for God's sake. This is supposed to be a day of *rest*," I grumbled, then reached up to yank the covers off my head. Roxy abandoned her bed and stood beside mine, her tail wagging at a pace that could only mean one thing: she sensed excitement. I reached out to pet her head as I stood.

To avoid the intrusion of a third ring of the doorbell, I thrust my feet into my slippers and made my way to the top of the stairs, my good-time Charlie of a dog plastered to my side.

I strode through the kitchen and rounded the corner to the hallway leading to the front door. I could clearly see my mother, MaryBeth, her forehead pressed against the glass of the sidelight, and the tall, thin outline of my father, Theo, could be seen through the etched-glass upper half of the front door.

This smells like trouble.

3

"ANOTHER STORY"
THE HEAD AND THE HEART

Roxy danced the four-step at my side, always up for company, especially from Grandma and Grandpa Turner. I could hear the soft pleadings of my bed calling to me as I trudged through the hallway toward the round, beaming face of my mother, unlocked the door, and swung it open.

My parents stepped into the foyer, and my father, ever the chivalrous gentleman, held the storm door to let my mother through first.

"Hi, Mom," I said as I hugged her. It was no mystery whose height gene I'd received.

"You feel thin," was her reply.

My dad patiently waited his turn, and when my mother released me from her grasp, he stepped into the space she'd made for him, bent severely at the waist, and wrapped his long, slender arms around me. "Good morning, Tiger," he rumbled into my ear. "Your mother insisted we stop by." As he unfolded his body, he gave my shoulders a squeeze and kissed my cheek. At that moment, I realized they were here to talk—at close range—and I hadn't brushed my teeth.

"I'm just getting out of bed. Let me put Roxy outside, run and brush my teeth, then we can sit in the kitchen. Sound good?"

We three made our way to the back of the house, where Roxy danced at the door. Mom began pulling mugs down from the cabinets she knew as well as her own. "Go right ahead and do what you need to do, and your Dad and I will take care of..." Her eyes scanned the room with a bit of sadness and a dash of judgment. "...everything down here."

My gaze traveled to the counter still strewn with last night's takeout menus, paper food containers trying to escape from the garbage can in the corner, and coffee cups in the sink piled as high as the Statue of Unity, and felt the burn of shame on my face.

"Okay, sorry about the mess. I was going to clean up a little today." I couldn't even meet their eyes before I turned and bolted up the stairs to the safety of my bedroom. I wondered how long I could hide out there before they came looking for me. That shoulder squeeze from my dad felt like a pre-apology, and I knew they weren't there for the lousy coffee.

After a quick run-through of my lengthy oral hygiene routine, I took a good look at myself in the mirror and found I was in a state similar to that of my kitchen. Somewhere along the line, the short brunette pixie cut I'd been so grateful for years ago had grown out to resemble the Gary Busey-inspired hairdo of a sheepdog that had escaped his groomer. The signature shock of white hair that had grown out above the center of my forehead after my son was born was down for the count, hanging limp like a white silk flag in a rainstorm. It had always given my round face some dimension, but after months of neglect, it just looked sad.

I sighed as a sad realization struck me. I'd stopped caring how I looked while no one was really looking at me.

For my first trick of the day, I stripped out of the comfortable, threadbare pajamas I'd had high hopes of staying in all day when I put them on the night before, then dragged my arms through the straps of a bra that had been hanging on my bathroom door knob for weeks. Next, I dug through the clean laundry pile that took up the 'other' half of my bed.

Wearing the first pair of sweats and t-shirt I found, I stood in front of the dressing mirror in the corner of my room and tried to get a sense of what my parents would see when I went back downstairs. Dressed to the nines? Ummmm no. Just the right side of homeless? Possibly. *"Good enough for whom it's for,"* I said to my reflection, hoping it agreed.

When I returned to the kitchen, the garbage had been taken out, the coffee mugs that had been vying for my attention for days were drying on a clean towel next to the sink, and my parents were already sitting side by side at the table, their hands strangling steaming cups of coffee. A third cup waited for me, marking my place directly across from them.

Clearly, this was going to be one of those *visits. Perfect.*

I sat where I'd been subliminally directed, picked up the mug, blew on it, and took a sip while peering over the top to see if my delay tactics were working.

Nope.

"So, what brings you to Casa del Rhiann this fine morning? Everyone is so chipper at eleven a.m. on a Sunday."

"I like what you've done with the place, honey," my dad joked. Much like me, he preferred to mask discomfort with humor. It irritated my mother endlessly to have both of us trying to clown our way out of every uncomfortable situation. Her voice of reason could only cut through so much sarcasm and ill-timed humor.

"Your Dad and I are worried about you, Paige. Your house is a state. You rarely go further than your front porch. Sometimes, I wish you worked in an actual office so you'd be forced to go out and socialize. It sounds like you've been going to yoga—"

Oh, so they've been talking to Kari. Nice.

"—but what else are you doing with your free time? These are the days we wish you had a sibling."

My mother paused and looked at my dad, who swallowed whatever thought was trying to escape and washed it down with a sip of his coffee.

"We love you, Paige. We understand what a huge adjustment it is when your last little bird leaves the nest," she continued, (I knew the "but" wasn't far behind) "but you can't lay idle in the feathers they've left behind. Anna left for school three years ago, and you need to get up and start making strides toward finding who *you* are now. You'll always be a mother, no matter where your children are. That doesn't end. Sure, they require less of your time, and you don't get to see them every day like you once did, but they need *you* as much as you need *them*. More, actually. The dynamics of your relationship have changed. Not the love."

I sat there trying so hard not to cry in front of my parents. Not that I couldn't. More so because I knew it would delay the conclusion of their little 'Come to Jesus' speech. The backs of my eyes were burning with the effort of holding it all in. I knew I couldn't trust my voice.

"Y-o-u gu-u-ys," I warbled in an off-key rendition of *All by Myself*. I cleared the blocked tears from my throat and tried again. "Okay, that's better. I appreciate you coming here, cleaning up my kitchen, and telling me what a mess I am. I'm sure that was difficult to do. I'm fine, and if I'm not fine, I'll be fine. I just need a little more time."

I looked at my dad, who was thoroughly inspecting his coffee to avoid making eye contact with me. I was certain *none* of that visit was his idea. While my mother had always been all business and to-do lists, he was more of a dance-around-the-topic when not reading a romance book kind of guy. In fact, he'd bruised his shins numerous times walking into furniture while holding some steamy bodice ripper in front of his face and simultaneously avoiding one sticky subject or another.

When I shifted focus to my mother, she looked me square in the eyes. "You're not fine. Anything but. However, we have seen the great things you can do. You're the most tenacious person I know when you put your mind to something, and I know *that something* is right around the corner, but sweetheart, you're never going to find it floating through your house like a ghost. Is there something you're interested in? Can we help you brainstorm some ideas?"

I wasn't really in the frame of mind to start airing my dirty laundry, but if I didn't, it would be dragged out of me regardless.

"I've been working on another book—"

Both my parents turned to look at one another, then back to me. The look they exchanged was as familiar to me as our current dialogue exchange was to them.

"—and it's not going as well as I'd hoped. I feel so uninspired, and I'm struggling to come up with much of anything. I don't even know if my idea is going to work. I am feeling a little blue about that, I guess."

"Well, Tiger," my dad chuckled, "you know I have a little bit of experience with literature. Maybe you could let me take a look at what you've got. If you're open to it, I have a few published friends from the English Department I could reach out to. Do you want me to see if someone has some time to sit down with you? I'm sure any one of them would be happy to."

"Thanks, Dad. I really appreciate that. Can I let you know when I get a little further along? It feels like pieces and fragments everywhere. I need to start pulling it together a little bit, and then it's a definite maybe. I appreciate it, though." I wiped an escaped tear with the heel of my hand and sat back in my chair. From that height, I felt like a kid again, sitting at the dinner table discussing our days—my dad sharing a tale or two about one of his English Literature students at the University of Madison, my mom chatting about who she ran into at the grocery store earlier, or a new recipe she was going to try out that week, and me trying to feign interest long enough to get back upstairs to whatever book I was reading.

Those were the easy days. My parents told me often enough when I was grumbling about some minor inconvenience or another, but back then, I was too kid-headed to listen. Why didn't I heed their warnings before it was too late to appreciate them? Fool that I was.

My mom wasn't finished, but I could tell she was starting to de-escalate based on the height of her shoulders. They were beginning to relax a little.

"We just worry. We're your parents. You understand, I'm sure. We want nothing more than for you to be happy, and if there's some way we can make that happen, we're all over it."

"Like hair on soap," my dad quipped.

I had always loved his sense of humor, especially at a moment like that. No one wants their parents to see them falling apart, and no one *definitely* wants their parents to come over first thing in the morning to point it out.

"Thank you. Sincerely. I do understand, and I know how all of this looks from the outside—"

"Since you mentioned it, your front yard is quite a sight."

"Thanks, Dad. Thank you for noticing. I have a feeling Kari's boys will be headed this way for some penance yard work soon. Anyway, I know how this all looks. I am taking everything you're saying to heart. I promise. I'm going to take some online quizzes, try a few new hobbies, and pray that, by some miracle, the path forward lights up in front of me. I know it will. I have nothing but faith that my days of wallowing—"

"Years."

"Yes, thank you, Mom. Ok, *years* of wallowing are almost over. Maybe a few more days. Maybe a week. A month, tops."

"Good grief. Another month of this. Baby Jesus, pray for us. Ok, we've said our piece, drank our coffee, and laid our eyes on you. Your dad and I are going to the fabric store. I'm making new curtains and a valance for the front room. I'll wash these mugs, and we'll get out of your hair. Theo, are you ready to go?"

"Oh yes, MaryBeth, I *cannot wait* to get to the fabric store. Can we spend hours there touching everything but leave with nothing?"

He handed my mom his empty mug, and as she got up from the table, she threw him a dirty look for good measure.

"You'll thank me when they're finished, and all the neighbors are stopping by to ask where I bought them."

I immediately sought out my dad's expression. He mouthed, "Pray for me," while his eyes betrayed his true feelings of contentment. Everyone knew there was nothing in the world my dad loved more than to spend a lazy afternoon with his wife. Lucky them. Lucky me.

My mom had finished scrubbing and drying our mugs and was standing by the front door with her purse under her arm before my dad and I had even risen from the table.

"Well, I better hurry up, Tiger, but promise me you'll call if you want to brainstorm some ideas. There's a big, wide-open future out there waiting for you. An adventure! I know you'll figure it out. I'm your number one cheerleader, and I can't wait to see what I'll cheer for next."

He ambled toward the door, and after bending to give Roxy a generous ear-flopping scratch, he opened the storm door, and they were off.

And I was once again alone with my dog and my thoughts.

"How do you feel about a walk, Rox?"

4

"ELEANOR RIGBY"

THE BEATLES

Two hours later, Kari found me sweating and swearing in the front yard. If I were being judged by the detritus of my efforts—a trowel, a hoe, a rake, two different shovels, three yard waste bags filled to the brim, and a golden retriever under a pear tree—it would seem as if I'd unearthed a botanical masterpiece. Unfortunately for me (and my neighbors), I'd barely made a dent. I was sitting in the middle of the lawn with my head resting on my knees when Kari's flip-flopped and impeccably maintained feet and Roxy's furry front paws came into view on my left.

"What's cookin', good lookin'?"

I lifted my head to the sight of her voluminous curls framed by the midday sun. Shielding my eyes, I stood, a symphony of stiffness echoing from my joints.

"Me. I'm cookin' out here. It's supposed to get up to ninety degrees later today, but it feels like we are there already."

Kari squatted down to bury her face in Roxy's neck, and because their hair was about the same color, it looked as if Roxy had grown an enormous goiter. I held in a laugh, knowing my friend would not appreciate the parallel as much as I.

"Basically. It's about eighty-nine right now, which makes me wish I owned something other than yoga pants. I was going to walk to the studio before I had to start teaching to try and get a little solo practice in before things get busy. I gave myself a few extra minutes so I could stop by and say hi, and here you are... So, *hi*."

"Hey there, sunshine." I wiped my filthy hands on my shorts and caught her in a hug as she stood, having lost Roxy's attention to a squirrel that had been evading her all morning.

As we stepped apart, she held out her right hand to give me a book I hadn't noticed she'd been holding, and I was instantly as excited as Roxy with a new tennis ball. I took it from her and flipped it over, groaning inwardly as I read the title. It sounded like a major snooze fest: *Gratitude Journal*.

"I saw an ad for that on Instagram and thought it would be good for you to do a little journaling. I know when I focus more on the positives in my life, they start to at least *feel* like they outweigh the negatives." She took a step back to get a better look at the mess I'd made in my front yard. "What have you got going on here?"

The journal in my hand felt like a bowling ball. "My parents stopped by this morning to read me the riot act about the state of my life. The front yard was a topic of conversation, and it felt like something I could tackle without too much psychological damage. I may have overestimated my abilities. And forgot that I'm fifty-five. Yeesh. I may have bitten off more than I can chew. Any chance the boys are free today? I have some cash burning a hole in my pocket."

Kari's laugh poured over me like cooling rain. It's always the one thing I can depend on to make everything at least *feel* better.

"Oh, you can bet they're free today. They need to finish their shopping lists before they head off to big boy school in a few weeks. They can go Christmas wrap their dorm rooms until they're blue in the face. Anyway, I'll text them as soon as I get to the studio and have them come over to help. Does your lawn mower have gas in it?"

The panicked look on my face probably answered that question.

"Never mind, they will come over fully loaded with everything they'll need to get this yard in tip-top condition. Do *not* pay them. This is a punishment."

I'd never been brave enough to argue with Kari, so I simply nodded my head. "You got it, boss. Am I allowed to feed them? Should I just throw some bread and water onto the porch?"

"Go ahead and joke, chucklehead. You know exactly what I'm going through. I was here to witness the shit show when your kids were teenagers, remember? So work them like rented mules and send them home when your yard is a contender for Home & Garden." She looked at her watch. "Okay, I've got to scoot, but I'll pray for you. Talk to you later?"

She was already walking backward toward the sidewalk before I could even reply, so I blew her a kiss. "Thank you, Bo Berry. I really appreciate this. Stop by later for coffee or a glass of wine—or both. And thanks for the journal. *So* great. I can't *wait* to write in it."

"I can see your face and *hear* your sarcasm, you know. Just try it. But you've got yourself a deal on the wine. See you at five," she said over her shoulder as she reached the sidewalk, turned, and speed-walked in the direction of the yoga studio.

"That's one scary but determined girl, Roxy. I wouldn't be surprised if she owns that place in a few years." I knelt on the ground and tried to hug Roxy, who was kind enough to sit still long enough for me to get one arm around her before she was off to stalk the squirrel again.

As I limped up the porch stairs to ditch the journal and refill my water, the music paused as my cell phone began to ring from its perch on the railing. A smile spread across my face when I saw the caller ID.

Uncle Mike. The fact that we talked every Sunday afternoon didn't make him my favorite relative, nor did the fact that his house in Dunedin, Florida, a neighboring town to Clearwater, was a built-in vacation destination for my family as long as I could remember—but those things certainly helped.

"Uncle Mike. How was your week? You caught me at the perfect time; I was just taking a break from yard work."

"Oh, sweetie, I have had the best week, and it's even better now that I hear your voice. But first, what are you doing with your yard? Something fabulous, I hope."

I sat on the top step and surveyed the day's progress. "Well, I wouldn't say fabulous yet, but it's somewhat improved. Matt and Alex will be over shortly to help me. They were up to their usual hijinx yesterday, so Kari's sending them here to work off the fourteen double rolls of Hallmark wrapping paper they used to cover her family room while she was at work."

Uncle Mike broke into one of his trademark laughs, and I could see him in my mind's eye, shoulders heaving up and down, eyes closed, head thrown back. In my family, laughter was a full-body experience. He and my dad grew up in a house that didn't inspire much joviality, and through their experiences, they'd learned that laughing was better than crying, and they had taught me the same mindset. While they employed a little off-color humor to lighten the mood, I'd taken that one step further to practical jokes. A laugh at your expense costs you nothing, right? Even one at my expense. That was fine, too.

"Those boys are the best, and their personalities are all yours. Kari must rue the day she decided to use your eggs," he added wryly once he'd gotten control of himself.

"Well, apparently, I was to blame for yesterday's prank, but I seem to have been forgiven. They're serving out their sentences behind a lawnmower and weed whacker in my yard, and not a moment too soon. It's a hell of a mess. Not unlike me."

My uncle cleared his throat.

Oh, shit. Here it comes.

"Let me tell you about my week, and then we'll get into all that. So, Chris and I are taking things to the next level, not to sound like I'm twenty-four. He's asked me to move in with him since I'm there all the time anyway, and his place is closer to the store."

Uncle Mike and his partner, Chris, are both clothes horses and, a year into their relationship, had opened up "A Dash of Flair", a haberdashery in downtown Dunedin. Chris resigned as VP of his bank and my uncle wheeled way back on his successful interior design business in order to give the store more of their attention, and their sacrifices and dedication had seemingly paid off.

"I guess by now he knows most of my quirks, and if two years together wasn't enough time to figure them all out, he'll just have to adjust."

"Uncle Mike! That is awesome news. I'm so happy for you guys. I have so many questions. When are you moving? When are you putting your house up for sale? Do I have time to come down for one last visit?"

"Take a beat there, Paige. Deep breaths. One question at a time. Ok, where do I begin? When? Ummm... soon-ish. I've got so much stuff in this house that I would basically need to start packing right this very minute and hope to be finished by next July. Every room is fully furnished. That's six bedroom sets. No. Eight. The third floor has two. On top of that, every bathroom is stocked with everything a person could possibly need. What would I even do with all this stuff? It's going to have to stay... Which brings me to the reason for my call. How long do you have?"

"I'm fine for right now. I'll need to hop off once Matt and

Alex get here, but that could be a while. They are seventeen and it is only one p.m. Practically the middle of the night for them."

"Ha. True true. Ok, so I wish we were having this conversation face to face, but... I don't even know where to start..."

I suddenly felt a knot in my stomach. "Eeeergh..."

"It's nothing bad, I promise. I'll share more soon, but what I really called for was to tell you I am moving in with Chris this weekend—"

Uncle Mike, that is incredible news! I'm so happy for you," I gushed.

"I knew you would be. But, I am also calling to ask—no. *Beg* you to come down here for an extended visit. I don't want to leave the house empty, and I have zero—I mean *zero*—interest in renting it to strangers. But no pressure."

Matt and Alex came huffing up the sidewalk at that moment, pushing and pulling an impressive collection of lawn equipment. I needed a moment to digest the (very one-sided) conversation I'd just had, so their timing could not have been more perfect.

"Uncle Mike, I... I don't even know what to say. Thank you? That sounds like a really awesome idea, but can I have a few days to think it over? I'd have to check with Kari to make sure she could keep an eye on things here. Honestly, my first instinct is to say, 'yes, please.' and hit the road, but this is a lot to digest. Actually, the boys just got here. Give me thirty seconds to get them set up, and then we can talk more about... this."

"Actually, honey, I pulled up in front of the store a few minutes ago and Chris is staring daggers out the window at me. I'd better go fold some socks. I know I just shocked you, and now I'm hanging up, but I wanted to give you a chance to marinate in the idea a bit, but hurry up. Oh, and say hi to the boys for me. Those two crack me up. Ok, I've got to run in. I'll talk to you soon. Love you."

"I love you, too, Uncle Mike, but what should I say? Thank you? I'm lost here."

His phone disconnected from his car's Bluetooth, and I could picture the huge smile on his face as he headed into the store, knowing he'd dropped a bomb on me. It was a good bomb, but explosive nonetheless. His voice came through again, clearer since he was speaking directly into the phone, but a little jilted and breathless from what was probably a hurried walk from the car to the store.

"Say you'll give it some serious thought. You'd be doing me a huge favor, but I have a feeling you're going to love it here and won't want to leave. Consider it an open-ended residency request. I wouldn't ask you to uproot your life if it wasn't important to me. On that note, I love you. I'm hanging up."

The shuffling on the line ended and I looked at my screen. He had indeed hung up.

What the hell was that?

5

"EVERYWHERE"
FLEETWOOD MAC

As I set my phone down next to me, I noticed right away the boys had wasted no time getting to work in the yard. Mature enough to realize I was on the phone and to wait on the loud gas-powered equipment, they were running back and forth across the yard, picking up the disaster I'd left behind during my fruitless efforts.

"Hi, Aunt Paige. We're here to help. We've gotten almost everything cleaned up, and we're ready to get to work," Matt said as they abandoned their yard waste bags and strode toward the porch in four big (for me) steps. They did not get their impossibly long legs from me, but many of their other physical characteristics had clearly hitched a ride with my penchant for pranks.

"We didn't want to bother you while you were on the phone," Alex said, finishing his brother's thought.

I stood and descended the paint-chipped steps to the walkway so I could hug my godsons. "Saw the aftermath of your Christmas in July. I've taught you well, young grasshoppers. I'm so proud." I gave them each a wholehearted squeeze around the waist and stood back to survey the current state of the yard.

"Well, I can't tell you how grateful I am to have your help, no matter how it came to be that you're here. I'm drowning in weeds, and the lawn is a sight. It's embarrassing, really. But not embarrassing enough to figure out where to begin. I'm so appreciative of you guys being here."

Alex, the quieter, more sensitive of the two, started unfolding a yard waste bag that had been laying near his feet. "It's no problem at all, Aunt Paige. We'd help you even if we weren't in trouble. Just say the word, and we'll be here. Now show us what you need done today, and we'll get it handled."

These boys.

I couldn't believe they were already adults, headed off to college at the end of the summer. Kari claimed they weren't mature enough to be too far away for months at a time, but as her closest friend for over four decades, I knew it was more that Kari wasn't ready. Until then, perhaps.

I was willing to bet at that very moment, she was mentally packing their bags. That's the beauty of raising adolescents. All the shit they put us through makes it so much easier to step aside and let them spread their wings.

"I was going to have your mom over later for wine and cheese, but I'm going run and see if I can catch her two o'clock class. I am trusting you both to behave while handling dangerous equipment with rotating blades and spinning strings, but if you need me just text me or call the studio. I'm only a phone call away. If there's blood, call 911." I gave them each a bit of side-eye, peering down (up) my nose at them to drive the point home. Not able to maintain any level of serious-ness with them for longer than a few seconds, I gave them my most reassuring smile and set my next statement on a tee. "This shouldn't take you too long."

"*That's what she said!*" they screamed in unison.

I shook my head in mock disgust, but my heart was filled with pride. "I walked right into that one, didn't I? I left twenty dollars for each of you on the counter. Don't tell your mom."

I gave them a hug and stood on tippy toes to deliver each a loud, obnoxious peck on the cheek, then turned and headed toward the sidewalk. As I looked over my shoulder right before walking out of view, I was just in time to see Alex give Matt a shove into one of the bushes in front of my porch railing.

A memory raced forward. A scene from a time not too long ago of my own kids pushing each other in a wheelbarrow around the front yard while I weeded and tended to the garden that had always filled me with such joy. Those days seemed to drag on forever. Until they didn't.

What I wouldn't give for one more day of fighting teenagers and Dorito-dust handprints on the walls.

AS LUCK WOULD HAVE IT, I arrived just in time for Kari's next yoga class. The room was pretty full, but after grabbing a mat from the shelves in the back, I found the perfect spot in the last row where I wouldn't be a spectacle to anyone except the people on either side of me. Kari stopped next to my mat as I started my stretches and raised her perfectly shaped eyebrows, a smile turning up one corner of her mouth.

"I didn't know you were coming to class."

"Well, here I am. I had nothing really going on, so I figured I'd come and namasté a little bit with you and then go out for that glass of wine after."

Kari looked at her Apple watch. "I'm so glad you did. It's nice to have your smiling face here when everybody else is sweating and grumbling." She turned and took a step toward the front of the room so she could begin class. She stopped when I began to speak again.

"While you're torturing all of us, you can wonder what my Uncle Mike had to say when he called an hour ago. Prepare to have your mind blown."

In one fluid motion, Kari put her hands on her hips, bent at the waist, and twirled around 180 degrees to face me again. I'd managed to stop her in her tracks. Mission accomplished.

"Oooohhhhh... Do tell," she breathed, inches from my face.

"I'll wait. It's more fun that way."

My dear, dear friend had never been a fan of not knowing all the information, and as an armchair psychologist, I was willing to bet it had a lot to do with how many times she'd had to be the new student in class while growing up a military brat. She opened her mouth to say something, then snapped it shut as she realized where we were (and why). "Who's ready to sweat?" she yelled as she looked at me with vengeance in her eyes, then stood, turned back around, and continued the way she'd been headed.

I was in so much trouble.

Class went by quicker than I expected, and my weak, rubbery muscles felt pretty good, so I decided to stay for the last session of the day. Kari was too busy chatting with the students coming and going to bother trying to get any information out of me in between sessions, but an hour and fifteen minutes later, we were headed down the street to the local wine and cheese establishment.

Walking into 'Better with Age' with Kari felt like coming home. I could safely assume that was their intention when designing it. Various seating areas were furnished with locally crafted wood tables and an eclectic mix of chairs upholstered in wildly varied, yet somehow still coordinating fabrics. Walls paneled with rough-hewn boards—none of which matched— mixed with fixtures of polished gold and handblown glass created the oxymoronic feeling of sitting in a swanky barn. After choosing our table and agreeing on our typical hummus toppings and merlot, we sat back facing one another in our favorite burgundy velvet chairs.

Kari got right to the point. "So... time's up. Tell me what the heck your uncle said. You're killing me, Smalls."

"Well," I began, "I got the shock of a lifetime. It's almost like the universe is listening to all of you tell me over and over again that I need to shake up my life, and it seems that it went and took that job on all by itself."

Kari leaned forward. "What on earth is it?"

As if on cue for dramatic effect, our usual waitress appeared with our usual bottle. "Your hummus will be right up, ladies. Extra olives, right?"

"Yes, please," I replied, and as she made her way to the table next to ours, I picked up the bottle of merlot and poured us each a glass, savoring the last few moments before the weight of what came next dropped onto the table between us.

I inhaled slowly and held it for a moment. Counted to ten. "Uncle Mike is moving in with Chris."

"That's great news. Why all the drama about that?"

"He doesn't want to sell his house and isn't thrilled about renting it out. He's asked me to come down there and stay for an extended visit to keep an eye on things."

Kari's mouth hung open, then snapped shut before delivering a rapid-fire series of questions. "Are you actually considering this? How long would you be gone? *Does Roxy even like sand?*" Her volume rose with each question until the last one was delivered in a near shout, drawing the attention of everyone seated around us.

She looked around and waved an apology to the dumbfounded couple seated in the mustard-yellow leather armchairs a few feet away, then turned her attention back to me. "Sorry. Sorry. I just—"

"Girl, I know." I rose from my chair and squeezed in next to her. I put my hand on her leg and gently patted it. My friend was struggling with the same thoughts I was. Other than my honeymoon and family vacations (mine, not hers, obviously), neither of us had been more than a few miles apart since we were ten years old. The idea of one of us being hundreds of miles away for any length of time without the other was inconceivable.

"Well—well—what does that mean?" she stammered.

"Well," I parroted, "it means I need to make a decision. I can either choose to let my uncle sell or rent out his house—which he really doesn't seem to want to do—or I can go down to Florida for a little bit to house-sit for him while he decides what he's going to do with it long term."

"What do you think you'll do?"

I sighed dramatically. "I'm really not sure. I haven't had time to process any of it. So at this point, I just keep playing the conversation over and over in my head, trying to figure out what in the world is happening today."

"I know whatever you decide, it'll end up being the right decision for you. You've always been great at figuring out what was best for you and your family, and this won't be any different."

"Thanks for the vote of confidence. I know this isn't an easy conversation, but at the end of the day, I know you're in my corner and you'll support me no matter what—and I really appreciate that. It's not forever. Maybe a few months and I'll be right back where I belong."

"You know I would do anything for you. You're my closest friend, and no matter where you are in the world, that will never change. And with today's technology, you and I can talk all the time. We can FaceTime, we can talk on the phone, we can text." She sniffed, belying the brave front she was suddenly putting on.

"I know, but I would still miss you all. I mean, how can I not see my godsons at least three times a week? How can I not walk down the street and take a yoga class with you and then drink merlot in these very chairs until we have to practically crawl home?" Emotion began to cloud my vision and squeeze my throat.

"Paige, honey, the good news is, your godsons are leaving for school soon, and if it does turn out that you are going to be in Florida for a little while, it becomes a vacation destination for me."

I tilted my head and shot her a look of disbelief. The word 'vacation' wasn't even part of her vocabulary. 'Staycation' was more her speed. "And if you're there and nothing is really keeping me here in Madison once the boys leave for college, who knows what will happen. Maybe I'll come keep you company while Nick is out of town for work."

"I won't hold my breath, but yes, please."

I hugged her around her shoulders before I moved back to my chair, and the rest of our time went by without another mention of Florida. We talked a little bit about the boys, how they were doing in the yard before I left, the classes they had registered to take that fall, where Nick was traveling next for work, and some drama he had with some of his co-workers. All surface stuff. Both of us completely avoided the initial topic.

We walked out of Better with Age lost in our own thoughts. Kari was headed in the opposite direction to pick up a few things from the local grocery store while I was headed toward home. We hugged and said, 'See you later,' but instead of our usual light-hearted banter, there was a heaviness around us. We both knew it was possible there was another "See you later" coming. One that would last longer than twelve hours.

What would life be like without my best friend two doors down? How would it feel to wake up every morning in a bed that isn't mine? How would uprooting the life I'd spend decades building here in

Madison affect me, emotionally? It's easy to point a finger at Kari's inability to travel away from our town, and not so easy to admit my own reluctance to start over, to face my own fears of failure head-on.

Who would I be if I stepped outside of the walls I'd built to shield myself from any more change?

6

"HANDLE WITH CARE"
THE TRAVELING WILBURYS

About a block away from Better with Age, I decided to call my dad. He picked up right away, as he usually did for me.

"What's up, Tiger?" I could hear water running and the clatter of dishes being stacked in the drying rack.

"Dad, I have had the strangest day."

"Well, any day that starts with your parents banging down the door at eleven a.m. is bound to be strange, sweetheart."

"Well, that too. But after you left, I went outside and did some gardening, and after Kari's boys showed up—oh, by the way, I totally called that one. They did end up having to do some penance yard work for me."

"That's good news. What on Earth did they do to deserve that severe a consequence?"

"Very funny."

I detailed the excellent job they'd done covering their family room with an entire Hallmark store's worth of gift wrap. My Dad's chuckle rumbled over the phone line.

"Anyway, right before they got there, Uncle Mike called."

"What did he have to say?"

"I don't even know where to start. But, basically, he called to tell me that he and Chris are moving in together."

"Isn't that the best news? Your mom and I are so happy for him. Both of them. I'm so happy to hear the contentment in his voice again."

"I feel the same way. Soooo... He had even more to talk about."

"Oh yeah?"

"Yeah," I laughed. "So, with him moving in with Chris, that big house full of furniture becomes quite a bit to deal with. And, um, the point of his call today was to ask me to come down to Florida and stay in his house while he decides what to do with it."

The clattering stopped. "Oh, wow. Wow. That's an exciting prospect. How long would you be in Florida?"

"I'm not really sure. He said it's an open-ended invitation."

"What do you think you're going to do?"

I switched my tote bag from one arm to the other and rolled the tension from my shoulders. "Well, the timing of his call is a little... coincidental considering all the *loving lectures* I've been getting lately about shaking things up in my life. I suppose it would be a good opportunity for me to get a change of scenery, and if I'm there long enough, avoid shoveling my driveway all winter."

"Florida definitely has its benefits. Which way are you leaning, Tiger?" The water turned off, and a moment later, I heard the clink of ice falling into a rock glass. It was time for his nightly dose of apple juice. So predictable.

"I'm not really sure. I've only had this information for a few hours now, and right after I got off the phone with him, I walked down and hopped into Kari's two o'clock class. I thought I'd work my way through it in between sun salutations, but I didn't get anywhere. I ended up staying for a second class, and then we walked over to Better with Age and talked for a little bit, but I don't know. I don't have a whole lot of clarity about it right now. I definitely think I'm gonna have to sleep on this."

"That seems like a good idea. Things always seem a bit clearer after a good night's rest. And remember, what the caterpillar calls the end of the world, the master calls the butterfly."

"You know I'm a sucker for a Richard Bach quote. That one always finds me right when I need it most. I do feel a bit like I'm in the second round of being a caterpillar, waiting for my wings to grow, but I don't know if I'm gonna stay put on this little... bush or if I'm gonna spread my wings and fly. And if I do, what will I be when I get there?"

"Here's the good news. You don't have to make a decision tonight. You don't even have to make a decision tomorrow. Did my brother tell you how long you have to think about it?"

"He said to take as long as I need, but I'm guessing he'd rather know what he's gonna have to deal with sooner rather than later."

"Yeah, he's not the most patient guy. He's probably waiting for you to call back right now."

As I got closer to my house and past the line of bushes, my yard came into view, illuminated by the two dozen solar lights I'd installed a few years before. "It looks like the boys did a pretty good job out here. Everything is cleaned up. They put all the equipment away and managed to not burn the place down."

"That's definitely a step in the right direction. Well, it sounds as if you have had yourself quite an interesting day, love. I'm glad you got some things accomplished today and Matt and Alex were able to come over and get that yard work done for you. I bet that feels like a huge weight off your shoulders."

"Huge. I'm no spring chicken, Dad. This was never more obvious than on this walk home. My quads are not cut out for back-to-back yoga classes. Especially with Kari leading them."

"If you're no spring chicken, what does that make me?"

I walked up the stairs to the porch, set my bag down on the table, sat down on the swing, and pulled my feet up next to me. "I don't even want to talk about it, but I'm so grateful that I always have you to bounce things off of, and you're always able to be a sounding board without trying to make my decision for me or pressure me one way or another. It's nice to have someone to talk to that can remain neutral. I do know one thing. If I end up staying in Florida for a while, I'm gonna miss you guys so much. I don't even know how I would begin to say goodbye."

My dad is quiet for a moment. "I'm thinking the very same thing. It definitely won't be easy, but I'll tell you this. I surely wouldn't mind having somewhere to visit over winter break. Who knows? We might be down there ringing your doorbell before you know it."

"Is that a promise or a threat?" I laughed. "Anyway, I think I'm gonna take the next few days to think everything through. God, I hate making big decisions on my own."

"While I've always been proud you inherited my madcap, devil-may-care view of the world, make jokes in light of serious situations, and laugh at inappropriate times, you are always careful to weigh all your options before making big decisions. And I know for certain this time is no exception. I'm confident you're going to make the best one for you this time, too. And if you hate it there and get homesick, you can always come back. My brother will understand. I'm certain of it."

"Kari actually said the same thing."

"That doesn't surprise me one bit. Great minds think alike."

"They certainly do. I've really appreciated picking your brain and talking through all of this tonight. And I know regardless of what I decide, I'm still going to be in a better position than I was when I woke up to the doorbell this morning."

"Oh, yeah, that reminds me. We need to put new pajamas on your Christmas list this year."

"Well, nice pajamas haven't been much of a focus of mine for a while, Dad. But, thank you for noticing—and caring."

"Hard not to notice the ancient potato sack you were wearing when you answered the door this morning. You have a good night, Tiger. And if you need any more perspective on this, you just call me right back and I'll be here for you.

"And maybe give your mom a call so she can give you her perspective as well. We tend to complement each other with our advice. I have a pretty good idea of what she's going to say, but I'm sure she'd like to say it to you herself."

"Thanks, Dad. I appreciate you more than you'll ever know."

"Oh, I think I do know, sweetheart. I'll talk to you later."

We said our goodbyes and hung up. After taking a few more moments for quiet reflection that resulted in very little insight, I unfolded myself from the swing, picked up my bag, and walked into the house. On the kitchen counter, I found the journal I'd left on the porch next to a note thanking me for the cash and telling me it wasn't as hard as they'd expected.

"That's what she said," I whispered to myself, my throat tight thinking about their impending departure and, very possibly, mine.

After letting Roxy out, I walked around the kitchen collecting the gardening gloves, empty glasses, and slightly damp paper towels the twins had left in their wake.

Even this. I'll even miss their mess. Ugh. This day has been wild. How do I make the decision whether to leave this house behind for months and live somewhere that until now has been a week-long vacation spot?

Within twenty-four hours, I had my answer.

7

"CRASH INTO ME"
DAVE MATTHEWS BAND

Because I had spent a little bit of time folding the mountain of laundry on my bed, when I woke up to sunshine streaming through the space between my blackout curtains, I decided to go golfing after I finished my work for the day.

I headed for the course at twelve-thirty and rolled up to the starter early for my last-minute tee time. The course was pretty empty, so I was lucky enough to be able to go off as a single, and as soon as he gave me the go-ahead, I was off and rolling for the first tee box. It was that gorgeous mild-mannered temperature that feels imperceptible on your skin, and it was late enough in the day that the gnats had gone off to wherever gnats go when they're done making our mornings miserable.

Things were going pretty well, considering I hadn't golfed in over a week, but by the third hole, my round had gone completely off the rails. So when my phone rang, and I saw that it was Kari, I put an AirPod in and answered right away. I could tell things were not going well at all based on the yelling in the background.

"What's up?" I asked, lining up my drive.

"*Well, they've finally gone and done it this time.*" she shrieked. Outside of her tone, her voice sounded a little frantic, and I assumed by 'they', she meant Matt and Alex.

"What happened now?" I was expecting more of their usual rubber band around the kitchen sprayer pranks. Boy, was I about to be surprised.

"The good news is, I've been saying for a few years that we need to replace our kitchen cabinets. The bad news is, at this very moment, there is a Camry in my lazy Susan. Or where it *used* to be, anyway."

"*What?*"

"Okay, I need to calm down." I heard my friend take a few shaky breaths in and blow them out slowly.

I took my swing and hit the ball, but had no idea where it went. I headed back to the golf cart, my mind racing.

"So apparently, Matt texted Alex and said I had asked them to move the car into the garage. When Alex got into the car and started pulling it into the garage, Matt jumped up from the back seat and scared the shit out of him."

"Oh. My. God. Are they ok? What happened?" I was standing behind the golf cart with my hand frozen on the grip of my driver which was halfway into my bag.

"They're fine. Alex stomped on the accelerator and the car jumped forward and is now in my kitchen. So, it looks as if we have a major rebuilding project on our hands. Exactly what I was hoping for right before I sent them off to college. It's perfect, actually, now that I think about it. I might start packing their bags now to calm myself down."

I got back in the cart and made my way toward where I thought the ball had gone. "What do the boys have to say for themselves?" I asked as I began my fruitless search.

"They're smart enough to have been mostly silent for the last half an hour. As soon as I heard the loud crash, I instantly knew it had something to do with them. When I ran downstairs and saw the front of the boys' Camry sticking out of my kitchen wall, I almost lost it right there. I think they knew at that point that they had definitely taken things too far because I just stood there staring at them through the windshield. Matt was speechless for once, and Alex looked like he was about to burst into tears.

"They have been sweeping and basically doing a bunch of nonsense that won't matter in a few days, but I think they're trying to keep busy so I don't drop them off at the fire station or smother them in their sleep."

"I guess the good news is they leave for school in a matter of weeks. At that point, they'll be the resident assistant's problem. Assuming, of course, they don't destroy anything while they're there."

"Don't even talk like that. I'm really hoping this is what teaches them to finally rein in the pranks. I'm all for putting plastic wrap over the toilet lid and rubber bands around the spray handle in the sink and all of that. I've grown used to it, but now we've gotten to the point where they're doing major damage to our home, and I am *over* it."

"I don't blame you one bit. I'm feeling a teensy bit guilty that I have been such a terrible influence with the pranks. It started out as a good way for me to bond with them, but I can see they have taken it way too far in the last few months."

"Don't blame yourself. They're old enough to know better."

"I don't even know what else to say, Kari. Have you spoken with anyone about what all of this is going to entail?"

"Well, I immediately called our insurance agent, and I'll be surprised if they don't drop us after this. They told me to get some quotes from a few construction companies and send them over. In the meantime, our house is uninhabitable.

"They will cover a hotel stay for us until the repairs are complete, but I'll be honest with you, there's zero chance I can be in a hotel room with these two right now. There's no way all four of us would come out alive. And I *just* replaced the kitchen appliances. I *cannot* believe this."

"Why don't you stay with me? I've got plenty of room."

Kari was silent for a moment. Only measured breathing could be heard from her end.

"While that sounds like boatloads of fun, you'd need to really consider all sides of that scenario, Paige. You have to concentrate on your work, and you're trying to write a book, and you've got your own things going on right now. I don't think it's the best idea for my entire family to be underfoot 24/7."

Fair point. I do like my kitchen the way it is. Sans car.

"Why don't you make some calls so you can get the estimates started, and we can catch up later tonight." I realized I'd been sitting next to my ball in the fairway for the last few minutes and looked behind me to make sure I wasn't holding anyone up, then got out of the cart, grabbed a club, and swung. The ball sailed into the rough along the right of the fairway, missing a sand trap by inches. "We'll figure it all out together. We always do, right?"

"What time is it? Two o'clock? Dammit, it's too early to open a bottle of wine."

"It's *never* too early for that when there are teenagers involved, but maybe get your calls done first. Look at me being the voice of reason."

"Terrifying. Ok, I'm going to go, but I'll catch up with you later, and I don't know, maybe I'll crash at your place tonight."

"No pun intended, I hope. But, yay. Sleepover. Actually, just head over now if you want to make phone calls from my house. Let yourself in and shut the alarm off, and I'll be home after my round. I'm on the third hole, and it's pretty slow here, so I imagine I'll be home by five at the latest."

"I might do that. I can't even look at these two right now, and I can't concentrate on what I need to do next with a

Camry sticking out of my kitchen wall. I'll see you in a few hours."

A small laugh escaped in response to the mental picture she'd painted, but I instantly realized the error of my ways. "I don't mean to laugh. It's... well, when it's not my house, it's funny."

"Be careful what you wish for because they might be *living* at your house."

"I'm not worried. They're probably going to tone it down a bit now that they've realized their actions have real consequences."

"Yeah, we'll see about that. Ok, get back to your round, and I'll see you when you get home. I'll be the one on the porch with the giant wine glass in my hand."

8

"EXILE"

TAYLOR SWIFT AND BON IVER

I spent the rest of my time at the course thinking about Kari, hoping she was getting through all her calls. I was a little distracted, but I was the only one out there on a Monday afternoon. I had some time to think about what it would be like having Kari and her family at my house while they were getting theirs repaired.

As strange as it was to even consider not so long ago, I had sort of gotten used to being alone. It had been a while since I had had teenagers in the house and all the chaos that comes with them. I started wondering if I had spoken too soon in offering to let them stay with me.

As I made my way through my round, one disastrous shot after another, it occurred to me how random life was. Sometimes, the universe sends you signs for the direction you're supposed to be going, but if you don't listen, the signs get bigger. Car-sized, one might say.

On the eighteenth hole, a text notification buzzed, then moments later, a second one. I checked for another golf cart behind me, then, finding I was still alone, pulled my phone out of its holder. Anna and Jason were texting in our group chat.

We had FaceTimed the night before and Anna had told us
she was still waiting to hear if the research project her co-op
had proposed would be approved for funding by the university.
My eyes scanned the first two texts before my fingers flew over
the keyboard in reply.

> Anna: My research co-op budget was
> approved!

> Jason: That's great news, sis. What's next,
> then?

> Oh, honey! I'm so proud of you. You're going
> to do great things, I know it. My daughter, the
> oncology researcher!

> Anna: Thanks, guys. The research director
> contacted me a few minutes ago and said we
> will be ready to begin our next trial as soon as
> the plan is approved. I'm going to be pretty
> busy for the next few months, but I'm so
> happy to finally be a part of something that
> could change people's lives for the better.

> Jason: Not just could. It will, especially with
> you on the team. So proud of you!

> You're going to make history, sweetheart. I
> wish I could give you a big hug! Have you told
> your dad?

> Anna: …

> Jason: Does he even know you applied for the
> co-op?

> Anna: I texted him about it in May and I got a
> thumb's up emoji. So…

> I'm sorry, honey. Your brother and I are
> insanely proud of you, as are Papa and
> Meema.

Anna: I know. It doesn't really bother me as
much anymore. He's the one missing out.

Jason: Yes he is. I don't even bother anymore.
It's not worth the emotional energy.

> I wish I were as emotionally mature as you
> two.

Anna: You're doing great, Mom. You're going
to write your book, it'll become a blockbuster
at the theaters, and you'll become the next
Nora Ephron.

> From your lips to God's ear.

We chatted for a little longer about Anna's upcoming clin-
ical trial and the new snag in Jason's current design project, but
I didn't feel ready to tell them about Uncle Mike's request. I
wanted to focus on Anna's news without turning our conversation into a "me" thing. But by the time I left the golf course, I
was pretty sure I knew what I was going to say to Kari when I
got home, but first I needed to call my mom.

She answered on the first ring, which she always had.
Sometimes it feels like they are sitting by the phone waiting for
me to need their help.

After our usual chatter about my morning, my golf round,
what she had for breakfast, and which to-do list item my dad
had successfully avoided all morning (it's a gift), I filled her in
on my conversation with Uncle Mike the day before.

"I'm sorry I'm just coming to you with this now. I called last
night, and you were at the food pantry, so I ended up talking to
Dad, but I wanted to get your take on this. I'm assuming he told
you about my conversation with Uncle Mike?"

"Yes, your dad was eyebrow-deep in one of his smut books
when I got home, but he eventually gave me a quick overview

on his way to get a snack, the benevolent prince that he is. So? What are you thinking?"

"If I'm being honest, an hour ago, I really wasn't sure what I wanted to do," I admitted. "It's so strange to think I have a six-bedroom waterfront house at my disposal for the foreseeable future, but do I really want to be away from my *home* for the next few months? And the twins... ugh. It's like losing another piece of myself."

One of the many things I'd always loved about my mom was her ability to sit patiently while I poured out every thought and then sifted through them as she waited.

"It would be really nice to have a change of scenery, though. And the boys are leaving for college in a few weeks, anyway. But after the call I got from Kari this morning, I think I may have already made up my mind. That being said, I wanted to talk it over with you because you understand me so well and I trust your opinion."

"I'm dying to hear what Kari could have possibly said to prompt you to make a decision so quickly."

"Let's just say that the boys have extended her garage by a few feet into their kitchen, and there's a good chance they'll all be staying at my house for the foreseeable future. And we all know how these major construction projects go. Considering the amount of damage she described, it could be a pretty long time, so I'm thinking I may head down to Florida now. Just until they're back in their house. If Kari stays at my house, I know everything will be taken care of, and I can concentrate on *myself* for a little while."

"Honey, I hate to think you might not be in the same town as us for a few months, but frankly, I'm relieved to hear you're thinking about your next steps; you've been frozen in the same place for so long. It was hard enough on you after Mark up and left out of nowhere. Your Dad and I loved spending all that time with Anna while you got your feet back under you, but...

Well, you've been particularly stagnant since she left for school. For three years, you've barely left the house other than to golf or occasionally do yoga with Kari. You'd always been so active. Social. Fun. I never thought I'd long for a little fake vomit on my kitchen floor. Your Dad and I miss you, honey. We miss the Paige from before that asshat walked out the door and stole your happiness. And you know you can never get around what you've got to go through."

"I know. I know." I shifted in my seat and yanked on the shoulder belt that suddenly felt like it was choking me. "I'm going to go home and check in on Kari. I would rather focus on her life right now."

"Okay, honey. You know we just get worried. But give us a call later. Your dad will be eager to get the details on what's going on with Kari once I get him caught up. Let us know if she needs any recommendations for a general contractor. We still have the number for the company we used when we finished the basement and converted the first-floor den into your dad's 'man cave' two years ago."

"Oh yes, the man cave. A.K.A. the giant Harlequin Romance library."

"Yeah," she laughed. "No matter what he wants to call it, that contractor took your dad's vision and carried it out beautifully. So, if Kari needs a builder she can trust, I would easily recommend ours. I'll text you his number this evening."

"Thanks, Mom. I appreciate you."

"You're welcome, honey. I'm going to let your dad in on what's going on. He's been hearing one side of this conversation, and he keeps gesturing and whispering. I have no idea what he's saying, but I'm going to go make a late lunch for Mr. Nosey, and I'll talk to you shortly. Funny what he can hear when I'm not asking him to *take the garbage out*." She said that last part in a way that made it obvious that it was a reminder of a previous request.

"If he's listening to one side of this conversation, he's probably coming unglued," I laughed. "Have a little fun with him first. Say hi to him for me, and feel free to stop by later if you want."

"Sounds good, honey. Talk to you soon. Love you."

9

"LANDSLIDE"
FLEETWOOD MAC

Before I went home, I drove by Kari's house so I could survey the damage. I saw Matt and Alex deep inside the garage, sweeping debris into enormous piles. It seemed like an impossible undertaking, but they were probably trying to stay busy and out from under their mother's eye.

The mangled, drywall-garnished Camry was backed up in the driveway, and I could see a large, jagged opening from the garage to the kitchen.

I beeped the horn as I rolled up, and the boys turned around and loped over to my car.

"I love what you've done with the place. Is this what they call an open-concept garage?"

"Hi, Aunt Paige," said a glum, unamused Matt. He took off his gloves and pulled the brim of his baseball cap down lower, then glanced back up at me. He looked morose. Humbled.

Alex couldn't even meet my eyes. "We really did it this time."

"Sounds like you did, but hopefully, this will be a learning experience for you—albeit an expensive one. And the good news is, you're leaving for college in a few weeks, so you'll be able to escape relatively soon."

Matt breathed out through pursed lips. "Yeah, our mom is super pissed."

"She can't even look at us," added Alex. "She wasn't even yelling at first. That was the worst part of all. When I crashed through the wall, the drywall slid off the windshield and my mom was staring right at me from the other side of the kitchen. You know that saying, 'if looks could kill'? It was the scariest thing I have ever seen."

I put my Jeep in park and hung my elbows out the window, resting my chin in my hands. "Oh, I can't even imagine. Your mom's pretty intense when she's mad, and you *know* you're in *big* trouble when she's silent."

"I think she's at your house right now. When you get home, can you just let her know that we were over here cleaning up, and there were sweat and tears and a little bit of blood? Maybe a few blisters?"

"Yes, I will definitely let her know that you're over here working your fingers to the bone, cleaning up your mess. If you need anything, just come over and grab it out of my garage. But maybe don't drive over."

Matt squeezed the brim of his hat, a nervous habit he shared with his brother. "Haha, you're hilarious. At least someone is able to joke about this. On that note, I'm getting back to work before she looks over here and sees us standing around." He turned and ambled back toward the garage, picking up a rogue piece of drywall along the way.

I looked back at Alex. "Luckily, I can joke about everything that doesn't directly pertain to my own life, so that's a blessing."

He finally made eye contact with me, his contrition evident. I hoped it would last for the few weeks they had remaining until they left for school. "We'll see you later, Aunt Paige. Thanks for not yelling at us."

"I have a feeling you'll be hearing plenty of that when your dad gets home."

"Oh, God, don't remind me. On that note, I'm going to get back to work."

As I pulled away from the curb and started a slow loop around the block, I had an epiphany.

MY ENTIRE ADULT life had been spent in loving service to others. Learning how to operate something more advanced than a hotplate (albeit, just as well) so I could cook dinner for my new husband. Sacrificing caffeine, alcohol, and my smooth, unlined skin so I could give my unborn babies the best start in life (which, of course, required me to satisfy my only craving—frozen cheese pizza). Breastfeeding for two years each. God, how I missed my young, perky breasts. Somewhere along the way, I had gone from a 34B to a 36Long, and although Mark had always assured me he loved the body that had grown and nurtured his children, *I did not.*

I had driven thousands upon thousands of miles to practices, games, matches, meets, sectionals, and state competitions. I had cheered on innumerable teams until my throat was shredded. I had hosted business dinners and birthday parties and Thanksgivings and Mark's loser sister who thanked us by stealing my prized first edition copy of *The Mists of Avalon.* I often hoped she choked when she got to that *one* scene. Not to death. Just enough to maybe throw up. I watched my husband—to whom I had given my youth, my body, and my trust—walk out the door without a word of explanation. He left me to slip through the surface that had once felt solid, but with the swoosh-click of our front door closing behind him, became a gossamer net at the top of a waterfall. Down I slid, tumbled, thrashed. Not caring about the sharp rocks at the bottom until a hand reached out to save me.

Anna.

She was sixteen, at the height of the awkward, sullen teenage years that had clouded our idyllic relationship, but emotionally mature enough to know she needed help, and most importantly, where she could find it. She spent so much time with my parents for those first two weeks, but one night after they dropped her off (and of course came in to scratch and cluck around our house and load the dishwasher), Anna climbed right into my bed. She laid facing me, her legs pulled up to her chest, mirroring me, and slid her hand into mine. My tumble down the waterfall, over, and while my identity had taken a critical hit, my purpose became clear. I was going to get my kids through whatever came next in as close to one piece as I could manage, and in doing so, would heal myself. Presto-chango. So super easy.

If only.

But, I could honestly say that the kids turned out pretty solid. Despite a few bumps and bruises, Jason and Anna grew up to be very loving *and* very driven. There's something to be said for overcompensating.

Fast forward four years, and while I'd poured out so much of myself into my children to fill the void left behind by their father's departure from our family unit, what remained was no longer enough to hold myself together. Pieces of me floated away unseen (but not unnoticed) every day.

And all of that was fine. Good. Expected (minus the loser sister). I sacrificed it all for the people I loved, and I would do it all over again. But seeing the wreckage in Kari's garage, pieces of sheetrock everywhere, spread from the kitchen to the drive-way, it opened up a little window somewhere inside of me. A breeze blew in, and on it came the whisper of a message.

"Time to find the pieces of you that were lost along the way."

So what had seemed unlikely, improbable, impossible a mere seventy-two hours before became my answer to the bidding of my soul. It was time to find out who I was in this phase of my life, and I was hoping that my new persona included *published author*.

There was only one way to find out. It was time to dress for my second act.

10

"BABE (I'M LEAVING)"
STYX

I headed home and found Kari sitting at the kitchen table with a pile of papers in front of her, her elbows on the table, and her head in her hands.

"How's it going there, love?"

Her head lifted. Her spirit, not so much. "I'm not even really sure where to begin. I called the insurance company back to update them. I have two builders who actually answered the phone and can give me an estimate next week."

"Oh, that reminds me; I stopped by your house and the boys are working their fingers to the bone."

She rolled her eyes, but did not respond.

"On the way home from the course, I called my mom and she is going to text me the number for the builder they used for their house. She wants to make sure you have someone you can trust."

"I really appreciate it. That guy was awesome. If I can find an estimate that isn't completely outrageous, we're going to have to get started right away, but I'm not really sure what the short term plan is for us." She started shuffling the papers in front of her from one side of the table to the other.

I took a deep breath and slowly let it out. "That's where the universe is working its magic here, Kari, because I've been thinking a lot about that call from my uncle yesterday and what I'm going to do. The boys' prank seems to have helped me make that decision."

Kari stopped shuffling papers and turned in her chair to face me.

"I think what I'm going to do is have you guys move in here while your repairs are underway. I'm going to head to Florida and see what I can make of my life in a different zip code."

"Paige, I—I hate to drive you out of your house, and I really hate the idea of you being so far away."

"The thing is, you're not really driving me out of my house. This whole situation is propelling me to make a decision, and maybe it's just inspiring me to make one sooner rather than later. And for me, that's never a bad thing. I do tend to suffer from a little decision paralysis."

Kari scoffed. "A *little?*"

"Fine. A lot. But why don't you talk to Nick and see how he feels about you guys staying here. And, look at it this way, at least you'll be able to keep an eye on the progress over at your own house. Maybe if you're two doors down, they'll be more likely to keep their foot on the gas. No pun intended."

Kari chuckled, but then quickly sobered. "I don't know what I would do without you. I can't even think about you not being here every day. *Especially* during the winter when you'll be lounging around in the Florida sun."

"I don't know how much time I'll have for lounging; I *do* still have to work. But you can always come and visit. I'm probably going to get lonely down there. I can't be hanging out in Uncle Mike's love nest with him and Chris every day."

Kari gave me a knowing look and tilted her head to the side, much like Roxy did every time I asked her if she wants a piece of cheese.

"I think we both know once you get down there, you're never going to want to leave. Not for any length of time anyway. So we'll see what happens, but I'm pretty certain you and I already know how this is going to play out."

"Kari, be serious. There's no way I'm staying in Florida. Especially not where my uncle lives. I'm a copywriter, not a tech CEO, remember? I'll probably be back before the end of September."

"By the end of September, it'll be fall, and there's no way you're coming back here for winter, but sure, okay, we'll see what happens." She sighed and put her head down on her arms folded on the table. "I'm going to miss you."

I reached over and rubbed her back. "I'm going to miss you too, but once the boys leave for school, you can escape and come visit me for as long as you want."

Kari lifted her head and looked at me; the rarest of tears shone in her green eyes. "Remind me how many bedrooms that house has."

I laughed, picturing an endless slumber party with my best friend. "Plenty, and you're welcome any time, assuming, of course, I end up staying that long."

"Mm-hmm," said an unconvinced Kari.

With that, a text notification chirped. My mother had sent over the number for their contractor.

"I'm going to send this number over to you, then I'm going to run upstairs and check my email, but you go ahead and make as many calls as you need to. When I come down, we'll figure out what we are going to do about dinner. I haven't cooked for more than myself in quite a while, so maybe we can make dinner together tonight."

"That sounds wonderful. Just like old times."

"I'd prefer to not eat burnt grilled cheese and watery tomato soup like old times, but we'll play it by ear." I laughed, remembering all the times Kari and I had tried—and failed—to cook on a hotplate in our dorm room. Back then, we thought we had it all figured out. We'd finish school, start our careers, get married, have a couple kids. Easy peasy, right?

What the hell did we *know?*

11

"WEIRD GOODBYES"
THE NATIONAL

Three days (and many tears) later, I had packed everything I thought I might need for several weeks and was standing on my driveway with Roxy, Kari, Matt, Alex, and my parents.

"Please be safe," my mom said in her standard-issue worried tone.

"If you run into any trouble, give us a call. Is your AAA membership up to date?"

"Yes, Dad. Thank you. I called and checked on it yesterday."

Kari looked at me, emotion clouding the dark ring around her army-green irises. "I don't know what I'm going to do without you being two doors down. We've lived within blocks of each other for almost half a century, and now you're going to be hundreds of miles away. I know it's what's best for you, so I'm trying to not be selfish and think only of my own needs. It's just going to be so hard."

I put my arms around her. I wished I could make both of us happy at the same time, but even though I could feel my heart clawing its way through my sternum to escape this fresh wave of loss, I knew I was making the right decision for me.

"We're going to miss you a lot, Aunt Paige. And who's going to protect us from our mom when our pranks go off the rails?" asked Matt.

"There won't *be* any more pranks," Kari said through her teeth.

"You boys are going to be leaving for college before you know it. Any pranks you have will be someone else's problem at that point, so you better be careful. Not everyone is going to be as patient with you as your mom and dad."

"I know," they said in unison.

"I knooow," I sing-songed back.

Kids always know, don't they? Until they don't.

My dad walked over to my Jeep and peered through the front passenger window. "Do you have snacks packed?"

"You know I do! Two kinds of cheese, three kinds of flavored water, four kinds of chips, six chocolate bars, three peanut butter and jelly sandwiches—"

"—and a partridge in a pear tree!" my dad cut in.

"Feels like it," I laughed. "I have bowls to give Roxy water. I have her leash. I have updated her tag on her collar, and I think we're ready to go, as hard as that is to say."

"I'm excited for you. Today could be the first day of the rest of your life, Tiger." My dad was back to his post next to my mom, rubbing his hand up and down her back.

She was standing statue-still at his side, uncharacteristically silent. I gave her a hug first because I could sympathize with how she was probably feeling. I'd been through it three times, if you counted when my ex-husband left. "I'll see you guys before you know it. And you can come and visit me anytime. There's nothing holding any of you back from a beach vacation in Florida!"

"You've got that right!" My dad bumped my mom with his hip and wiggled his eyebrows up and down at her. "We have a cruise coming up here soon, but we will be down shortly after that."

Alex knelt and put his arms around Roxy. "Are we invited, too? We'll be good, right, Matt?"

"Yes. We *promise* to keep our shit together."

"Language!" chided Kari.

I couldn't help but laugh. "Yes, you can come down whenever you want. *Please* do. I'm not going to know anyone down there other than my uncle and Chris, so I'm going to need some visitors."

"You can count on us," said my mom. "Like your dad said, we will be down there after our cruise. We leave as soon as his summer session at the university is over. Once we get down to Florida, we can help you meet some people."

I could picture my mom bossing perfect strangers into a super awkward friendship with me.

"That sounds great, Mom. Let me get settled, and then you can begin your campaign."

My Dad chuckled quietly behind his hand, but not quiet enough to escape notice. My mother shot him a look that could melt titanium, but her gaze softened as she looked back at me.

"We are so excited for you, honey. Truly."

"Thanks, Mom." I wrapped my arms around her and squeezed. She relaxed in my embrace, which I took as my cue. "Okay, guys, I'd better hit the road before Roxy has to stop and go potty in an hour."

My dad stepped forward and wrapped me in his familiar embrace. "Are you going to stop anywhere along the way?"

"Yeah, I think I'll stop at Mammoth Cave and maybe again somewhere in Georgia, but I'm not sure. I'm going to get as far as I can when I leave Kentucky tomorrow. I am just hoping to make it to Paducah tonight before it's too late. I don't love driving in unfamiliar places in the dark."

"Please keep us updated on your progress, and we will be

thinking of you. Turn your location on so we can keep track of where you are." My mom's voice broke and her eyes started to well up with tears. I hated doing this to them, but for the first time in a really long time, I felt completely in control of my own life, despite all the lingering questions hanging over my future steps.

"Will do," I assured them.

I gave each one of them a hug, ruffling Matt and Alex's hair as I let them go.

What a difference a week can make.

One Saturday, I woke up with nothing but more of the same ahead of me. By the next Saturday, I had a whole new adventure laid out before me, and it was starting at that very moment.

12

"LEARNING TO FLY"

TOM PETTY & THE HEARTBREAKERS

By that night, I had made it to Mammoth Cave in Kentucky, and checked into a hotel that had fallen into some disrepair since I'd stayed in it twenty-five years earlier. I laid away half the night, jumping at every sound, convinced the room was haunted. Roxy growled at what I hoped was nothing in the corner until the sun finally came up and we could reasonably hit the road for the day.

Once I was through the drive thru of the first fast food restaurant I could find, I pulled around into the parking lot and called my kids to let them know I was ok. When we'd hung up a few days before, I could tell they were concerned about my state of mind; I didn't normally make rash decisions to pack up and leave town for an unknown period of time.

Once we were all on the line, Anna was first to speak. "Mom, what is going on? Are you really on your way to Florida?"

"I am, honey. I'm in Kentucky right now and I'll probably stop for the night somewhere in Georgia. I didn't get a whole lot of sleep last night. I'm pretty sure the ghost in my room was happy to see us leave."

Jason couldn't mask his concern. "Ghost? *What?* Mom, seriously. What is going on? Is this some kind of midlife crisis? We talked to Papa and Meema last night and they told us you were fine, but I—*we*—can't help but wonder what the heck is going on."

"You guys. I love you so much, and I appreciate your concern, but I'm perfectly fine, or at least I think I'm on my way to being fine. It was well past time for a change, and this opportunity felt like divine intervention. I'm trying to be positive and I'd love it if you could have a little faith in your old mom. Ok?"

Anna sighed. "Fine. Fine. We have all the faith in the world in you, but we worry about you just the same. Jason and I love you and want you to be happy, but this just feels a little extreme. Jay? Do you have anything to add?"

Jason took his typical beat before responding, then sighed. "We love you, Mom. If you're happy, I'm happy. We are worried, but you've always made pretty solid decisions and we all need to let you have some space to make this one if you feel like it's the right one for you."

"I *do* feel like it's the right one for me at this point. And, honestly, what could it hurt? If I get down there and realize I hate it, I can go back to Madison. I haven't made any permanent decisions. I'm just staying in Uncle Mike's house for a little bit, not permanently leaving the country. It's going to be ok. *I'm* going to be ok."

Anna, my little worrier, finally relented. "Then we will keep our worrying to ourselves, but will you please keep us updated throughout your trip and let us know when you get to Uncle Mike's?"

"Of course. Now tell me what you've both got going on this week."

We resumed the cadence of our typical Sunday call, and we hung up after I expressly promised to keep them apprised of my progress for the rest of the trip. I polished off my breakfast sandwich and washed it down with the coffee that had cooled while I soothed my children's nerves. After taking Roxy for her last walk for the next two hundred miles or so and climbing back into my Jeep, I adjusted my rearview mirror and stopped for a moment to look at the woman in the reflection.

There were lines on my face that hadn't been there when I said "I do." Or when I wrestled a ramrod-straight toddler into a carseat. Or when I strapped butter-soft pink leather shoes onto a tiny ballerina's foot, moments before her first recital. Those days seemed endless at the time. All I'd ever known was raising kids, and it was the only way I identified myself that even mattered. That badge of honor had been worn alongside that of 'wife', and in the happier days of my marriage to their dad, we'd shared the responsibilities of raising them. Not always evenly, but joyfully, and we'd felt like a team. I thought we were happy.

How easily those happier times were discounted. Easily cast aside for... I still don't know what.

But, in the end, that loss had taught me a lesson, one that was reinforced as I dropped my second, and last, college freshman off at the airport. The only person I could count on to always be there was staring at me in the mirror in a Hardee's parking lot, but I didn't even know the person I was looking at. My marriage had spontaneously combusted and I'd been carrying its ashes around for... too many years. My children were off living their lives; I'd done my job.

But what have I lost in the process? If I got it back, would it even fit me anymore?

13

"I CAN SEE CLEARLY NOW"

JOHNNY NASH

Two days and thirteen hundred miles after my journey began, I was driving over the Courtney Campbell Causeway, headed into Clearwater. Roxy sat in the passenger seat with her blonde head out the window, her eyes half closed in obvious bliss, her ears blowing wild in the fresh, saltwater air. Her front feet tap danced on her seat, and her pink tongue hung free, catching endless sun rays as they fell unencumbered all around us. To my left, a multi-colored patchwork of towels and bathing suit-clad beachgoers flashed by as jet skis zipped back and forth along the coastline, sea spray momentarily occluding their riders with each turn.

It felt apropos to end this long journey by crossing a bridge, and I prayed the joy that swelled in my chest with each mile was a sign of things to come. It felt like a beginning. Of what, I wasn't sure. But in the center of that joy was a sense of peace, and from that peace, a new confidence grew. I switched from my audiobook to a local classic rock station, and as I drove across the Causeway, the feelings of fear and loss I'd carried around for years began to fall away, and in their place was something new... hope.

As the monument at the end of the Causeway welcomed me to Clearwater, I knew I'd find some clarity during my time there. Perhaps I'd even find the Paige I was meant to be next.

I was excited to meet her.

ROXY COULD CLEARLY SENSE my nervous energy as I drove down the gravel road that separated my uncle's house from the Intracoastal Waterway. The dance she'd perfected on the drive over the Causeway had reached a frenetic 'Dog of the Dance' pace, and I had been forced to strong-arm her off my seat and back into her zone multiple times.

"We're here, Rox. What do you think? Could you see yourself here for the next few months? Are you a beach puppy?"

She gave a short bark in reply and relocated to the back seat for only a moment (of course, slapping me in the face with her tail in the process) before returning to her co-pilot position.

I picked a few of her tail hairs out of my mouth and laughed. "I'm going to need to get my Jeep detailed next week, so get all the hair and drool out of you now, please."

Three city blocks down the road, I could see my uncle's house. The patina of the copper gutters and downspouts, which had always been my favorite part of the exterior, complemented the pale pink siding. Mature palm trees shaded Chinese Hibiscus along the edges of his property, and crepe myrtle wrapped around the patios and sunroom that faced the water. The symphony of their unique (yet somehow related) scents swirled through my open window and surrounded me. The salt from the air settled on my tongue. That, I knew. That felt familiar.

When I reached the private road that led to their driveway, I could see Uncle Mike and Chris standing at the back of the house. Tipped off by my location I'd shared with them that morning, they were waiting to serve as my official welcoming committee.

I pulled in and put the Jeep in park as Uncle Mike sprinted around the passenger side to let Roxy out. She jumped down from her co-pilot chair and landed at his feet, a frantically waving tail demonstrating her excitement. The stillness of the Jeep let in a blast of heat and humidity, and I took a deep breath, relishing the briny, aromatic notes on the breeze that drifted through.

"I'll never get tired of that smell!" I exclaimed.

"Never say never," my uncle laughed, "remember, it changes with low tide."

"Ohhhh... right. Well, it's a fair trade in my book."

Uncle Mike stepped around Roxy who spun in circles at his feet, and placed his hands on the passenger seat. I cringed, looking at the layer of golden retriever hair his hands were resting in, but he didn't seem to notice.

"Welcome to Florida, sweetheart! We are so happy you decided to come down for a bit. I give it one week before you decide you'll never leave! Now, let's get in the house before we all melt into a puddle in the driveway." He reached down and grabbed my purse, and when he closed the door, I took a moment to let the moment wash over me.

This is the first day of the rest of my life.

14

"TODAY MY LIFE BEGINS"

BRUNO MARS

Stepping down into my new world, I found myself face-to-face with Uncle Mike and Chris. It never ceased to amaze me how different they were, both in personality and appearance. Where my uncle was tall and thin with a clean-shaven face, brown wavy hair, an easy, breathless laugh, and green eyes identical to my dad's, Chris was... softer. Quieter. He stood at my uncle's side, his freshly shaven head barely clearing his shoulder. His thin, Roman nose crinkled above a wide smile, and his brown eyes sparkled under the glorious bushy eyebrows that had apparently made the rest of his hair hide in shame. They were, of course, both dressed to the nines.

"We are so delighted you're here, Paige!" Chris said, stepping forward first to wrap his arms around me.

I returned the hug. "I'm thrilled to be here. I'm still a little shocked, I'll be honest, but I'm excited to at least spend some time here with you. I really have no idea how long I'm staying, but I plan on exploring as much as I can while I am here."

Uncle Mike, not one to be left out of a hug session, stepped in between Chris and I and enveloped me in an embrace that rivaled a cozy blanket and felt like home. "I am so happy you're here," he whispered as he rubbed my back. "You're in for the adventure of a lifetime. Are you ready?"

We separated a bit, but he gripped my shoulders and looked into my eyes. The love I saw there caused a ball of emotion to bubble up and settle behind my eyes.

"I am," I choked out, and he released me just before my emotions spilled over. I swallowed hard as I looked around for Roxy, who was surely going out of her mind in her new environment.

She was running back and forth across the coarse grass, inspecting the myriad of new smells at her disposal. When she started chasing a lizard that wasn't looking to spend his last moments as a chew toy, we took it as a sign to move our little reunion indoors.

We made our way down the Unilock paver walkway, past the explosion of tropical foliage and expansive stamped concrete patio that surrounded the in-ground pool and hot tub. Uncle Mike held the back door open for us and we all walked into the house. Roxy bounded off to explore the new environment, while I was not quite as impervious to my immediate surroundings.

No matter how often I visited, the sight from the foyer never failed to take my breath away. A custom-painted three-dimensional mural covered every wall in the foyer, down to the other end of the long, bright hallway we were standing in, and continued up the stairs. Hand painted in tropical colors and featuring graceful herons, realistic flowers, and lush greenery, the walls were an endless expanse of art that changed with each new Easter egg I had discovered since it was finished ten years before. Stealthy lizards hiding under leaves. Nests bursting with downy-feathered baby birds, yellow beaks open wide in anticipation of their next slithery meal. Shadows that camouflaged a sleeping squirrel.

The thick, gleaming dark walnut banisters curved up the staircase to my left, and the floors that led to the front of the house shone with a fresh coat of wax. I could see the bay sparkling through the glass-paned door at the end of the wide hallway we were standing in.

Uncle Mike, seemingly immune to the charm he'd lovingly crafted, was the one to break the spell. "Let's go sit in the kitchen. Are you hungry?"

"I could eat," I replied. "We drove the last two hundred miles without stopping so we could get here. Let me run to the bathroom real quick. I'll let you decide on lunch while I'm gone."

"You got it, stinker. Grilled cheese and tomato soup work for you?"

"Ummmm have we met? Melted cheese and buttery carbs are my love language."

"Three grilled cheese sandwiches and soup coming right up. You know where the powder room is."

I stepped into the tiny bathroom off the kitchen, and not a minute too soon. My bladder had been protesting against all the coffee I'd been drinking during the final thirty miles of our journey, and was well aware that we'd arrived. After relieving myself, I took a good look in the mirror. The sight that greeted me was familiar, but not at all the same as the one I'd last seen in Madison.

Despite the two-day journey and fitful sleep in an unfamiliar hotel bed the night before, I looked refreshed. My cheeks had a glow I hadn't seen in many moons.

Who am I kidding? Years. What kind of witchcraft is this?

I ran my hands through my newly tamed hair. My pixie cut had returned to some semblance of an actual style. I hadn't realized how much the neglect of my appearance had affected my mental health. It seemed the further I sunk into my apathy, the less I cared about how I looked, and the focus I placed on looking like the Paige I recognized in the mirror, the less I cared about anything else. I had caught myself in a vicious cycle of physical and psychological neglect, but with a few snips of the shears and a few (dozen) strips of wax, I was finally starting to recognize my reflection. I couldn't honestly say my mental state was back to that of the old Paige, but I felt a lightness in my chest that was vaguely familiar. It was fighting for space amid my self-doubt and my anxiety over being neck-deep in the unfamiliar—and it was swiftly gaining ground.

I bent to splash water on my face, then put my hands on either side of the sink and looked myself square in the eyes.

At every pivotal moment of my life, my dad had always given me the same advice. "Take the next right step," he'd say, as if it were that easy. It wasn't until my ears were old enough to listen that I understood.

In that bathroom mirror, I was Paige, but changing. I had taken the next right step and found myself there. Where would the next right step take me?

I was ready to find out.

But first, grilled cheese.

15

"A HEAD FULL OF DREAMS"
COLDPLAY

We sat around the enormous white marble counter in the center of the kitchen. I immediately noticed that my uncle had made some updates, and I was sitting on one of them.

"I am a fan of these new chairs!" I said as I spun on my high-back bamboo barstool. "This palm leaf print is so chic. I approve."

Chris turned from the Viking range (also new) and held his arms out. "Your uncle was so excited for you to see everything he's done. He's too modest to brag, but this kitchen has been short-listed for ELLE Decor's 'Coastal Chic' 35th Anniversary Edition coming out next spring. He's hoping to hear back in the next couple of weeks."

"Uncle Mike! This is incredible news. I am so, so proud of you. I love the clean white with pops of color." I turned in my chair more slowly to take it all in. My eyes landed on the back-splash that separated the glass-fronted white cabinets and expansive countertops that flowed around the walls of the twenty-by-fifteen-foot kitchen. I could see from where I sat the textured glass tiles were custom—and expensive. A gasp slipped through my lips. "Are these Tiffany blue?"

My uncle had always had an eye for design and had built a successful business using that talent, but never liked to brag about it. He blushed a light pink that perfectly matched the background on the artwork that hung behind him next to the window above the copper farmhouse sink.

"It is. These are just a few ideas I threw together on Pinterest. It's no big deal."

"No big deal? Are you kidding me? Look at this place! This is going in the Yelp review. 'Ten out of ten. Highly recommend.'"

I had a true gift for making people squirm, but I thought it best to not bite the hand that was literally feeding me, so I changed the subject. Instead, I filled them in on my journey to Florida and the creepy hotel I'd stayed at in Kentucky, and how Roxy had barked at basically nothing in the corner all night and scared the shit out of me.

After lunch, Chris walked around the counter and started picking up our plates.

"Why don't you guys go out and walk the property and chat while I clean all this up?"

"That's a great idea. Lunch was perfect, by the way," Uncle Mike said, then walked around the island to give an unsuspecting Chris a bear hug as he washed our dishes.

Back outside, we spent several quiet moments watching Roxy revel in the sunshine and fresh air. As the three of us passed the fragrant jasmine that climbed the trellis on the side of the house, I raised my arms above my head and turned around in a slow twirl. "This is so beautiful. Every time I come here, I hate to leave."

My uncle paused as I twirled one last time, picked a gardenia bloom from one of the planters that lined the stone walkway, and tucked it behind my ear once I came to a stop. "And now you don't have to for a long time. This is an open-ended invitation and I want you to stay as long as you would like. I was thinking maybe you could get acquainted with some people and make a few friends here. It should help you feel a little more settled. And while I'm on that subject, you living in my house gives you full access to my membership at the country club."

"*Squee!* I love it there. Do you think we'll have a chance to golf together this week?"

Roxy barked in response to my high-pitched reaction, and Uncle Mike laughed. "We've got a pretty full schedule at the store. New fall apparel is starting to come in; a few collections from a new bespoke brand Chris found last time we went to Chicago Collective at the Merchandise Mart. But I think I can carve out a few hours to golf with you."

"That would be so great! You can introduce me to everyone there, and I won't feel quite so awkward."

"I have a feeling you're going to fit right in there, honey. I actually know a few of the members of the ladies league; a couple of them run businesses by the shop. But let me talk to Chris and see what day I can sneak out for a few hours. I'll call the pro shop tomorrow morning. Actually, I'll call them on my way back to Chris'—whoops. *Home.* That's going to take some getting used to. Anyway, I'll call the pro shop and let him know you're staying here in case you want to go before you and I have a chance to."

The conversation about the country club membership reminded me of another less-fun topic we needed to address. I looked around to make sure Roxy was still nearby (she was shoulders-deep in a lavender bush along the front porch). I breathed in slowly through my nose to clear my anxiety, then let it out in a rush of words. "*Idon'tfeelrightaboutstayinghereforfreewhileyoucoveralltheexpenses.*" Uncle Mike stopped short and spun to face me where I stood. Frozen. I took another, more controlled breath and began again. "The electric bill must be through the roof. Please let me at least cover my own utilities. I'll still be working while I'm here, and I have some money in savings. It will help me feel less like an interloper."

His blue eyes crinkled at the corners as he flashed his trademark boyish grin. "Sometimes I forget you're a big girl now. If you think you can handle it, I won't argue with you. I'll leave some past bills on the counter. Take a look and then we'll talk. On that note, let's walk down to the water and then back to the pool. I need to point out a few things you need to keep an eye out for. For starters, the new maintenance guy will be by. He usually cleans up the yard and checks for any damage and wear and tear from the salt water that beats on this house nonstop."

We walked the rest of the property and chatted here and there, interspersed with me calling for Roxy when her exploration took her beyond my line of vision and Uncle Mike pointing out things I needed to be aware of. This plant needed coffee grounds and frequent pep talks. That board at the end of the pier was getting loose. Those bushes hid the most lizards, and the herons knew it. "And from the looks of it, Roxy knows it too." Uncle Mike wheezed as he propped his hands on his knees and bent over with laughter. I didn't need to search long for what had set him off; a blonde streak of fur passed us by, in hot pursuit of an iguana whose afternoon nap had been disturbed by a black snuffling nose.

We followed their trail around the pool and sank down into the plush lounge chairs along its edge.

I kicked off my flip flops and laid back with my arms behind my head. "I will definitely be enjoying this pool."

"That is a huge benefit of living in the South. You get a lot more use out of things like pools and country club memberships." My uncle threw caution to the wind, swung his Louboutin-clad feet onto his cushion, and sat back.

As we sat there listening to the fountain trickle into the pool, Chris came out.

"Are you ready to go home?"

Uncle Mike looked at me. "Are you ready for me to leave you alone here? Maybe you can get your stuff unpacked. We'll help you carry everything up to the master bedroom, then we'll be out of your hair."

"You'd never be in my hair, but yes, I'll be fine here. I'll probably order some dinner and head to the grocery store later."

Uncle Mike stood and stretched. "Okay, sweetheart. Can I just say how happy I am to see you sitting here with me, knowing you're staying for a long, long while?"

I shielded my eyes from the sun as I looked up at him. He was positively beaming, and his joy fell all around me.

"I am thrilled to be here."

From a bush next to the garage, Roxy barked.

"Sounds like Roxy is thrilled as well. Let's get your bags upstairs so you two can get settled."

UNCLE MIKE and Chris left for Dash of Flair, but not before carrying all three of my sixty-pound suitcases upstairs and leaving the number for the country club and a few utility bills on the counter.

With nothing but time on my hands, I headed upstairs to get myself unpacked. The closet, bureau, and chest of drawers were all empty, and I didn't even want to think about how long it must have taken my uncle to move his extensive wardrobe. While Roxy dashed around in a haphazard figure eight, investigating every corner, I took a moment to appreciate all the changes to the main bedroom.

It was apparent that Uncle Mike's redecorating had extended beyond the kitchen; the bedroom that had once been a vibrant salmon color with splashes of white and green against white rattan furniture now gave off a 'den of relaxation' vibe. The tall windows that met in the corner of the room were covered in heavy navy blue velvet curtains, pulled back to expose pristine, bright white sheers. Beyond the window directly across from me was a veranda that comfortably held a bistro table and two chairs. The impossibly tall mattress on the ornately carved dark mahogany four-poster bed was topped with a plush sand-colored linen duvet. The bed was clearly hand-constructed and perfectly matched the heavy wooden desk, dresser, and chest of drawers. The walls were painted a shade of blue so dark the night itself could disappear into them.

Avoiding the temptation to curl up on the bed and bury myself in the sea of navy, light blue, and white pillows that beckoned me like lazy early-morning waves rolling onto an empty beach, I was able to get myself unpacked and organized without much fuss. Within thirty minutes, I was back in the kitchen, going through the fridge and pantry to see what I needed from the store.

I looked around and found a list on the counter with nearby places I might need, such as the libraries (yay!), a few independent book sellers in town, and the grocery stores. I'd seen one of the names on the list plastered all over the reusable shopping bags in the pantry, which made my decision a lot easier.

After a quick trip to the store for the essentials, I unpacked everything into the fridge and pantry, loaded my golf clubs back into the Jeep, put the country club into my GPS, and off I went.

As soon as I walked into the pro shop, I knew exactly why my uncle had chosen this club. Rather than the typical 'Aunt Gertrude's couch' patterned carpeting, the floors were mahogany, waxed to a high shine. Each breath carried with it a whisper of orange, and modern, copper light fixtures shone down on tables of well-merchandised, branded golf apparel. I was thrilled to see a large section for the ladies (which any female golfer knows is a rarity).

After a quick spin through the racks, I walked up to the pro behind the counter. He was about my age with salt and pepper hair covered in a navy Titleist hat that matched his polo. It was clear he took full advantage of his employee discount.

"Hi, I'm Mike Turner's niece, Paige. I'm staying at his house, and he mentioned he'd called to add me to his membership."

A flash of recognition and a smile passed over his face and settled in his denim blue eyes. "Nice to meet you, Paige. I'm Dan, the assistant pro here." He reached across the counter and shook my hand. "Yes, I spoke to your uncle myself. Welcome to the club! If you have a few minutes, I can show you around the facilities, the women's locker room, and the grill." He walked around the counter and beckoned to a young man to take over for him. "How long have you been playing?"

"About twenty years, and I'm very active in my ladies' league. Do you have many female golfers here?"

"First, remind me to get you a card for range balls. Feel free to come by anytime to hit a bucket of balls. And to answer your question, we do have a very active ladies' league. Actually, our Tuesday league plays at seven a.m. tomorrow. Interested?"

I couldn't believe my luck! Golfing with the ladies' league on my first full day in Florida. "Absolutely. Sign me up."

We continued the tour, and Dan stopped occasionally to introduce me to a few members and employees of the club. By the time we made it back to the pro shop, I was ecstatic. "What do I need to do to play with the league tomorrow?"

"There are some forms you'll need to fill out," Dan explained. "They're all online, so if you give me your email address, I can get them over to you. Here's your range card." He handed me an emerald green plastic card with an ornate palm-tree-themed logo on the front. "I hope we see you tomorrow. It's a great group of women. You're going to fit in perfectly."

"I will definitely be here tomorrow. I'll get the forms filled out as soon as I get home, but I'm going to hit the range first."

"Absolutely. Have fun out there, and I'll see you tomorrow morning."

After writing my email address down on a notepad he handed me, I thanked Dan for his helpfulness and headed out to hit some balls.

As I set my golf bag against the rack behind my station at the range, excitement quivered low in my belly.

Less than twenty-four hours into this little adventure and I already have something to add to my dance card.

THE REST of the day was relatively uneventful. I took Roxy for another walk, then flipped through the utility bills my uncle had left for me on the counter. Once I had a good idea of what I would need to cover every month, the afternoon stretched endlessly in front of me. The call of the pool was growing louder, but it was almost five o'clock. In the spirit of bucking tradition, I decided I would turn the tables and call Kari. I needed to catch her up.

"*Hey there,*" I practically shouted when she answered the phone.

"*Well, hey there, yourself,*" she shouted back with equal enthusiasm. "I was just sitting down to call you. I almost forgot you're in a different time zone. How are you, new Floridian?"

"I'm mostly settled in. I unpacked, went to the grocery store, and stopped by the golf course."

"Wow! It sounds like you're all set then. Did the grocery store have Pop Tarts and Hot Pockets?"

"Har de har har. I actually bought some of these weird

green leafy things. And cheese. But, yeah, it's been pretty smooth so far. I'm thinking I'll spend the next few days trying to get acclimated and hopefully meet some people. I don't have to work for the rest of the week, and the ladies' league meets tomorrow, so I think I'm going to join them. How are things going on your end?"

"First, let me say I'm so proud of you for jumping in with both feet. You'll have to let me know how things go with the league tomorrow. As for what's going on here, we've gotten a few estimates, and the insurance company is just waiting for us to choose a contractor. The timeline they've given me is two to three months, but we all know what that means."

"Two to three years?"

"Pretty much. I don't know how long we're going to be here, though, Paige. That's what I'm most worried about."

"Honestly, it doesn't really matter. You stay there as long as you need to, and if I decide to come back from Florida before they're finished, I'll be more than happy to just slide right into the spare bedroom. With the boys leaving for school soon, it'll just be you, me, and Nick anyway, so I wouldn't even worry about it."

"Okay, well, I do worry about it, but thank you for everything you're doing for us right now. Allstate will be covering the cost of our interim housing, so I'll send you that money every month. And no, it's not up for debate."

"Whatever makes you feel better, but you're my best friend. This is what we do. And besides, I feel a little responsible for teaching the boys all those pranks. Who knew my mischievous nature would transfer over with my eggs?"

"If only we'd known..." Kari quipped, but I knew it wouldn't have made a difference. "No, this is *not* your fault. These are two seventeen-year-old boys who let something go a little bit too far, and that's just how seventeen-year-old boys are. Their frontal lobes aren't quite developed yet, and we *all* have to suffer the consequences. They're going to be busy paying off the deductible on this insurance claim, as well as the difference in our new premium. It's going to take them a while to do that, but we gave them through next summer to pay it back because right now, we want them to concentrate on school."

"When are they leaving?"

"Twelve days. I can't even believe it. It's going to be so quiet around here once they go."

"You're preaching to the choir. I am staying in a house hundreds of miles away because of how quiet my own house was."

"Who knows. Maybe you'll decide to stay, and I'll pack us up and follow you."

"I wouldn't complain about that."

I felt a nudge on the back of my leg and looked down to see Roxy's sweet little face looking back up at me. "I'm going to take Roxy for a walk. She's giving me the eye, and I'm sure there are a few salamanders she'd like to chase outside, so let me know if you need anything, and I will talk to you soon."

We hung up and after convincing Roxy everything she'd found to chase would still be here when we returned, I took her for a long walk down our road and back. We came back hot and sweaty, and unable to wait for one more minute, I rinsed off under the outdoor shower and dove into the deep end of the pool, shorts and all. I rolled onto my back and with my arms leading the way, kicked to the other side. When my fingertips touched the edge, I let my lower body sink until my feet touched bottom and only my head remained above the water. I rubbed my arms, the salt slick under my hands. I breathed in.

Low tide was coming.

16

"KODACHROME"

PAUL SIMON

Unable to contain my excitement, I was up and out the door at six the next morning. I hadn't swung a golf club in nearly a week, so I decided to go a little early and hit some balls on the range before jumping into a cart to show three women I didn't know how rusty I was.

The golf club was only twenty minutes away, and when I pulled into the driveway, I turned off the radio after an American Idol-worthy duet with Stevie Nicks (as Tom Petty of course). I hopped down, grabbed my clubs from the back, and headed around the back of the building to look for the pro shop.

After about thirty minutes on the driving range, I decided to roll some balls to check out the speed of the greens. When I turned around a few minutes later, there were a couple ladies already chatting and putting their clubs in their carts.

I figured it was as good a time as any to meet some of them.

One of the women putting her clubs in the second cart back in the line looked to be about my age and the other a little older, so I walked up and introduced myself.

"Hi, I'm Paige." I mentally shook my head. For someone who was paid for her choice of words, that skill did not translate well to in-person communication.

The older woman turned toward me. She began tucking her bright, multicolored floral top into her equally bright pink golf skirt. "Hi, Paige. Are you new here?" Her gravelly voice threw me for a moment. It was equal parts chain smoker and phone sex operator.

"I'm visiting kind of on a long-term basis, and I decided to join the ladies' league so I could meet a few people."

"It's nice to see a new face around here. I'm Grace Thompson. I've lived in this area all my life, and right now, I'm in one of the condominiums along Clearwater Beach. This is Elyse," she said, putting her hand on the shoulder of a woman who looked to be about ten years younger and almost a foot taller than me. "She's riding with another of our friends, Cat, who usually runs up to the first tee box at five after seven. She owns a café that she needs to open in the morning, so we give her a little bit of grace."

Elyse turned and faced me, raising her right hand in greeting. She was wearing a sleeveless golf polo and the artwork on the arm she'd raised was on full display, although I was only able to catch a few pieces—a tree and a fireman's axe—without looking like I was staring. "It's nice to meet you, Paige. Grace was our third wheel today, so why don't you throw your clubs in her cart, and we'll roll as a foursome."

I put my hand out and shook Elyse's while Grace picked up my clubs and strapped them in behind the passenger side of the cart. Within a few minutes, twenty or so women were paired up in golf carts, ready to go. Grace and I climbed into our cart and turned to continue chatting with Elyse while we waited. She sat in the driver's seat, alone.

"Dan usually lets us go off on hole one," Elyse explained.

"He knows Cat will be here just in time to tee off, and he doesn't want her dodging everyone else's golf balls to get to us. How long have you been playing?"

"About twenty years; I started when my kids were little. It was a great excuse to get out of the house for a bit on the weekends, then a few years later I was able to sneak out while they were both in school. It's been a love-hate relationship ever since."

Elyse nodded her head in agreement. "I hear you loud and clear on that last part. Lately, it's been more hate-hate for me, but I'm trying to push through the pain. It's the one time my stubbornness pays off."

The starter motioned us over, and we headed to the first tee box, climbed out, and grabbed our drivers. Grace pulled a neon yellow sun hat down over her spiky, platinum hair. I couldn't help but picture it looking like a tinfoil hat after a round in Florida's heat and humidity. I stifled a giggle just as I saw Elyse driving up to the tee box behind us, with a woman I could only assume was Cat in hot pursuit. I knew we were going to be fast friends when I saw the devious smile on Elyse's face as she looked over her shoulder while rolling to a stop.

"I've had some periods when I didn't golf as much," I continued as I looked back to Grace, "but since my kids have left for college over the last several years, I've definitely been golfing a lot more than usual."

Grace briefly broke eye contact with me to glance back at our playing partners, who were engaged in a playful shoving match now that Cat had caught up.

"Children!" she chided, then turned back to me, probably realizing it was hopeless to rein them in at that point. "Well, my kids left for college a few *decades* ago, but I'm typically out here on league day, and I also play two or three rounds throughout the rest of the week. I keep myself pretty busy."

Elyse had disengaged from Cat and was walking up to meet

us on the tee box while forcing wavy hair that didn't appear interested in cooperating into a ponytail. She was followed by Cat who was holding both of their drivers and trying to goose her with one of them.

"Good grief, you two. Cat, this is Paige. She's staying in Dunedin for a while and trying to meet a few people while she's visiting. Luckily, you two knuckleheads are on your best behavior." She rolled her eyes, but her sarcastic tone was dressed in affection.

"Hey, nice to meet you, Paige. How long will you be visiting?" Cat reached into the back pocket of her yellow golf shorts (which coordinated perfectly with her yellow and white striped shirt), pulled out a matching bandana, and tied it around her head, topping the whole ensemble with a baseball cap that was a lovely pastel green... just kidding. It was yellow.

"I'm not a hundred percent sure how long I'm staying, but I'm trying to get the lay of the land and meet a few people in the process. I work remotely, which will help a lot. Oh my gosh, we've been standing here forever. How do you decide who tees off first?"

Elyse bent over, holding her sides as she laughed. "This day could *not* get any better!" she squeaked out as she stood up straight. "Grace, Paige *mustache* you a question!" She and Cat doubled over with laughter as Grace fought off her amusement, the left side of her mouth quivering upwards. "I try not to engage when they're like this, or it takes us five hours to finish a round, and we hold up the entire field. So, to answer your question, whoever hasn't waxed their mustache in the longest time starts us off. It's a real honor."

Cat snorted. "The competition gets really hairy!"

Grace huffed and then chuckled. "Well?" she prompted, looking back at me.

"I'm going out on a limb here, but I'm guessing I'm not first," I said as I looked at each of the other three women. I didn't feel like we'd reached a point where I could examine them for facial hair, but I did mentally thank one-week-ago-me who had taken care of all personal grooming appointments before leaving Madison.

"It's always me," said Grace. She stepped up to the front of the tee box, then put her tee in the ground and left a ball behind on top of it in one smooth motion. "These two have a laugh at my expense every week, but I've embraced my menopausal mustache. These two have apparently never heard of that old adage that begins, 'She who laughs first....' You can go after me, and we'll let these two duke it out next."

Grace swung the club, sending her ball into the air straight toward the green. "Looks like you're my good luck charm today, Paige. You're up."

My first shot and every shot after it was as smooth and easy as the conversation between Grace and me as we made our way through eighteen holes. I filled her in on the higher-level details of my life: the kids, my chosen singleness, my parents, and Kari. We talked about her daughter, Sarah, who was thirty-five, married with two small kids, and worked as a social worker at a local middle school. She told me about her son, Bill, who was thirty-three, also married with two kids, and owned a successful business, Bill's Body Shop, in Dunedin.

"Raising the kids with William was an adventure, but he was always so supportive of my career. I turned my love of books into thirty-eight years of running a few of our local libraries. William and I got married the same year I started behind the desk as a staff librarian, and there were times he practically raised our kids on his own while I worked on a few of my passion projects. My dreams were always as important to him as they were to me."

She paused as we pulled up to our next tee box and kept her eyes on the group ahead of us as we waited for them to make it to the green. "He's been gone five years now, and I miss him every day." Her husky voice broke as she continued. "I stayed on as the head librarian for three more years, but my heart wasn't in it anymore. I've been retired for two years, and it was a big adjustment, but I eventually returned to the hobby I'd taken up when the kids were younger, and that's been keeping me pretty busy."

I didn't have the opportunity to ask her to elaborate as the group ahead of us was finally putting, and she changed the subject back to me as soon as we returned to the cart. As we pulled up in front of the cart barn forty-five minutes later, she turned to me and smiled. "Are you in a hurry to get home? We usually stay for lunch afterward. You're welcome to join us."

"I'm off work until next week, and I love lunch. Actually, I don't discriminate against any mealtimes; they're all my favorite. You've sold me." I was grateful for a chance to get to know them better. I'd been enjoying their company and wasn't in a hurry to get back to the house for a staring contest with my dog.

We settled around a table in the grill and, one by one, took off our hats and giggled like school girls at the state of our hair. Nothing is more humbling than removing your hat in public after eighteen holes in the heat and humidity. It turned out my prediction about Grace's tinfoil hat was a hundred percent accurate, and, having just met her, I fought off the urge to share my observation.

When Elyse took hers off, the ponytail holder that had been straining to maintain some sense of control over her mass of hair saw it as its cue to split, and while most of it was weighed down with sweat and settled across her shoulders, the rest was waving and dancing to rave music only it could hear. Other than being brown instead of blonde, it reminded me of Kari's mop of thick, wild hair. I'd been watching her try to tame that beast for forty-five years, and she'd recently given up the fight and let it live in whatever dimension it had been intended to.

Elyse gave up trying to turn the volume down and pulled a turquoise ponytail holder off her wrist. "I always have a few backups," she told me with a wink. "What brought you to the Clearwater area? I'm sure you already told Grace while we were out there, but she doesn't allow a lot of time for chatting."

"Well, it's kind of a long story."

"We love long stories," said Cat, who had removed her own hat, leaving the folded bandana covering her close-cropped hair. "I don't have to be back at the café until one, so as long as it's not two hours long, I've got plenty of time."

"Ok. My kids, Jason and Anna, are mostly grown. Jason lives in Boston and works for an architectural firm, and Anna is a junior at Washington State. She's studying to go into Oncology research. It's been hard having them so far away, especially being single, but we make time every Sunday to catch up with each other via FaceTime."

The ladies all nodded in understanding. I continued, "My uncle, Mike, owns a home here, and he called me last week with a bit of a bombshell. He's moved in with his life and business partner, Chris, and he asked me to come down and stay in his house for a bit. As luck would have it, the very next day, my friend-slash-neighbor in Madison had a little teenager-related incident involving a car and a new entrance to her kitchen from the garage—"

There was a collective gasp from my captive audience and a muffled chuckle from Cat.

"—and I took that as my cue to accept his offer. My friend and her family are staying at my house for the time being. And here I am. I have no idea how long I'm going to stay, but with the kids all grown and living in other states, I'm not in any hurry to get back."

Elyse's jaw hung loose before replying, "Ummmmm... that seems like an easy decision to me. You don't have to shovel sunshine," to which Grace and Cat nodded their heads in agreement. Elyse slapped the table in front of her. "Do your uncle and his partner happen to own a clothing store?"

"Yes! They own Dash of Flair in downtown Dunedin."

"I know them well. The bookstore I run is right across the street from their shop. They're good people."

"The best. I'll stop in your bookstore next time I visit them."

"Please do! There's a lot to do in the area and I've got some maps I like to hand out to visitors and new residents. Stop in any time."

We paused to peruse the menu, but Grace, Cat, and Elyse seemed to already know what they wanted. Luckily, it was mostly standard golf club fare, and I was able to find my trusty stand-by lunch choice within moments.

"Yeah, the Wisconsin winters are pretty rough, but I've been there all my life, so I should be used to it. But, I'm getting a little tired of the winter weather now that it's just me; if I ever see a snow blower again, it'll be too soon. Aside from that, my family seems to think I need to make some major changes in my life, and my well-intentioned mother is probably home in Madison right now crafting lists of all the ways I could improve my life. So, yeah. I've been a little unmoored since my kids—and husband—left."

Cat picked up her menu, took a picture of the bottom of it, and moved it to the pile formed by Grace and Elyse's on a corner of the table. "When my son, Sam, left for college almost ten years ago, I was in the same position. I'd been a single mom for a few years at that point and had no idea what to do with all the time I suddenly had on my hands. I ended up opening the café within a few months, and it has been an adventure. Over the last few years, I've been able to hire some local women who really needed a job, and that freed me up to do some traveling. Sam eventually moved back to the area and opened up his own law practice, but I can completely understand the feeling of being washed out to sea. I'm glad you decided to give things a go in Florida. I think you're going to love it here."

"Who's your friend?" asked the waitress who had just arrived at our table.

"Laci, this is Paige. She's staying in Dunedin for a bit and hopefully—" Elyse looked pointedly at me, "will be joining us on Tuesdays. Paige, Laci is another local native. You'll probably be seeing a lot of her."

I awkwardly raised my hand in greeting. "It's nice to meet you."

"Likewise! What can I get you for lunch? And before you ask, everything on the menu is my favorite. Our chef is one of Cat's former cooks and she is a wizard in the kitchen!" She winked at Cat who nodded her head and beamed with pride.

"I think I'll have the club sandwich this time," I said. "On sourdough if you have it. And an ice water."

Laci nodded and scribbled down my order.

"Good choice. I'll have the same, as usual," agreed Grace.

"And Caesar salads for the two of us," said Cat, motioning to herself and Elyse. "And no lemon in Elyse's water."

"Of course. You know, Elyse, we don't actually let the lemons roll around on the floor of the kitchen."

Elyse chuckled. "I don't know that for sure, and I am not taking any chances."

The corner of Laci's mouth bent upwards in a barely concealed grin. "Three ice waters with floor lemons and one without. Got it." She pretended to pick something up and dust it off, winked at me, and left the table, returning a few moments later.

"How did you ladies play today?" she asked as she set four sweating glasses down on the table. She counted out straws from the pocket on her crisp, green apron and set them where our menus had been stacked.

Cat stretched her arms above her and leaned back. "Only lost eight balls today. Two better than last week."

"That's good to hear. You're probably paying one of the pro's salaries with all the golf balls you buy here." She winked at Cat who beamed with pride. "I have to ask," she continued, turning her attention to Grace, "have you received any alien communication today? That's quite a hat you've got there," she deadpanned. Then, as if she hadn't just thrown a shot at my playing partner, she turned on her heel and walked back toward the kitchen. "Those will be right up for you," I heard her say over her shoulder.

Grace ran her fingers through her hair in a fruitless attempt to return it to its full, spiky, platinum glory. "Laci's a real sweetheart, but she's got a sarcastic streak that would make Vince Vaughn blush. I wish she golfed, because she'd fit right in with us out there."

"Luckily she's a reader because we also get to enjoy that sense of humor at book club," pointed out Cat.

"I definitely want to come back to that topic, but first, I have to ask. It seems like everyone knows everyone else around here." I swept my pointer finger around the table. "How are you all connected?"

Elyse spoke up first. "My bookstore is down the street from Cat's café. I met her when I was picking up a catering order for a book signing several years ago, and we hit it off immediately. When I found out she golfed in college, I invited her to league *several times* and she finally relented. She's been an enormous pain in my ass ever since." She dodged a balled-up straw wrapper Cat threw at her. "You missed. Anyway, I met Grace here at the club; we've been golfing together for years."

"And I met Cat the same way, at the café. I was picking up a lunch order for William and me shortly after she opened almost ten years ago and she was running back and forth manning the register while cooking. I was so impressed with her moxie, I instantly knew we would be friends, whether she wanted to or not. I'd been trying to get her to the golf course for a few years when Elyse finally showed up with her."

My curiosity got the best of me. "What changed your mind?"

Cat's face clouded over for a moment, but quickly recovered.

"It's hard enough being a female golfer, let alone a Black female golfer." She looked across the table at Elyse. "But she was relentless, and—"

"I'm like water on a rock," Elyse cut in.

"You'd give an aspirin a headache." Cat spun back to me. "Like I was saying, she was relentless, and would stop in every single Monday, pick up a Caesar salad, and invite me to league the next day. One Monday, as she left with her lunch, I decided I couldn't take it anymore. I'm tenacious, but Elyse takes it to a whole new level.

"So, the next Monday, there she was with her twenty-dollar bill and her damn puppy-dog eyes. I wish I had cameras in the café just to play back her expression when I finally said, 'Fine. I'll come, but only if you promise to let it go after this.'"

"I was stoked. I knew she'd fit right in if she'd give us a chance. And was I right?"

"You were. As usual."

They shared a smile that began in their eyes, any involvement of the rest of their face was completely extraneous. I could see the depth of their friendship in that one look.

Cat picked up her phone and began tapping away on it. We sat watching her, waiting to see if she had more to say on the subject. She must have registered the silence because she looked up and set her phone down on the table. "I noticed some new items on the menu and I was texting the chef to tell her how damn proud I am of her. She's come a long way in the last six years."

"And she has you to thank for that," Grace said, then covered Cat's hand with her own, her blue eyes softening. "You've changed quite a few young women's lives through your mission at the café."

Cat looked down at an imaginary spot somewhere near her edge of the table. She slid the bandana over the back of her head, refolded it, put it back on. When she looked up, her dark green eyes pooled with emotion. "It's been pretty great, hasn't it? I love seeing them light up during the interview when they realize I'm going to give them a chance with little to no experience. They've been kicked around by life for so long, an outstretched hand is a rare but welcome sight."

Grace gave Cat's arm a gentle squeeze, then sat back in her chair. "And now you're doing the same for our sweet Jenna." She looked across at me. "The young lady that runs the register and does the baking at Cat's is a longtime Dunedin resident who's had a not-so-easy life."

Elyse crossed her arms and scoffed. "That's putting it mildly."

"She's almost painfully quiet and reserved, but found her way to Cat's open interviews after her last cashier left to maitre de at our local Italian restaurant, Café Alfresco. Yet another of Cat's success stories. So, back to Jenna, who walked in for an open interview and won over Cat's heart within five minutes."

"She drew the rest of us in just as quick. I love that kid," added Elyse.

"What are you, a hundred? She's twenty-six, hardly a kid." That sarcastic jab earned Cat a bit of delayed retribution in the form of her own balled-up straw wrapper. A direct hit to the left cheek. Elyse snorted, then slapped the table so hard our silverware jumped and clattered back down.

Grace put her palms together and thrust her arms between their faces. "You two are in your forties and behave like toddlers. Cat, you need to learn to take a compliment." She turned to her left. "Elyse... excellent aim." She looked at me and shrugged as if to say, *If you can't beat 'em, join 'em.*

Elyse stuck out her tongue at Cat, who rolled her eyes and flicked a sugar packet back her way. It landed short, slid across the table, and dropped into Elyse's lap. "Missed again."

"Anyway...," Cat said, drawing out the last syllable, "When she told me she'd gone from her parents' house to her marital home and had never had her own money, I was done. A few months after she started, my baker left to open her own catering business, and when Jenna saw me struggling to find her replacement, she offered to help out. She'd been baking at home since she was a young girl, and let me tell you. That woman knows her way around a springform pan. My business has grown by fifteen percent since she put that apron on."

"Sugar, you lucked out with that one. What a dynamo," said Grace. "She's been opening up a little at book club, too."

"Okay, tell me more about this book club." Again, I couldn't believe my luck. I'd met and golfed with three fun people I could see myself spending time with, *and* they were readers?

"We meet on the third Thursday of every month in various locations," replied Grace as she pulled a compact from her kelly green crossbody bag and wiped off the runaway eyeliner that had not held up to the humidity. "My daughter, Sarah, is also a member, as is Jenna. If you're a book lover, you have to join. We're actually meeting at the library this Thursday night at six. Do you like to read? Are you free Thursday night?"

"I am an avid reader," I assured her. "I pretty much read every spare minute I have, and I have absolutely nothing on my calendar for the foreseeable future."

"Then it's settled," said Cat. "Give me your phone and I'll put my number in it."

I dug my phone out of my bag and handed it to her while we talked about the book they'd be discussing that week. I was relieved to find I'd already read it and had more than a few points I'd love the opportunity to discuss. A few moments later Cat handed my phone back to me and hers began to ring.

"I called myself from your phone; save my number as Cat St. James. I'll text you later with the details for this week's meeting. So, what do you like to do for fun other than reading and golf?"

At that moment, Laci returned with our food. After depositing each of our choices in front of us, she took a deep bow, swept her arm in front of her, and said, "League and Lunch Ladies, please enjoy your meals. I will leave you to it."

She straightened up again. "Grace, how did your hair get worse? I think I hear the mothership calling me." As she started walking back toward the kitchen, she called back, "Love you guys."

"*Love you, Laci,*" they all sang in reply, then as everyone else began eating, Cat returned to the topic we'd begun before lunch arrived.

"Okay, back to you, Paige. What else do you do in your spare time?"

I quickly swallowed my hastily chewed bite of sandwich. I was starving and had dug right in, forgetting we were in the middle of a conversation. I took a quick drink of water to wash down the last bit of razor-sharp toast. "That seems to be the problem these days. I'm not really sure what I want to do now that the kids are grown. I know what I'd like to do, I guess, but I'm not a hundred percent sure I'm going to be able to pull it off."

"Well, color me intrigued," said Elyse. "What is it?"

"I'm actually trying to write a book. *Trying* being the operative word. This is my third *try* and I'm really struggling to get anywhere with it."

Elyse's light green eyes lit up, turning them almost blue. "I can't believe this. It's like divine intervention. Grace here is our resident author. She's written six or seven books already and she's always working on something new. Cat and I are certain we are fodder for her stories."

"That's the risk you take hanging with an author." She turned to me. "Yes, I do a fair amount of writing myself. I've published six romance novels and I am working on my seventh. It's hard to keep that momentum going. Believe me, I understand the struggle. I wrestled my way through quite a few of my first drafts, but I have some tricks up my sleeve I'd be happy to share with you."

"I'd *love* to pick your brain one of these days. I wonder if my Dad has read any of your books. He loves a good romance."

"Pick away. And as for your dad, I actually have quite a few male readers. Way more than I would have expected."

We spent the next ten minutes inhaling our food, and finished within seconds of one another. After stacking our plates and bowls on the corner of the table, Grace took her napkin from her lap and placed it on top. "Are you ladies ready to go? I need to stop over at the café and check on an order I placed. Cat, I'll see you there shortly. Is Jenna in today?"

"She is, and she was hard at work on getting everything together for you when I left. I don't know what I'd do without that woman."

A look of pure affection softened Grace's features. "You're a blessing to her as well, sugar."

We paid our checks, and as we stood to leave, I felt as if I were getting ready to say goodbye to three friends I'd had for ages.

Grace turned to me as she slung her purse strap over her shoulder. "Will I be seeing you on Thursday?"

"I don't see why not. I have nothing going on, and I really need to start meeting people in this town if I'm going to be here for a while."

"I think book club would be a great place to start now that

you've joined the golf club. We'll all hopefully see you Thursday."

We walked out to the parking lot together, said our "goodbyes" and "nice to meet yous" and I got into my Jeep. I couldn't seem to wipe the perma-smile off my face all the way back to Victoria Drive.

What started out just a simple round of golf seemed to have become a potential doorway to a whole new life in Dunedin. I hoped it wasn't too good to be true.

17

"TO FIND A FRIEND"

TOM PETTY

The next few days passed without much ado. Roxy and I took a lot of walks exploring the neighborhood, Uncle Mike and I made it out for a round of golf, I hosted a four-course dinner for him and Chris on Wednesday night, and on Thursday morning, I decided I was ready to go back to work. It was nice to return to some semblance of my regular routine and feel productive again. Well, productive at my job, anyway. I hadn't even touched my book since I'd arrived. I told myself I was waiting for some kind of inspiration to strike, but the same old anxiety started creeping up every time I thought about sitting at the beautiful desk in my third-floor office to write.

As Thursday evening approached, a long-forgotten feeling of anticipation and excitement boiled in my stomach. I was grateful for the opportunity to get to know a few more people there, even though I had a teensy bit of anxiety about meeting numerous people all at once. As soon as I hung up with Kari, I said goodbye to Roxy and headed out to the Jeep.

At five forty-five, I was driving through downtown Dunedin. I passed Pioneer Park and smiled at all the families milling around in the grass. I made a mental note to stop by Skip's Bar (Pet friendly!) with Roxy later and check out the pet mural on the side of their building.

I rolled past the Dunedin History Museum, the Crown and Bull Bistro, and turned around after Back in the Day Books across from Dash of Flair. I slowed to a crawl and peered through the window of the bookstore. I pictured a line out the door as I sat behind a table inside signing copies of my book.

Someday.

After heading back down toward the library, I pulled into an open parking spot along the bushes at the far end of the lot and was just sliding out of my Jeep when I heard a familiar voice.

"Hey there, you."

I turned around and saw Grace standing behind the pearl-white Range Rover in the parking spot next to mine.

"I'm so glad you made it. You're really going to love everyone you'll meet tonight. Most of the time we talk about the book, but a good part of it is spent catching up and general chit-chat."

"I'm always down for chit-chat. I'm glad I've already read the book we are talking about tonight."

"Well, I'm excited to hear a new perspective. Are you ready to head in?" She smoothed down her white linen straight-leg pants and held out a hot-pink-cardigan-covered elbow. She seemed to have an eye for fashion; there was no way my t-shirt and jeans wardrobe was going to pass muster if she was setting the bar.

"Yes. I'm excited." I looped my arm through hers, and we walked toward the building. Separating at the top of the stairs, I held the door for Grace, who then led the way to the community room where the meeting was being held.

As I followed her through the room to the circle formed by soft brown leather chairs that were worn just enough to make them cozy, I was relieved to see another familiar face—Elyse. She had on a Fleetwood Mac concert t-shirt and jeans and her beautiful, art-filled right arm was waving wildly in the air. She was talking to a sundress-clad Laci who was attempting—and failing—to contain her laughter behind her hand. It was clear that Grace had also seen Elyse; she was already making a beeline toward her.

"Look who I found in the parking lot."

Laci and Elyse turned toward us at the same time, tears from laughter streaming down their cheeks.

Laci swiped at her eyes, raised a hand in greeting. "Nice to see you again, Paige. Ok, ladies, the room is starting to fill up. I'm going to head back over to my seat." She walked off to the other side of the circle shaking her head, our symphony of goodbyes following her.

"Hey there, Paige. Nice to see you could make it," said Elyse. "Cat texted a few minutes ago to let me know she's running a little late, so I threw my bag on a chair to save it for her." She nodded her head toward the chair next to her, which currently held an orange leather backpack I would have picked out myself. I loved her style. "I was just telling Laci about the children's reading circle at the bookstore today. We don't have time for me to tell the whole story again, but suffice it to say, little kids pronounce "dump truck" in all sorts of interesting and amusing ways, none of them G rated. Anyway, do we need to save seats for Sarah and Jenna?"

Grace turned and looked around the room. "Depends how fast they can walk and how many times Sarah stops to chat. They're strolling in right now."

I followed Grace's eye line and saw two women winding their way through the others still milling around.

While at first glance, one might assume they shopped off of different racks at the same department store—one decked out head to toe in pastel and tan business casual and the other in a long baby blue skirt and pink sweater set—but the smile that erupted from the woman on the left when her eyes landed on our little group instantly set her apart. "Hi, Mom." she exclaimed, quick-stepping over and throwing her arms around Grace.

Grace returned her hug with gusto. "Hey there, Sar Bear. I'm glad you could make it." She stepped back from Sarah, who smiled at me curiously then turned and walked toward Elyse. Grace took a half step to her right, and stood on her tiptoes to hug the young woman who'd walked in with her daughter. "Jenna, you look lovely as always," she said. "I had one of your apple walnut muffins this morning and it might have actually been better than the blueberry lemon muffin I had on Tuesday! Anyway, I'm glad Sarah had time to pick you up because there's someone here I'd like you to meet. Sarah? Can I have a moment of your time?"

Sarah, who was sitting on the edge of a chair, already deep in conversation with Elyse, stood and smoothened imagined wrinkles from the front of her pants, then put her arm around her mother's waist. She used her free hand to straighten the headband holding back her shoulder-length ash blonde hair. "I couldn't wait one more minute to update Elyse on what happened at the meeting with that student's parents. Mom, you have to ask her about what happened at the children's reading circle today. I will never look at a dump truck the same ever again."

She turned to me, and her eyes caught mine. I'd read about eyes 'sparkling', but had never seen it firsthand. At first glance, Sarah's eyes were brown; however, when I looked directly into them, I could see flecks of gold that caught the light. They were captivating and I wished at that moment I were a painter.

"Sarah, this is Paige," Grace began. "She is visiting Dunedin —indefinitely. Maybe forever?" She looked at me with the last two words, and I felt a warmth spread through my chest. "Elyse,

Cat, and I golfed with her on Tuesday. She's a big reader and needs to meet some new people, so we invited her to join us tonight. I have a feeling she's going to fit right in."

"Nice to meet you, Paige, and welcome to Florida," said Sarah. I put my hand out to shake hers, and was pulled in for a hug instead. "I'm a hugger. I hope that's ok."

"Hug away," I assured her. "My entire family is filled with huggers, so it's pretty much my default."

After a few moments, she released me and spun around to pull Jenna into the circle. "This is Jenna. She works at Cat's café, and she's quite the baker. I call her my Maven of Muffins. I get to taste test all her new creations, and I might actually turn into a muffin eventually, but I don't even care. I bring some into the school once a week and leave them in the staff lunchroom. It's not specifically mentioned in any school social worker handbook, but it's my professional opinion that cupcakes and muffins can raise your serotonin levels for at least eight hours. Long enough to make it through an IEP meeting, at any rate."

While Sarah extolled the indisputable virtues of baked goods, my gaze rose to Jenna, who was staring somewhere near my feet, her face nearly covered by the curtain of her neat brown bob. I was willing to bet she wasn't a hugger. Deciding to play it safe, I put my hand out in her line of vision. Jenna's eyes followed it up to the space just below my chin. They were the same color as her hair... and sad.

"Nice to meet you, Jenna," I said as she returned my handshake. "I've heard all about your talent. I am also a lover of baked goods, so clearly, we are going to be best friends." I gave her my warmest smile and squeezed her hand a bit before releasing it.

"It's nice to meet you too," Jenna replied in a voice that could barely be heard above the excited chatter in the room.

"Have you read this book?" Sarah pulled that night's selection from her tote bag and held it in front of her chest.

"I read it a few months ago, and I skimmed through it again last night, so I should be okay."

"Oh, that's a relief. What kinds of books do you usually read?"

"I read everything but horror. My Goodreads is packed with everything under the sun. I try to keep it updated, so feel free to friend me if you're looking for inspiration."

"I'll do that right now. What's your last name?" She scrolled through her phone, then paused, waiting.

Within seconds of saying, "Rhiann. R-h-i-a-n-n," I had a Goodreads notification on my screen.

Jenna stood next to Sarah and listened as we discussed some of our favorite (and not-so-favorite) books and a few on our To Be Read piles, but did not say a word. I wondered if she was shy, or had social anxiety. Demure had been the 'word of the day' from my desk calendar the week before, and it fit her perfectly.

As the rest of the book club members filed in and the seats were nearly all claimed, Grace turned back to me. "Let's head to our chairs. It looks like we're almost ready to start."

The five of us spread out in a curved line to the right of Elyse, and moments later, Cat sprinted through the door. After stopping to quickly scan the circle, she made her way over, a ray of sunshine headed our way.

She sat down and placed Elye's bag between them at their feet just as a woman in the center of the circle started talking. Leaning over, she whispered to me, "I'm glad you could make it. We'll chat after, ok?" Then she sat back, took a deep breath through her nose, and let it out slowly. It was a move I knew all too well.

After the meeting was over, we made our way out to the parking lot together while continuing the discussion we'd had with the group. Sarah and Jenna stopped at a vehicle that had seen more miles than Forrest Gump, but was still as clean as if it had just driven off the lot. "Will you be at our next book club meeting?" Sarah asked as she plucked her keys from a hook on the inside of her sensible brown leather tote bag. "Did you enjoy yourself tonight?"

"I really liked some of the questions a few of the members came up with," I replied. "I had looked up some questions online to see if I was prepared for the meeting, and the ones that were asked tonight were well thought out and really made me consider what I had read and what I would do in each character's situation."

"That's the beauty of our book club," said Grace. "There are no standard-issue questions here. All our members think outside of the box, so when it comes time for our meeting, we never know if we're fully prepared or not."

"I love that; I need to think more outside the box myself, so I enjoyed the conversation tonight and learned a lot. I would definitely come back again. I'll be here for at least a few more months, so I'll be at next month's meeting for sure. Have they decided on a book yet?"

"Not yet, but I'm going to add you to the Facebook group where we will discuss next month's meeting and the book we'll read beforehand."

"I look forward to it."

Sarah glanced at the time on her phone. "Ladies, it's been fun, but I need to get Jenna home now. I'm sure I'll see you soon. It was great to meet you, Paige." She stepped forward and hugged each of us briefly, then chirped her car locks and turned one more time before opening her door and climbing inside. "If you're ever up for a visitor or a glass of wine, I'm your girl."

"I think we're all her girls if that's the criteria, Sarah." Cat chuckled and winked at me.

"True. Ok, I need to get home to the kids. Mom, Ethan and Lily told me to say hi to Nana for them. They're looking forward to seeing you at dinner tomorrow night. I'm making beef bourguignon, so if you could bring a bottle of red, that would be perfect. Ready, Jenna?"

Jenna sent a nervous glance my way. "I need to get going, I've been here way too long as it is, but I really did enjoy meeting you, Paige." And with that, she opened the passenger door, climbed in, and gently closed it.

The other ladies walked with me toward the back of the parking lot where I was parked.

Elyse stopped behind a black Audi convertible parked next to Grace's Range Rover. "Come by any time," I offered. "It's the pink house on Victoria Drive. You can't miss it. Or my yellow Jeep."

Elyse's eyes lit up. "I've driven by those houses a thousand times. I'd love to see the inside of one of them. I'll stop by soon."

"Any time," I said. "Truly. It's just me and my golden retriever, Roxy, floating around in that huge house by ourselves."

"Golden retriever? Would she be interested in making friends with a German Shepherd? Eden is huge but a total sweetheart."

"Yeah, Roxy could stand to make a few friends herself."

"Awesome. It's a date. You'll be seeing us soon."

"Sounds perfect."

Cat took a pair of fingerless black leather gloves out of her back pocket and slapped them on the palm of her left hand. "Count me in for drinks as well. My bike is in the lot next door, so I'll see you all soon. Someday, I'll be able to leave the café on time and get here before all these spots are filled." She raised her hand in a brief goodbye, then walked between our vehicles and through the bushes they were parked against. We heard the roar of an engine, then, moments later, a flash of yellow as her motorcycle pulled out of the parking lot next door and took off down the street in front of us.

Grace and I chatted for a few more minutes before we each got into our vehicles and pulled out of the parking lot. My trip back to the house took fifteen minutes, but I was so lost in thought, it felt like seconds. I pulled into the driveway with a huge smile on my face. I'd had a big week, one of my biggest, and the roots I'd tenuously coaxed from their slumber up in Madison were already starting to grow in their new little corner of the world. My second act was really starting to take shape. Of my life, anyway.

My book? That was a whole other story.

18

"THE HEART OF LIFE"
JOHN MAYER

The next day, after completing some work projects, I decided I would try to make some progress on my novel. After I took Roxy for a walk, of course. And made lunch. And threw in a load of laundry. And ran the dishwasher. And anything else I could do to avoid sitting in front of my computer.

Two hours later, I finally gave up procrastinating, reluctantly made my way to my office, and opened up the document that contained chapter one of my latest unfinished manuscript. I had no idea where I wanted to go with my story. I was hoping that by sitting there, some inspiration would strike, but after an hour of typing and deleting... nothing.

I walked around the house for a bit. Walked down to the kitchen to get myself a snack. Took Roxy for another walk. Came back.

As I walked by the pool upon my (most recent) return, I theorized that inspiration would certainly find me in the water. I quickly changed into my suit and once back outside, dove in and took some easy-ish strokes back and forth several times across the pool. Ok, fine, three. It was three. Exhausted after an embarrassingly small amount of physical exertion, I trudged heavy-legged up the stairs at the shallow end and flopped down in one of the huge teal cushions on the lounge chairs. Inspiration had missed its chance for a water landing. Water-adjacent would have to do.

What do I want to happen in my book? What do I want this story to be about?

I had made no progress in the last six months, and I was banking on the hope that being in Florida would clear my head, but so far, chapter two had still evaded me. I went inside and grabbed my Kindle, thinking maybe some reading would help, and started downloading the newest book from one of my favorite thriller authors. When Kari made her nightly call two hours later, I was a quarter of the way through the book, but had made no progress on my own.

Another day gone with not a thing to show for it but a slight sunburn and a lot of avoidance. Nothing new there but the sunburn.

By Saturday, I was mostly settled in and had somewhat of a routine down. I had met Grace, Cat, and Elyse at the golf course for one of the early tee times, and had come straight home after. I was thinking about heading out for a walk when I heard a knock at the back door. Roxy gave a half-hearted bark, but she never was much of a guard dog.

I opened the door to find Elyse standing there, still dressed in her super adorable, totally on-trend zebra striped golf dress and a pair of silver Olukai flip-flops. An enormous sable German Shepherd sat at her feet. She stood when she saw Roxy, and they wasted no time at all sniffing each other from head to... butt. It was clear they liked what they smelled, because within thirty seconds, they were off and running in circles through the yard.

"Well, that was easy." Then, a simultaneous clap and *woo!* erupted from Elyse who was bouncing on her toes. "I have walked past this house a hundred times and always wondered what it looked like on the inside. I just love that it's pink, and these copper downspouts and gutters are stunning. Do you just *love* it here?" Elyse gushed.

I stepped aside to let her in. "I've always loved this house. I'm still in shock that I'm here, but I *am* starting to get more comfortable with the idea. Do you want a tour?"

"Do I?" Her voice was one click short of a shriek.

We entered the foyer, and when her jaw dropped, I knew what she was seeing. "This place is gorgeous."

"Wait until you see upstairs."

We called the dogs in through the mud room, and while they slopped water all over the rubber mat on the floor, I took her on a quick tour through each of the six bedrooms on the second and third floors and then up to the two-bedroom suite in what used to be the attic.

"This place is awesome." she said, spinning in a circle with her arms held out to her sides like that scene from The Sound of Music. "Can I vacation here?"

I chuckled, understanding the sentiment entirely. "You're welcome anytime. I imagine I'm going to get lonely in a house this big."

We returned to the first floor and settled across from each other at the kitchen island.

"Coffee? Tea? Sparkling water? Pick your poison," I offered.

"Coffee, please. The early tee times slay me. I am *not* a morning person. So, tell me a little bit more about yourself," she said as I busied myself with the Nespresso machine.

After turning on Spotify and pairing my phone to the outside speakers, I filled her in on the higher-level details of my life beyond what I'd already shared on Tuesday: My parents, Kari, the twins. We took our mugs out to the back patio, and settled in to watch the dogs run around the yard from the loungers next to the pool.

My eyes drifted to her arm that held her mug. "Can I ask about your tattoos? I've never had the courage to get one myself, but I love hearing the stories behind everyone else's."

"Of course!" She set her coffee down on the table between us and stretched out her right arm. As she pointed them out—a tree with four tiny stars above it, a calla lily, a golf flag, a baby bunny, a fireman's axe, a snail, a fish, a microphone, a camera, a chef's hat, and a globe and anchor—she told me the story behind each or the person they represented.

As she finished and sat back, her face took on a dreamy slackness as her eyes settled on the water flowing over from the built-in hot tub. "If I had a house like this, I would never leave. It's so quiet and peaceful out here, and the sound of the waterfall flowing into the pool. Oh, it's like heaven. Have you tried writing out here? I'm inspired just sitting in this chair."

"Well, so far, I have made zero headway on the *one* book I'm trying to write. I'm not really sure what I need to do at this point, but I know something is going to happen. I feel different here. I wasn't doing much more than floating through life in Madison, but something about this place is changing me already. I feel a little less 'unsettled' if that makes sense."

"It makes perfect sense." She took a careful sip of her still-steaming coffee and stared at the water. I waited, sensing she had more to say. "I've known my husband, Drew, for almost thirty years, and we've been married for seven. We are still honeymoon-level in love with each other, and he's by far the best friend I've ever had. That's a whole story in itself, but I'll save it for another day. Anyway, it's always been my dream to own a bookstore. I work at Back in the Day Books in downtown Dunedin, and Drew and I have been saving for the day the current owners decide to retire. But in the meantime, I feel like I'm in limbo, waiting. You can only feel fulfilled by so many trips to the airport, you know?"

I understood what she meant but decided to assume her question was rhetorical. She yanked the ponytail holder out of her hair, letting the unruly waves tumble to her shoulders. Running her fingers through it to smooth the flyaways, she sighed. "I rock babies in the hospital nursery twice a week, and during my downtime at the store, I've made it through a ton of research for an idea I had for a historical fiction novel. I golf two to three times per week. I visit my parents in Boca once a month, and Drew and I travel and golf several times a year..." She trailed off, leaned back against the cushion, and closed her eyes.

I waited and sipped my cooling espresso.

When she spoke again, her voice was strangled by emotion. Sensing her distress and being opportunistic to the core, Roxy wandered over from her spot in front of my lounger and sprawled across the stamped concrete between us, offering her soft blonde waves for therapeutic petting. Elyse reached down with her left hand and stroked the fluffy ear closest to her, and I found myself mirroring her action when Eden settled next to me. "When you look at my life from the outside, it seems perfect. Hell, it looks perfect to *me*. But there are times when I feel like I'm always waiting for something. I'm not a patient person by nature, so this makes me feel unsettled. Instead of feeling grateful for all the ways I've been blessed, and all I have to look forward to, when I get in a mood, I focus on what hasn't happened for me at all." Her one flip-flopped foot dangled from the side of her lounger closest to me, bouncing as she spoke. Stilled. Bounced again. Her legs were so long, her toes nearly touched the ground next to her.

After a few moments with only the crooning of John Mayer in the background, her hand stilled on Roxy's head. She smoothed her golf skirt over her tanned, toned thighs and turned to look at me, her dark brown eyes wide and clear. She shook her head, almost imperceptibly. "Good grief. Here I go getting all emotional on you right out of the gate. I'm so sorry." She shifted her body to face me, kicked off her flip-flops, drew her legs up, and criss crossed them in front of her. "I came here to get to know you better, and here I sit blubbering about my own silly problems. Please continue. What do you see when you imagine your future?"

I set my empty coffee cup down next to hers on the table. "Please don't apologize. I'm enjoying your company and getting to know you. This is good for me. Honest. I basically isolated myself once my kids had both left for college. I only interacted with my parents, coworkers, and friend, Kari, whom I've known so long I might as well call her my sister. Her twin boys have been influenced by my sense of humor and love of practical jokes, which I suspect is a lot for her to handle. She's all peace and love and namasté to the rest of the world, but the people closest to her know she's as serious as a heart attack. Having three of us who were down to clown at all times has been more than she can handle most days. She's threatened on numerous occasions to drop us all at the fire station.

"My parents were concerned about my stasis, and they managed to get her on the 'save Paige' bandwagon. I was never more lost than I was at the moment I started over the Causeway, but I can honestly say I haven't felt this good in months. Years. Not to be all Debbie Downer, but the emptiness that opened up in my life when my daughter left for college was swallowing me whole. I was existing, but barely. It must have been difficult to watch as it unfolded." I shifted and put my feet down on the ground next to Eden, stretching my arms up above my head.

"But since I've been here, I feel lighter. I can sit next to this pool, see the dance of the sun's reflection, and feel its warmth again, if that makes sense."

Elyse's head nodded. She reached over to scratch Roxy's back as she rose and left her station to commence her lizard hunting duties, her emotional support duties fulfilled. "It makes perfect sense to me. But I can tell from what I've learned about you so far that you're a good person, and I know you'll find your way here." She looked across the yard to the garage where Roxy was teaching Eden the finer points of lizard hunting, then continued. "I'm going to be fifty in two years, and I don't have a single thing to point at and say, 'this is how I bettered the world. This is my contribution to humanity.' But I feel it out there somewhere. Waiting for me."

"And I hope I'm here when it happens," I said, reaching across the space between us to put a hand on her forearm. "I'm glad you came over today."

Elyse's eyes smiled as she turned her arm over to gasp the underside of mine and squeezed. "I am, too. To both. I don't usually spill my guts so soon after I meet someone. It must be the water."

"I think it's something in Roxy's fur because it happens all the time when people are petting her. I've told my entire life story at the vet's office."

We both cracked up at that, injecting some much-needed levity into the moment. I stood up to stretch my legs, and Elyse did the same before we moved to sit on the side of the pool to swish our feet back and forth in the cool water. We talked a little longer, swapping stories and highlights, conversation flowing as easily as the water slipping over the cobalt wall into the rippling pool. The time slid by as it always does on Saturdays. Roxy strolled over to check in, snuffled our necks, and tried to climb into my lap. As I put my arm around her belly to stop her from tumbling into the pool, Elyse laughed and stood, her joints making familiar snap, crackle, and pops of protest.

"On that note, I'd better get Eden and head home. Drew's tee time was about two hours after ours, so he'll probably be getting back soon. We are headed to Home Depot today. I can't seem to go more than a month in between home improvement projects."

I stood, stretched my back, and silently cursed younger '*I can do whatever I want*' Paige.

Youth isn't just wasted on the young. We are foolishly trusted with it.

"I really am so glad you stopped by today. I enjoyed talking to you; it felt natural. Please don't be a stranger, and next time, bring your bathing suit."

"Oh, I'll be sure to do that," she said, slipping on her flip-flops. "I can't wait for Cat to see this place. She's always so busy with the café, but we do our best to drag her out as often as we can. I'll have to bust her out of there one day and we can have a pool day."

"I'd love that." I walked over to the driveway with her. "I'll see you Tuesday then?"

"You absolutely will. Thank you for the coffee and for listening to me whine."

I laughed and assured her it was no trouble and extended an open invitation for her to return for more of either. After she left, I gathered up our coffee cups and headed inside to slip into the new bathing suit that had arrived the day before. The pool had been calling my name since I'd gotten home.

Home. Hmmm. Interesting.

19

"YOU ARE THE BEST THING"
RAY LAMONTAGNE

Five o'clock on the dot that same night, my phone rang as I was getting settled into my favorite lounge chair next to the pool. You could time an Olympic race with Kari's accuracy.

My first instinct was to make some sarcastic comment, but the boys were leaving for college in a week and I did have *some* couth.

"How's it goin', Mama?"

"They are all packed up and itching to go. And I have to say, I'm right along with them. I never thought the day would come when I would be ready to drop them off somewhere else and not see them for months. But if the last several weeks have taught me anything, it's that there's a 'just right' time to let your little birds fly from the nest... and this is definitely ours."

"It's not easy, Kar, and you may feel this way now that you're ready to let go a little bit. But your emotions are going to change, and they'll keep changing over time. You know if you need someone to talk to next weekend, I've been through it, and I'm always here for you." I did not envy her the mechanical bull ride of emotions that was ahead.

"I know you are. And I know there will be some tough days ahead, but right now, I'm ready."

"Seven days will fly by in a blink, so enjoy as much as you can with them. Later, when they're too busy to call and check in, and you're standing in the doorway of their empty rooms wondering where eighteen years went, you'll be glad you did."

"Pray for me next weekend," she said, a sobering hitch in her voice.

"It's gonna be a mixed bag for sure, hun, but you can do it. Every time you want to stop your car and run back to drag them home, just think about wrapping paper gate."

"Don't remind me. I have enough to keep my memory fresh every time I go and check on the progress at my house. Sometimes I wonder if my hair has gotten curlier from shock with all the crap they've pulled. I know you're right, though. I'll try my best to be patient and present for the next week. No one warns you how hard it is to raise teenagers."

"Ahem... I–"

"—Shut up. I know. I thought you were being dramatic. You made it look so easy."

"None of it was easy, Kar. But it was all worth it."

"Yeah, well..."

I decided to let it go. I knew Kari well enough to realize she was masking her true feelings, and her irritation was a defense mechanism to get her through the next few weeks. We caught up on the progress on the house (not much), and the progress on my book (not much), and after a few more minutes of pointless chatter, we said "see you soon," and sat breathing into the silence, both of us feeling the weight of the words that had ended every call and visit for the last forty-five years. "Soon" had become relative in the wake of my departure, and for the first time, our customary promise had become a figure of speech.

After we eventually ended the call a few moments later, I

moved over to the side of the pool and sat, dangling my legs into the cool water. As I swished them back and forth, I felt the resistance of the water, then the release as they pushed through the swirling wake they created.

I reflected on my journey to get there. My scrolling memories glanced off the key moments in my adult life when the end result of a difficult decision had profoundly impacted me. Shaped me into the person I was at that moment. Increasingly difficult choices I made as an adolescent, a wife, a mother, a friend, a *person*.

Do I major in business or English?

Do I go on a date with this guy… or that one?

Do I marry him?

Do I end my marriage when I've tired of someone else telling me who I am and what I'm capable of?

Do I take a chance and apply for a job that I'm wholly under-qualified for but is exactly what I'd dreamt of?

Do I dress up or down for my first day?

Do I move into the city with Kari?

Do I accept a date from the cute new guy in accounting?

Do I move in with Mark?

Do I marry him?

Do we start our family now?

Do I work from home or bring Jason to daycare?

Do we have another baby?

Do I put our strong-willed Anna in time out… or myself?

Do I donate my eggs so Kari can experience the sleepless nights and swells of joy that accompany motherhood?

Do we buy a house in the more-family-friendly neighborhood Kari discovered?

Do we redo the kitchen or slap another coat of paint on it?

Do I go to Jason's soccer match or Anna's?

Do I try to hide myself in Jason's luggage when he leaves for college tomorrow?

Do I start writing a book now?

Do I beg Mark to stay?

Do I absolutely have to get out of bed?

Do I try to write a different story?

Do I fly out to the Pacific Northwest with Anna or let her be her independent self and leave for Washington State on her own? Without me?

Do I have to?

Do I get a puppy?

Do I try to write yet another story?

Do I want pizza or Chinese for dinner tonight?

Do I sell this house and all the memories it contains and start over somewhere else?

Do I let my parents in or pretend I never came downstairs and go back to bed?

Do I pack a bag and stay in Uncle Mike's house for a few months to see if I can break out of this funk?

Do I take I-65 toward Louisville or I-55 through Memphis?

Do I go to Clearwater Beach or Honeymoon Beach today?

Do I want to make myself chicken marsala or beef and broccoli?

Do I need a new pair of golf shoes? (The answer to this question is always yes.)

Do I keep trying to write this book or throw in the towel altogether?

Do I need help with better strategies for getting words on the page?

Do I find someone who can help me?

Thirteen hundred miles away, someone who watched—and when asked, helped—me make most of those decisions was working on the answer to the one that was currently weighing on me. And as usual, his guidance would change everything.

～

SUNDAY MORNING, the phone rang at nine a.m. I saw the call was coming from my mother's number. Living in the Eastern time zone meant I was an hour ahead of my parents, bringing our acceptable time for phone calls into closer alignment.

I tapped the green button to accept the call. "Hey, mom."

"Hey there, Tiger." I could hear my father yell.

Speakerphone. Of course. What is it with parents and speaker-phone? "Hi, Mom. Hi, Dad. What are you up to today?"

"Well, we were coming back from the grocery store, and we drove by your house and saw the twins outside mowing your lawn. It's nice to see Kari's got them busy," my mom replied.

"I'm happy to hear they're maintaining the grass. They do such a nice job with it."

"Yes, they do. We stopped by there earlier in the week to talk to Kari, and it seems like she's chosen a contractor from the estimates that came in," my mom continued.

My dad's voice came over the phone next. "Sounds like they might be done within two to three months. She showed us the plans for the kitchen. They're trying to make lemonade out of Camry lemons and drew out all the changes to the kitchen they've been dreaming about since they moved in. The contractor they like best had 3D drawings and presented them with a feasible plan. It's really going to be something."

"That's great news. I'm sure I'll get the update when she calls later."

My dad cleared his throat. "I've been thinking, sweetheart."

My throat seized.

Here we go. More thinking for them spells more change for me.

"As I mentioned, I've still got those university contacts. My former colleague, Caleb, is actually living in Tampa, not too far from you. I was wondering if it might be helpful for you to sit down and talk to him. He has written quite a few books himself, and I remember when he was getting started with them while we were working together. He struggled with writer's block quite a bit with the first few."

I felt my breath escape, unaware I'd been holding it. Had I not just given in to this very idea the night before? "That might work, Dad. I really appreciate it. But I'd hate to take up a bunch of someone else's time."

"Oh, no. He loves mentoring new authors. Trust me, he will absolutely love this."

"And I really think you're going to like him," my mom interjected. "I've met him several times at different university events when your dad was teaching full time, and he is a very energetic and likable guy. You'd learn a lot from him."

"Why don't I send you his number and you can decide what you want to do with it?"

"I'd appreciate that, Dad. I'll let you know if anything comes of it."

"You do that, sweetheart. Well, we just wanted to check in, and talk to you about reaching out to Caleb. I'm going to have a chat with him today and see if he's got some availability. We'll talk to you later, okay?"

"Sounds good. Thank you both for calling. I'll talk to you soon."

"Bye, sweetheart," they said in unison.

I tapped the red button to end the call and smiled to myself, touched by how adorable they were together. My mind slid to our conversation, and I considered how I would feel about being mentored. I knew I could use the help, but had no idea how the process would even work. I'd taken creative writing courses in college, and they'd been an expensive waste of time.

"I guess I'll wait and see what happens, if and when he calls," I said to Roxy, who was standing next to my bed wagging her tail in what I could only assume was encouragement. "Let's go, furball. It's time to start thinking about breakfast."

I sat in the sunroom with my 'second lunch' of cheese and crackers balanced on my knees, ready for service. A huge ficus sat to my left, its leaves reaching for the sunlight that streamed freely through the wall of white plantation-shuttered windows across from me.

When my phone began to ring, I moved the plate to the glass-topped table next to my glass of iced tea. I settled into the plush, muted turquoise velvet cushions that covered the white rattan couch and answered the call.

"Hi, Grace."

"Hey Paige. Will you be at league this week?"

"I absolutely will. I'm looking forward to it. I actually bought a new glove, and a new pair of shoes mysteriously arrived in the mail yesterday. Wink, wink."

"Oh, I can't wait to see them. Ok, so, full disclosure, I wasn't calling to ask about league."

"Okay... what's up?" I sat up and took a sip of my iced tea, then settled back into the couch.

"The leader of our book club is looking for a place to host the next meeting," Grace began, "and I was hoping you would be interested in opening up your home for the evening. A little birdie mentioned you've got a lot of space, and it would be a great excuse for me to come and see your house."

"That would probably work. What day is it?"

"It's three weeks from this Thursday."

"I don't really have a whole lot planned as of yet, so I'm going to have to say that chances are good it would work for me." I eyed the cheese on my plate. It was already starting to sweat.

"Really? Oh, that would be so great. From what Elyse tells me, your house is gorgeous. I can't wait to see it, and I bet the other ladies will be just as thrilled. We've all talked about the houses along Victoria Drive."

"I'm happy to host. What do I need to do?"

"We typically bring snacks when we meet somewhere other than the library, so if you want to have a couple hors d'oeuvres in place, we'll each bring one snack with us. It's a bit of a potluck."

"Sounds great. I love reading and eating, so that works for me."

"Fabulous. I'll let the other ladies know. Thank you so much, Paige. I'm looking forward to seeing you at league this week."

"Me too. I'll be the one in the hot pink golf shoes."

"Alright. Thank you, Sugar. I will talk to you soon."

We hung up a moment later, leaving me to my cheese and a breathtaking view of the bay.

ON THE WAY into the house after our nightly walk, my phone began to sing.

"My milkshake brings all the boys to the yard—"

I scrambled to extract it from my pocket, eager to share the week's developments with Anna. "Hi. I'm so happy you called." I said calmly. Ok, fine. I pretty much shouted it. While I'd eventually *accepted* that my contact with the kids had gradually slowed from the constant neediness of infancy and toddlerhood to a weekly phone call, I knew in my heart I'd never really get *used to* it. Every Sunday, I answered their calls like a retiree waiting for a call from Publisher's Clearinghouse.

"Hi, Mom. How is Florida? Wait. Don't answer that yet. Jason is waiting for me to dial him in. Do you want to FaceTime?"

"Yes. That would be great. Roxy would love to see you."

"Just Roxy, huh?" Her tone was teasing, but she followed it up with a laugh that hadn't changed since she was a girl. A quick, high-pitched burst that ended with a sigh. It never failed to make my heart squeeze a little tighter every time I heard it.

"I suppose I wouldn't mind seeing you too. If I must."

"Silly. Ok, hang on. I'll FaceTime you right back."

She disconnected the call. While I waited, I got myself settled in the sunroom. Within moments of sitting down, her face flashed across the screen, and I answered before the 'milkshake' even had a chance.

There they were, smiling back at me. Seeing their faces never got old. While Jason had inherited Mark's height, deep blue eyes, and dark blonde hair, Anna was the spitting image of her mother—sans the hairstyle and skunk stripe... but only time would tell.

"Okay, now you can answer," prompted Anna. "How is Florida? Do you love it? Are you making tons of friends? Have you pranked any of them yet? How is Roxy handling her new environment?"

"You look great, Mom," Jason said in the deep baritone voice that had come seemingly out of nowhere in between his Sophomore and Junior years of high school. "The saltwater and sunshine agree with you."

"It's so wonderful to hear your voices and see your faces," I gushed. "I miss you both a ton. Things are great here; Roxy spends her days chasing lizards, I've joined the ladies' league and a book club, and I've already made some friends. It sounds like I might also be hosting the book club meeting in a few weeks."

Both of my kids were completely still and uncharacteristically silent.

"Did I lose you? I wonder if the WiFi went out. Blink if you can hear me."

Anna was the first to break out of her stupor and her wide

smile overtook the top half of my phone screen. "Mom, that's incredible. I'm... Wow. I'm impressed."

Jason, typically a man of fewer words than the ladies in his life, seemed to shake off his temporary speechlessness. "You've been busy. I'm so happy to hear you've made friends already, Mom, although that doesn't shock me at all."

"Oooohhhh, Aunt Kari isn't going to like that one bit," chuckled Anna.

"Well then, she can get her butt on a plane and come visit me."

"Good luck with that," replied Jason. "It's a good thing she's managing that construction project, or she probably would have hung on your leg like a puppy while you got in the Jeep to leave."

That mental image brought up a bubble of laughter, and soon, the three of us were roaring.

"She might already be there. Have you checked under your beds?" quipped Anna, wiping tears from her eyes with the back of her hand, not holding her phone. "You being in another state might be the only thing that will ever get her to leave that zip code for more than an errand."

"I'm sure it's far too dusty under the beds for her. She'd be out in a flash looking for a dust mop."

That set off another round of giggles, which we all capped off with a simultaneous sigh—as usual. No matter how many miles were between us, one undeniable truth remained. Distance could not break the bonds we'd formed through the laughter that had been ever-present throughout their child-hoods. Humor was a basic tenet of our relationship, and it had gotten us through some pretty tough times.

"Enough about me. And Aunt Kari. You guys tell me about your week."

Jason and Anna took turns filling me in on what had happened since we'd talked on my way to Florida. Jason briefly outlined the skyscraper project his firm had successfully bid on and won, after which Anna went into great detail about the progress her university research team had made on their summer internship project. Both of them beamed with pride—for themselves *and* each other. The bond they shared was evident, even over a video call on a five-inch screen. Our relationship—and theirs—was a source of pride for me. I'd known many families that had folded under the devastation caused by teenage years and divorce. Somehow, the three of us had weathered the one-two punch and come out stronger for it.

We stayed on the call for another twenty minutes, each of them taking turns asking Roxy for her opinion on her new digs and accepting her tail wag as a matter of opinion. When it was time to hang up, instead of the crushing sadness that typically accompanied our goodbyes, my heart was full. For the first time in as long as I could remember, our call had filled my emotional batteries instead of leaving me feeling the need to crawl into bed.

We said goodbye, and I set my phone down on the counter.

"Who's ready for dinner?" I asked Roxy. "I'll cook. You get too much hair in our food." I'm fairly certain she rolled her eyes, but I didn't mind. Not everyone got my sense of humor.

20

"DREAMS"

FLEETWOOD MAC

Hot and steamy July turned to a hotter and steamier August. Three weeks passed by in a flash of nightly check-ins from Kari, sometimes afternoon check-ins from me after the boys left for college, FaceTiming with the kids, speakerphone chats with my parents, dinners with Uncle Mike and Chris, copywriting, walking Roxy, trips to the beach, ladies league, and cooking for myself, which was an activity I hadn't realized I missed. I still tended to cook too much food, as transitioning from cooking for a family to cooking for one had proven more challenging than one would think. But, the way I saw it, I was saving a ton of money on lunches, so it all came out in the wash.

Late in the morning, on the day I was to host the book club meeting, I was in my office getting a few work projects done before the cleaning crew arrived. Even though I had been keeping up with general cleaning by doing a little bit every day, with a dozen-plus people expected to come through, I wanted to have a few extra hands to make sure the house was dressed to impress. Just as I posted my last project for the day, Grace called.

"Hey, Grace. Perfect timing; I was just finishing up work for the day. What's up?"

"Hi, Paige. Elyse, Jenna, Sarah, Cat, and I thought we would come by a little before the meeting to help you greet people as they arrive. You don't know many of them yet, so maybe that would help relieve some of the stress. Everyone showing up all at once could be a little overwhelming."

"Oh, that would be wonderful. What time are you thinking you'll be here?"

"Probably about five-thirty."

"Okay, that sounds great. I'll see you then."

After we hung up, I set my phone down on the counter, then ran my hands across the cool, smooth white marble. That was how everything had felt since I arrived. Smooth. Comforting. In stark contrast to the emotional fortress I'd built around myself in Madison, this house had become a launching pad— and a safe place to land. I wondered how it would feel to have eleven *(or more)* other people in the house. I still hadn't met half of them, which meant that would happen as they were all descending on me while I was in my cushiony landing spot.

I headed into the powder room to throw some water on my face, and when I finished drying off and saw my pink-cheeked reflection in the mirror above the sink, I gave myself a mental pep talk.

If you don't know who you are anymore, just be the version of yourself your kids adored when they thought you hung the moon; the one you hope to see every time you look in the mirror. Become the person you were in that little girl's hopes and dreams. Be brave.

I had surprised myself so much in the last few weeks; perhaps I had a few more surprises left in me.

~

A FEW HOURS LATER, Roxy's cold, wet nose reminded me we hadn't taken our twice-sometimes-thrice-daily walk. Feeling compelled to enjoy the beautiful weather and sunshine, I slipped a lead over her head and off we went. I still couldn't wrap my mind around the possibility that was blooming in me. Staying. The more I felt that long-forgotten sense of belonging and the more people I met, the more I couldn't picture myself living in Madison anymore. I wasn't ready to make a concrete decision, but in my head and heart, I felt like Clearwater, Dunedin, or some other nearby town would end up being my home.

With that thought, my heart gave an extra squeeze. I was so used to Kari stopping over all the time, having a glass of wine after yoga, and having dinners together with her family. Now, I had to settle for a phone call with someone I was used to seeing on a daily basis.

I missed my friend.

I scrolled to her last update on her house and the boys and read through it, smiling. When I scrolled back up and clicked the 'Call' icon, the phone rang three times before she picked up, heaving. "Is everything okay?" she panted into the phone. I could picture her in my kitchen, folded in half, holding her side.

"Take a breath, girl. You sound like you just raced an Arizona Cardinals tight end for the last water bottle at the end of a preseason home game. Yeah, everything's fine. I was just walking with Roxy and thinking about how much I miss you. Tell me what's going on around the house." She took a shaky breath in, then let it out in a rush.

"Well, the contractors are making progress, but you know how that goes. Two steps forward, four steps back. Four steps forward, one step back. We're trying to be patient throughout this process, but it's difficult. We're so grateful to be able to stay in your house instead of a hotel, but it's just not home, you know? Everything just feels a little different."

I could relate. I was still feeling a teensy bit off-kilter myself. "I understand that feeling, Kari. Believe me, I do."

"I know. It's so nice to just hear your voice. I miss talking to you. I miss being able to just stop by on my way to the studio. Knowing you were mere steps away made life so much easier..." She trailed off for a moment, and a sniff gave away the reason for her momentary silence. "I just... I miss my friend."

"I miss you too, Kar Bear. When are you coming to visit?"

"I was going to try to keep it a secret for a little while longer—"

"Squeeeeeee! Tell me. Tell me." I shrieked over her.

"—but I'm just not capable of keeping secrets from you, especially one like this. How would you like to have a house guest in two weeks?"

"Are you serious?" I screamed. Roxy stopped in her tracks, alarmed by the tone of my voice. I was suddenly aware of my surroundings. A quick look around reassured me that there were no witnesses to my meltdown. Other than Roxy, of course.

"Aunt Kari's coming for a visit, Rox. What do you think about that?"

She yipped her approval, turned, and kept walking, leading us along the path toward Honeymoon Island.

"When do you get here?" I was able to exercise more restraint that time.

"The boys have been at school for almost three weeks and I'm ready for an adventure. I'm going to wrap up a few things around here, and Nick has agreed to closely monitor the contractors and subcontractors and ensure the project stays on track. But it looks as if I am arriving two Saturdays from this weekend."

I counted on my fingers. "*In seventeen days?*" I screamed again. Decorum was out the window.

"Yep."

"Gah. I can barely contain my excitement. Okay, well, I'll pick you up from Tampa airport, and we'll come back here so you can unpack, and we can do anything you want and if you want to go to dinner we can or we can stay in and—"

"Paige, breathe, honey."

"—I can cook for you. How long are you staying?" I took a deep breath in, having expelled every free oxygen molecule during my outburst.

"I'm going to stay for a week. I took time off from the studio, and I'm really looking forward to seeing you. I think it will ease some of my loneliness. Your house is papered in post-it notes and lists, and I need a break from it all."

"Well, I'll be here to ease your troubles and soothe your heart, and you being here will certainly ease mine. I love it here, Kari. I really do. But it will sure be nice to have a piece of home in this house, and I can just see us sitting out by the water with a bottle of wine and four kinds of cheese."

"Ooh, cheese. Say no more."

"I'm proud of you. This is a big step, leaving home for a week."

"I know. Nick was shocked. I'm a *lot* shocked. But I really miss you and need a change of scenery."

"I think that's the first time I've ever heard you say that, Kari."

"I think it's the first time I've ever said it, but it's the truth. Any chance you have a yoga studio nearby?"

"Oh, there are quite a few. I'll ask around and see which one is the best, and you and I can go together. It'll be a great gas-perience after all that cheese."

We both laughed at the same time, Kari's staccato *HA* assaulting my eardrums in that old familiar way.

We talked for a few more minutes about her visit, I gave her a short list of items I needed her to bring down with her, and by the time we hung up, I was sporting a smile as big as my heart.

"Let's head home, Roxy."

Home. Hm. There it was again.

PROMPTLY AT FIVE-THIRTY, there was a knock at the back door. I could hear people talking from the kitchen as I wiped down the counters one last time before everybody arrived. Five women stood outside with an array of Corningware dishes, crock pots, and Tupperware containers, each with a bright yellow book under her arm and a huge smile on her face. Elyse was leading the pack, and I could hear her excited voice through the door. "Just wait until you see this foyer."

With an excited Roxy spinning at my heels, I swung the door open. "Welcome to book club, ladies."

Elyse led Grace, Jenna, Sarah, and Cat through the back door, past me, and into the foyer. Each of them slowly turned in a circle to look around. Cat was the first to speak, and every thought tumbled out at once. "Look at this wallpaper. Is this wallpaper?" She closed her eyes and ran her hand soft as a wind-swept feather over the wall. Then, in a whisper, "I think this is actually paint. It's glorious."

I laughed, remembering how I felt the first time I had walked through that door. "It is indeed paint. This is a custom-painted mural that my uncle had commissioned years ago."

"It is gorgeous. Look at these floors. How on Earth do you maintain all this wood?" Grace marveled.

The twelve-year-old in me giggled, which set off Cat and Elyse. Sarah and Grace looked straight-faced at one another and rolled their eyes, but they couldn't hide their affection.

"Sorry, sometimes I can't help myself. But as for the *floors,*

I've yet to find out. I've been Swiffering them every day to pick up Roxy's tumbleweeds."

This prompted a quick snort from Elyse.

Jenna looked down the hall at the postcard-worthy scene on the other side of the front door. "Is that the bay?"

"Beautiful, isn't it? Let's get all this stuff out of your hands, and we can go on a tour if you'd like."

Sarah was still spinning a slow circle, taking it all in. "Yes, please," she said in a voice that had disappeared and left behind an exhale.

The ladies walked further into the foyer, and I led them into the kitchen, where we set up the food they had brought.

"Okay, are we ready? How many more are we expecting? Should I leave a note on the door?"

"I can run down and let people in," offered Elyse. "I had the pleasure of seeing your house a few weeks ago, so I can be the official doorwoman."

"I appreciate that. Alright, ladies, let's go through the first floor. Clearly, this is the kitchen, and if we go back out into the hallway and walk toward the front door, you can see the yard and, as you've already seen, the bay. To our left is the sitting room with an attached sunroom, and to our right is the dining room which opens into the front of the kitchen." I led them into the sunroom, arguably my favorite room in the house, and gave them a moment to soak it in.

"This is gorgeous," said Grace.

Jenna nodded her head in agreement.

"Are you ready to head upstairs?" Without waiting for a response, I turned back around, headed back up the hallway toward the foyer, and up the staircase to the first landing.

"How many floors does this house have?" asked Jenna.

"Well, there's the first floor we were just on," I replied as we made the turn at the landing and headed up the next set of steps to the second floor, "This floor has two full bedrooms, and the third floor has four. My uncle had each one converted to en-suites about ten years ago. He was hoping to turn this into a bed and breakfast, then realized it was way more work than he wanted to commit to."

I led them into the bedroom across the hall from mine, and the ladies wasted no time gasping and touching everything.

Grace ran her hand over the emerald brocade duvet that covered the white-washed four-poster bed. "Which room do you sleep in? How did you even choose?"

"I'm on this level. Here, let me show you my room. I'm not sure if the bed is made, so no judgment."

The ladies filed into my room one by one.

"Is that a balcony? What is your view from here?" asked Sarah.

"Yep. It looks out onto the parking lot of the businesses one block over. But, I actually don't mind. There's a birthing center over there and sometimes I'll sit out there with a cup of coffee and watch people coming and going. I love when I'm out here at the perfect time to see a couple leaving with a brand new baby. That always makes me so happy. I love being able to witness the joy of a new life together just beginning."

"Oh, that would be wonderful. I love babies," said Jenna almost breathlessly.

"Me too," said Elyse. "I wonder if they're looking for any baby rockers once they get home."

"Sounds like you've got yourself a new business idea, Elyse." Cat laughed and punched her shoulder playfully. "Rockin' with Elyse."

A thoughtful look crossed Elyse's face. "That's actually got a nice ring to it."

"It's so wonderful that each of these rooms has their own bathroom," said Sarah.

"Yeah, no kidding, except I'm the one that has to clean all of them. Well, I'm actually *dusting* most of them. I don't have a whole lot of overnight guests at this point."

"Who knows? That could change," said Elyse with a conspiratorial wink at Grace.

I decided to let the wink go as I'd likely find out the reason behind it soon enough with that crew. They tended to say exactly what was on (most of) their minds. There was very little beating around the proverbial bush. "Let's go see the rooms on the third floor."

Elyse took over the tour at that point and led the rest of the women up to the third floor and through each of those suites, then continued up the steep, narrow staircase to the fourth floor. As Elyse opened the door at the top, the light that came in from the skylight and both bedroom windows on each side of the apartment splashed over us. She stepped through the door and moved aside so we could all file in.

Grace stepped into the center of the room and spun in place. "This is beautiful. Is there a bathroom up here too?"

"There sure is. Right through that door." Elyse pointed to the door to the right of the one we'd just walked through, and gushed, "There's a bedroom over here and a bedroom directly across from it, and we're standing in the living room."

To my left, I heard Jenna sigh. "I would love to live here."

"You know," said Grace, "I could see myself sitting in one of these rooms writing my next book. Wouldn't that be wonderful to have a place where you could just go and be creative? You should really think about opening this house up to some kind of writer's retreat."

And there it is.

I stopped rearranging already perfectly placed pillows on the couch and stood straight up. She had my attention, and I turned toward her as she continued.

"You could do it on the weekends and have the house to yourself during the week."

"Hm," I said. "I hadn't really considered anything like that, but you really think that would work? This isn't even my house, so I'm not sure about the legalities of it all."

"Oh, absolutely. There are so many writers in this town and the surrounding areas. You'd have women beating down your door to stay here. And I happen to know a few people on the zoning board... but what do you think your uncle would say?"

With that thought and follow-up question bouncing through my head, the doorbell rang, and we all headed back downstairs to let in the rest of the book club members.

The meeting progressed as expected, and I thoroughly enjoyed the company of everyone who attended that night. At the end of the meeting, as everyone was sitting around in the sunroom chatting, Grace piped up, "Hey ladies, what would you think about the possibility of having a writer's retreat here? Someone could come for the weekend, work on their book, and go home at the end of the weekend refreshed and ready to take on the week."

I could see some of the women around me nodding their heads. One by one, they voiced their opinions and ideas.

"I would love that."

"Oh my gosh, that sounds amazing. There is nothing more inspiring than other women walking the same path."

"I've always wanted to write a book."

"Me too. Oh, maybe you could have morning sessions available for people to learn more about writing in general. There are so many people who want to write a book but have no idea where to start."

Is this something I could see myself doing? I mean, I like people and all, and I would definitely love to have another source of income, but is this something that would actually be feasible? I can barely keep a grocery list.

My new friends, probably sensing my rising panic, jumped in.

"We could help you," said Elyse.

Jenna nodded. "I'd love to help."

Sarah raised her right hand. "I'm in."

"Yep, absolutely," agreed Cat.

"Well, there you have it," said Grace.

"I don't know how long I'm going to be staying here. I don't even own this house, so I can't imagine it would even be approved."

"Just consider it," Grace urged. "Talk to your uncle. If he says it's ok, and you think it's something you could do, you'd have plenty of help."

It was definitely something to think about, and I didn't know where I would even start, but in the famous words of Mary Poppins, it's always best to start at the beginning. And it's even better with friends.

21

"TUESDAY'S GONE"

LYNYRD SKYNYRD

The next week at ladies' league, I was paired with Grace again. I had a sneaky suspicion that it was by design. *Her* design. Cat and Elyse had prior obligations, so Grace and I were on our own.

She wasted no time getting to the point as soon as my clubs were strapped into our cart. "Have you given any thought to what we talked about at book club?"

"I have, but I don't know where to even start. I'd have to run it past my uncle and I'm certain I would need some kind of licensing, insurance, zoning. I mean, it's a little overwhelming."

Grace rolled up to the first tee box and pulled to the side so the rest of the carts could pass us. "Here's some good news for you, my dear. I'm retired and have all the time in the world to help you figure out your first steps. If you want my help, I would be more than happy to jump in wherever I'm needed. Come to think of it, Elyse has a friend who has helped out numerous local small businesses with their marketing. If you'd like, I bet she could set up a meeting for you once you figure out if this is something you can and want to do. She'd also have a lot of the market information you'd need to get started."

"That would be good. I'd do fine writing the marketing pieces, but the design side of things isn't my strength."

"Totally understandable. You're only one person. Elyse and Cat also know quite a few members of the Economic Development Committee. They could probably talk to them without giving any details and try to get an idea of what this whole endeavor would entail from their standpoint. But take a few more days and give this some thought while I start asking around. Take the first step and reach out to your uncle. See what he says."

As we watched the last of the carts make its way down the cart path in front of us, I got out and put my glove on and pulled three golf balls from the front pouch of my bag. Grace straightened up beside me. "Okay, fine. Take all the time you need, but hurry up, would you?" Grace teased with a wink. She put her ball on the tee and swung, then walked to the back of the tee box. "I was talking to Elyse and Jenna. Both are pretty excited about this and have tons of ideas. Would it be okay if we all met at your house and brainstormed with you?"

I stepped into the space she left and repeated her actions, sending my ball into the rough on the left side of the fairway. "That would be great, but give me a chance to talk to my uncle first."

"Oh, I'm so excited. Let me know what he says. If he's on board, you can count on us to come prepared to plan. I love a project to work on, plus, I think it could really benefit a lot of newer writers as well as those of us who already have an established career but need a change of scenery. There are quite a few of us who like having other people around; it boosts creativity. Speaking of which, how is your book coming along? I haven't wanted to ask in case you're still struggling, but you haven't mentioned it lately."

"Ugh. I have not written a single word since I've been here. I've moved my office into a different room. I've sat down and tried to force the words. I've tried to not think about it. I've basically tried everything. But, there is actually some hope for me. My dad called last week and gave me the number of a former colleague of his who is living in Tampa. He said he might be interested in mentoring me, and I'm at the point where I think I'm going to reach out to him and see if he's equipped to take me on."

"I think that would be a great idea. Sometimes, getting somebody else's perspective, especially somebody who has been there and has a few books under their belt, can help get you moving. He might even have some resources to help you break through this block.

"It would be a good idea to at least meet with him. Just be open to anything he has to say. And don't forget, I'm always here for you, too. If you need some advice or want me to read something over—"

"If there was something to read over, I would definitely give it to you. But right now, it's just a whole bunch of blank paper."

"I've been there, girl. Don't worry. Between your dad's friend and your new friends here in town, I have a feeling you're going to have quite a bit of inspiration headed your way."

I laughed. "From your lips to God's ear."

We finished our round and left for the parking lot together.

"I'm going to put us all in a group text if you don't mind. Once you get the green light from your uncle, we can come up with a day and time that works best for us to get together for a chat," said Grace as she swung her clubs into the back of her SUV like they weighed less than a pound.

"See you later, Grace."

"Not if I see you first, sugar."

We parted ways, and I put my golf clubs in the back of my Jeep and drove home with my mind racing, wondering if the retreat concept was a possibility.

Being surrounded by writers for days at a time—I couldn't help but be inspired, right?

Before I reached my driveway, I decided that before I talked to my uncle, my first step should really be reaching out to Caleb to see if he was willing to mentor me.

His advice couldn't possibly make it any worse.

As if the universe heard my thoughts, I unplugged my phone from the charging cord before I got out of the Jeep, and it began to ring in my hand. I didn't recognize the number, but the area code was local, and I decided to save the caller from the endless abyss of my voicemail inbox.

"Hello?"

"Hi, is this Paige?" asked a voice I didn't recognize.

"Um, yes, this is Paige. May I ask who's calling?"

"Hi Paige, it's Caleb. I used to work with your dad at the University of Wisconsin. He gave me your number and a little bit of information about what's been going on with your work in progress."

"Hi, Caleb. My dad gave me your contact information, but I have yet to call. I appreciate you taking the initiative. And let's call it what it is, a lot of work and no progress."

"Believe me, I understand. I've been at this for years, and while it does get easier, I still face some struggles with each book. I think I can help you get unstuck. So what do you think? Do you have some time next week to get together?"

"I will make time."

"Great. Do you mind if I text you some dates and times I have available? You can pick whichever one works best for you. Your dad told me you're working full time, so my schedule is a little bit more flexible than yours."

"That would be wonderful. Should we meet at one of the

libraries in Dunedin? And thanks a lot for agreeing to do this. I really appreciate it."

"First, yes, the library works for me. I'll reserve a meeting room at the one downtown. And, honestly, your dad helped me so much when I was getting started at the university. Even though I was only a couple years behind him, he gave me the lay of the land and mentored me until I was settled. I would love to repay his kindness by helping you."

"Yeah, that sounds like my dad. I feel like if this was something he could help me with, he would do it in a heartbeat."

"That's for sure. Ok, I'll send you a text within the hour with some possible days and times, and we'll talk soon."

Less than five minutes after we hung up, a text came through from Caleb. I stored his number in my phone and, after checking my calendar, replied back confirming a time for the following Wednesday at noon.

Next, it was time to call my uncle.

22

"DON'T STOP"

FLEETWOOD MAC

"Hey, Paige. I'm in the car on my way to pick up some wooden hangers, and I've got the top down. Can you hear me, ok?"

"Gorgeous day for that. Yep, I can hear you just fine."

"Excellent. What's up, honey?"

"First, I wanted to tell you that Kari is coming for a visit next weekend. I'm sure you'll want to come over and say 'hi', so I'll probably plan a dinner for the four of us.

"Oh, honey, I'm so happy for you. I'm shocked she's traveling, but so thrilled for you both. So... what's second?"

"I'm not sure where to start, so I'm going to just jump right in. I hosted that book club meeting at the house last week and a few of the ladies have got it in their heads that your house would be the perfect place to host a writer's retreat. It's not my house to say yes or no to the idea..." I trailed off, letting him fill in the blanks.

"Wow. That's huge."

"That's what she said."

"Okay, knucklehead. Try to be serious for five minutes," my

uncle retorted, but the crack in his voice gave him away. He never could resist my twelve-year-old humor.

"I mean, there would definitely be some hoops to jump through, but I think it's a great idea. A question comes to mind, however. And it's a big one—"

"Th—"

"—don't even try it. I walked right into that one twice in two minutes. Anyway, the question. Do you think you'll be staying here long enough to host a retreat? Don't get me wrong, I'd love for you to stay forever, and some of that is because I don't want to have to pack up that beast of a house." We both laughed at the truth of his statement. He could run a booming antique resale business out of his house. "But I know your home, your parents, and your lifelong best friend are all in Madison. What do you think?"

He wasn't wrong. The life that had taken me three decades to build was thirteen hundred miles away.

So... what? Really. Who's to say I can't build a new life? Who's to say 'from this day forward' only applies to a marriage? I've said it under that context—twice—and look how that ended up. From this day forward, I have only myself to think about, only my future stretching out in front of me, and I alone control my journey through it. From this day forward, I am going to set my course and sail through whatever comes next.

A lightness I had missed for years filled my chest. "How long can I stay?"

AFTER A BRIEF EXCHANGE in our group chat, Grace, Elyse, Sarah, Jenna, and I settled on meeting at my house on Saturday at three o'clock. Cat would be at the café, but I assumed the girls would fill her in later. "I have news," I'd texted to the group, then braced for the tsunami I knew was coming.

By the Grace of our Maker, the rest of the week flew by. I had tried to sit down three or four times to strong-arm some words onto the page, but it was obvious it wasn't happening. Before I even blinked, it was Saturday at three, and my new friends were at the door.

They filed in one by one, each with a hand free to greet Roxy (which she appreciated) and the other holding some kind of snack (which I appreciated).

"Well, you certainly know the way to my heart," I said as I scanned their haul on the way to the kitchen.

"If it's one thing we know how to do, it's eat," said Grace.

"That's the whole reason I golf sometimes... just to get out and away from my fridge. Otherwise, I'd sit at home and eat all day."

Jenna set a large paper shopping bag on the counter. "Cat packed up a few things to send with me. Grace just picked me up from the café, so everything is still fresh."

"First things first," began Grace, "I wanted to tell you face to face how thrilled I am that you're staying for the foreseeable future. You fit into our little group so well. It's like you've always been here."

Elyse jumped in before Grace could take a breath. "You're killing us, here. What did your uncle say about the retreat?"

The rest of the women stared a hole through me, hands clasped on the table in front of them, their faces doing nothing to mask their anticipation.

"He said he'd think about it..."

Four sets of shoulders slumped.

"..and then three seconds later he said, 'gotcha.'—and now I get to say it... Gotcha."

Four sets of hands flew into the air in celebration, and what ensued next could only be borrowed from one of my favorite children's books. One I had read to my kids at least once a week for a decade.

Let the wild rumpus start.

As soon as the chaos died down, each of the four women sat back in her chair around the glass-topped table, bent down and pulled a notebook out of her bag, set it on the table in front of her, and placed a pen on top of it—all at the same time.

"Is this a synchronized planning team? Did you all rehearse?" I joked. "You came prepared for good news, I see." Anxiety roiled in my belly. More change. More unknowns. More meeting large groups of people at one time.

I stopped. Placed my hand over my belly to calm it.

From this day forward.

There was no going back, only forward, and the first step in this giant leap of faith was in front of me. I rolled my shoulders back. "Should we get started?"

Sarah, the saint that she is, jumped in first. "Let's walk around and take notes as we go."

Elyse stood in the hallway between the two rooms on the second floor. "Why don't we plan on leaving this floor out so you have a little bit of privacy." We all agreed the third floor would be perfect for the bulk of the guests.

"Let's take a look at the top floor," said Grace as she led us back to the staircase that led to the attic apartment.

Once we'd all filed in, all four of the women began writing furiously in their notebooks.

Elyse was the first to comment. "You could charge the same for this space and still put two women up here, because there's more room to spread out."

"This space would be good for a situation like mine and Sarah's," said Grace. "Or two friends traveling together. You could really make these rooms work for a lot of different situations. So right now, you have availability for up to six people. Let's go back downstairs and get to work."

We settled around the kitchen table again, this time with plates full of food.

"Insurance is going to be a must," pointed out Elyse. "You might want to start there to ensure it won't price you right out of business before you even start. Let's add that to the list."

We all bent over our notebooks and began to write.

"You are going to need some help with marketing. I had a chance to talk to my friend, Raina, and I will put you in contact with her. She seemed very excited about the idea and had a few great ideas while we were talking. I think she's going to be a big asset."

"Yes, definitely put me in contact with her," I said to Elyse, who was typing away on her phone. My phone buzzed on the table. "You are *very* efficient."

"Guilty as charged."

Jenna cleared her throat and set her pen down on the table next to her notebook. "I was wondering what you thought about food."

"Great point. That's going to be a necessity."

Grace added to the list she'd started. "One thing is for certain, writers are going to need a lot of snacks."

"And you could probably have some kind of sandwiches or salads or things like that, just grab and go where people could either take it back to their room or sit in a common area and chat while they eat their lunch," added Sarah.

Grace looked up from her notebook. "Everyone should be on their own for dinner. They could either get together and order takeout, go off in groups to dinner, or go separately and get some alone time. It would be completely up to them."

"I think that's a great idea," agreed Elyse. "I could see myself getting tired of being around other people all the time. It would also help keep your costs down."

If the entire conversation had been recorded on video, I would have played it back later to see my mouth hanging open in shock. The women were so invested in the idea and had considered so many things I would never have thought of until it was upon me. "I think these are all great ideas, assuming I can get this off the ground. What do you all think I need to do as far as getting approval from the city?"

My question prompted a flurry of paper flipping from my shockingly prepared planning committee. By four-thirty, we each had a to-do list. Mine included a list of people I needed to call, including an insurance agent and the zoning department.

"You guys are awesome."

Grace clicked her pen closed and slid it into a pocket of her purse. "We're extremely motivated to help you make this happen."

"My friend Kari is coming in next weekend. I bet she's going to have some ideas too."

"Oh, I can't wait to meet her." Grace slid her notebook into her tote bag, then looked up suddenly. "Did anything come from your conversation with your dad's colleague?"

"Oh yes, Caleb. We're actually meeting at the library next Wednesday."

"That's great news."

"Who's Caleb?" asked Elyse.

"He's an old colleague of my dad's who is going to mentor me."

Sarah pushed her chair back and stood, prompting the other ladies to follow suit. "Let us know how that goes, would you?"

"I sure will."

We stood around the kitchen counter for a few more minutes, picking at the snacks that lay in shambles, then, they trickled out one by one. After they left, I finished cleaning up the detritus of our meeting and headed out to the back patio with Roxy to wait for Kari's call. I thought about how grateful I was that they had found their way into my life. It was nice to feel the companionship of these women around me. For so long, it had basically been me and Kari.

"Roxy, this time next week, Kari will be sitting right here with us."

She wagged her tail as if she understood, but she might have been eyeing a lizard.

As I HUNG up with Kari after filling her in on the developments from our ad hoc planning committee meeting, my phone rang again.

My dad's number came up, and a warm happiness spread through me. They'd been on a cruise they had planned in May, and it had been a while since we'd spoken. My smile quickly changed to a grimace when I realized what my ears were in for.

"Hey, Dad." I said, cringing.

"Krrrssssht krrrsssssht" The crackle of the speakerphone assaulted my ears.

Yep. Speakerphone. Called it.

"Hiiiii, honeeeeeey. It's u-uuuus." My mom and my dad sang in unison.

"I kind of assumed from the name on the caller ID. How are you guys doing? How was your cruise?"

"It was great, honey. Your Dad will send some pictures over later. Theo, move over so I can sit down next to the phone."

"Good grief, woman. Get your ass out of my face."

"Just scoot over."

I was thrilled to be listening to my parents bicker over speakerphone. Again. Someone should arrive at every sixty-year-old person's house the day after their birthday and disable their speakerphone function altogether. People in restaurants and airplanes everywhere would cheer. Wars would end. Babies would sleep through the night from birth.

My mom's far away-even-though-she's-inches-from-the-phone speakerphone voice came through next. "We stopped by your house yesterday and saw Kari. She said they're making progress, but when we drove by, everyone was sitting around on the grass with coolers."

"Yeah, they probably take breaks once in a while, Mom," I laughed. "It's August."

"I know that, silly. I just wish for your sake they would work a little faster."

"I'm in no hurry, Mom. I'm enjoying myself here, and I don't know... every day, this feels a little more like home to me."

"Hmmm... How was your book club meeting at the house?" my dad asked.

"It went better than expected, and I've been wanting to talk to you about a conversation we had at that meeting, but I'm still trying to process it a bit."

"Well, let's hear it, Tiger. No time like the present. Maybe we can help you process it faster."

So I laid it all out. The book club pre-meeting with the league ladies, the other book club members' enthusiastic agreement. My conversation with Uncle Mike. The 'planning' meeting that day. The constant undercurrent of anxiety that I would try and fail and waste everyone's time.

"Sweetheart, this sounds like a *fantastic* idea," my dad exclaimed. "A place where like-minded women can go to write without distractions. I know how hard it is for me to concentrate with this woman constantly distracting me with yard work, errands, grocery shopping, and eye doctor appointments."

"It's not my fault you keep us so busy," My mom interjected.

Here they go again...

My parents communicated in a playful fusion of snark and guilt trips that could alarm the casual observer. However, I was not a casual observer. To me, their playful banter sounded like home.

"I would be just as happy sitting in my recliner with a book and a tall glass of iced tea. Anyway, sweetheart, continue."

"If you're sure you guys are finished..." I waited for a rebuttal from the other side, then continued. "I don't know how I would make it all happen. Sounds like a lot of paperwork, and you know that's not my strength."

"You can do anything you put your mind to," said my mom. "Look at how far you've gotten in life. You have a successful career in marketing. You have two successful children—"

"—two very unsuccessful marriages."

"We won't count those against you, honey," quipped my dad.

"I've got Kari coming here next weekend, and I'm sure she'll be armed with enough lined paper, pens, and highlighters to outfit an entire sixth-grade class. We apparently have big plans to put together a pros and cons list."

"Oh good, you know. We didn't want to ruin the surprise, so we've been keeping it to ourselves, but we're very excited for you both. How wonderful that she's decided to travel a bit," said my mom.

"I think this might be her first vacation since her honeymoon, and that was only to Milwaukee. She's not much of a jet-setter."

"That's understandable, though, given all the moving around she did as a kid," my dad mused. "Those roots are firmly planted. Speaking of roots, those boys were taking good care of your yard. I saw them out there every weekend mowing and weed-whacking. Kari had them working like rented mules."

"We're so happy that she's going to be there. She's been a little morose since the boys left. You'll be able to help each other," added my mom. Her voice sounded like it was coming from across the room.

"With that, I believe your mom has already gotten a head

start on some fun household chores she's planned for us today, so we're going to get going. But we wanted to check in with you and see how you were doing. We're going to give your uncle a call next and check in on him. Seems like it's going good from what I hear. He seems very happy, and that makes *me* very happy. We're going to be making a plan to come down to visit all of you."

We chatted for a few more minutes, then said our goodbyes. I heard the clatter of the phone as they picked it up and their muffled conversation through what must be the fabric of my dad's pants pocket.

"Do we have any more laundry detergent?"

"Yes, we have a whole bottle in the basement."

"I'm thinking about maybe going to get the car washed."

"*After* we're done with the laundry."

I left them to their domestic bliss and did them the favor of ending our call before I heard something that would scar me forever. It could be said my parents were set in their ways and sometimes seemed like polar opposites, but one thing they knew how to do was love one another.

I just didn't need to hear the evidence of it.

23

"GO THROUGH IT"
GRIFFIN HOUSE

Before I knew it, Wednesday arrived, and I was going to meet with Caleb. I wasn't sure what to expect, but I figured I might as well have an open mind. If it was someone that my dad thought could be helpful to me, then I was going to give it everything I had, and consider it a great opportunity to learn something from someone who was not only doing what I wanted to do, but had done it *successfully*.

My Dad had texted me a description that morning, so I knew who to look for. When I walked in, I saw an older gentleman with white, shoulder-length hair sitting at a table who kind of looked like one of the Beach Boys. He waved in my direction, so I walked over and sat down, swinging my backpack around to set it on the floor next to me.

Caleb reached across the table and shook my hand. "Paige. As you probably guessed, I'm Caleb. It's so nice to meet you. After hearing so much about you over the years of working with your dad. You are the apple of his eye if I can use such an antiquated phrase."

"Oh, believe me, I know. My dad is the best. I am really

appreciative of him introducing us; he thinks very highly of you."

"The feeling is mutual. Now why don't you tell me a little bit about yourself, and let me get a better sense of who you are aside from the virtual saint your dad used to talk about, of course."

I went through the highlights of my life: the kids, the marriage, my career as a marketing writer, my kids going off to college. I very briefly touched on the divorce and capped it all off with the borderline unbelievable story of how I came to be sitting in a Florida library.

He took out a notebook and pen. "I'm going to write some things down if you don't mind." He tapped his pen on the blank page in front of him. "You've had a very full life so far. Why don't you tell me what you've been working on."

I shifted in my seat and fiddled with the pen I'd set on the table in front of me. "That's where it gets a little sticky. I'm not really sure. I've started two novels before this one and got to about five thousand words written for each before I lost interest. I don't know... I would just start over with another idea that felt half-baked, and I didn't really *connect* with it, even though it seemed like it would be something someone would like to read."

"And what are you working on now?" Caleb bent over his notebook to jot something down.

"I am working on my third story, and it's more of the same. I just sit in front of my computer and that damn cursor just blinks at me. I can hear it in my head. 'You're failing.' 'You're failing.' 'You're failing.'"

"First of all, let me stop you right there. Not getting words on the page is not failing. You just haven't found the story that you *want* to write. The one that keeps you up at night with characters that make their opinions about their next move known at the most inconvenient of times. There's nothing wrong with that. Many, many, many successful authors go through a phase where they start and stop numerous times before the one *great* story lands right in their lap."

I sat up abruptly and knocked my pen off the table. "Great. How do I make that happen? I'll do it." I bent over to pick up my pen, and blood rushed to my head.

Caleb chuckled at what must have been a beet-red face of wide-eyed desperation. "I'll be honest, you don't make it happen. It just *happens*," he explained, then picked up his notebook and skimmed over what he'd written. "But, I think we could change the course of your writing by altering your perspective a bit. You said you get five thousand words in, and you aren't connecting with the story anymore, but you feel confident other people would want to read it?"

"Yes, I have this vision of women sitting around at a book club talking about *my* book. That's what I picture when I want to give up."

"Perfect. I know exactly where you need to start. Unfortunately, it's not going to be as easy as it sounds, but it's going to be a lot easier than what you're doing now. Instead of trying to think about a story that other people would want to read, why don't you think about a story *you* would want to read? Do you read a lot?"

"A lot is putting it mildly. I probably read at least one book per week."

"Okay, well, then we have a lot to work with. What kinds of books are you reading?"

"I'm a mood reader, so they're typically books that reflect where I am in my life. I mix in some mysteries and thrillers because I do like a little bit of excitement, but right now, they're all about women who are having some kind of struggle in their lives, and the path forward just opens up in front of her... or something like that."

"Those sound like perfect stories for you then, Paige. Why

don't you do this: Build a main character you can identify with. Don't worry about your reader as much. Make it a story *you* want to read. Start with a short story about someone like you, someone who's going through some changes in her life and isn't really sure what she's going to do next. Give her a conflict, give her a way to resolve it, and then find your way there. Why don't we make it five thousand words, since that's where you seem to be stopping with other stories. See if you get to five thousand words and still feel a spark. If you can identify with this woman, you may instinctively know where her next steps should land. Give her some friends and family. People the reader can connect with. Make sense?"

I would like to say that at that moment, a story took shape in my mind. But it wasn't a magical library meeting room, and I wasn't a magical author. What I did feel was a little more sense of direction than I had that morning, and that felt pretty good. I was going to stop writing for those imagined book club readers and start writing for *myself*.

"So what do you think?" asked Caleb, breaking me out of my reverie. "You look like you're deep in thought."

"I have a pretty good idea of what I need to do next. This was so helpful. I didn't know what to expect, but everything you said made so much sense, and for the first time in a long time, I think I can make this work."

"I'm so happy to hear it. What do you think? When would you like to meet again?"

After a brief scuffle with my cell phone on its way out of my bag, I consulted my calendar and we agreed to meet at the same library in two weeks.

Caleb began packing up his things, but paused to look up at me. "Do you enjoy walking on the beach?"

For one brief moment I thought things were about to get weird, but he must have read the panic on my face because he quickly added, "Go sit by the water today. Spread a blanket out on the beach. Bring a couple bottles of water with you. Bring lunch, some snacks, and start looking at the people around you. Try to imagine what their stories are. See a family sitting there? Put a story together in your mind. If you see something interesting, write it down. Do that for a couple hours, and for the next couple of days, every time you go somewhere, make a point of really looking at the people surrounding you. Listen to conversations. Don't eavesdrop, necessarily—or at least don't be obvious about it." We both chuckled. "But if you happen to hear a word or two," he raised his hands in the universal 'oh well' position, "try to put a story together in your mind based on that conversation. If you see someone sitting alone, ask yourself, 'Who are they waiting for? What's their story?' You see what I'm getting at here?

"Stories don't come from thin air. They come from experiences, even if they're not *our* experiences. Put a story together *you* would want to read, something that would inspire you, something that would make you want to know the characters, maybe even be their friend."

My mouth said, "I can do that," while my brain grumbled, *Not this again.*

"I know you can. Do you think two weeks will be enough?"

I wasn't sure if it would be enough, but I could feel something boiling up from the bottom of my belly. That old familiar feeling—hope—that had been having some trouble ignoring my internal naysayer. I couldn't wait to get started.

"I think two weeks will be plenty. I really appreciate this."

"You're very welcome." He slid his pen into his backpack and stood. I followed suit.

"I've got another meeting in about an hour, and I want to take a walk through the town, see what kind of people I can create stories for. I'll probably take a stroll past your uncle's shop. Their window displays are ingenious. I'll see you in two weeks, Paige." We shook hands briefly, and he clapped me on the shoulder like an old rugby teammate. "Say 'Hi' to your dad for me, would ya? Tell him I'm expecting him to visit soon. I'd love to see your mom as well. She's a spitfire, that one," he said with a twinkle in his eye.

With that, he transferred his backpack from the table to his shoulder, turned, and left, leaving behind a glimmering trail of confidence.

∽

As soon as I returned from the library, I inventoried the contents of the fridge. It was nice to once again feel the urge to cook something more than pasta and jarred marinara. I was enjoying getting my hands dirty and flour all over the kitchen. Making something that required at least an hour of clean up after all was said and done.

I planned out a few days' worth of meals for myself, and after I'd scheduled my Instacart order for later that afternoon,

What a time to be alive!

I decided to take Caleb's suggestion and head to the beach for some light stalking. When I arrived at Honeymoon Beach, it was packed.

What do all these people do for work that allows them to sit around at the beach all day on a Wednesday?

Up to that point, I had never really thought about the people around me being fodder for stories. But it seemed all you needed were some warm bodies and a little bit of creativity.

I plopped myself down in a four-by-four area of the sand, put on some sunscreen, and got to work observing. There was a family directly in front of me. Looked like a mom and a dad with two little kids. Mom sat in a low beach chair with her long, freckled legs stretched out in the shade of her umbrella and a book propped up in her hands. The dad was off to the side, building sand castles and making the kids run back and forth

with buckets of water as he attempted to erect a masterpiece—
or at least a masterpiece of a memory.

I started crafting a story about their lives.

Mom stays at home taking care of the kids while Dad travels for work. She's exhausted by the weekend, and Dad is kind enough to take over so his wife can take a break. He enjoys this time; he misses his kids so much while he's gone. But, he enjoys his sales job as well. The time apart during the week gives them a chance to miss each other. Their marriage is still fresh after five years, and they have a deep appreciation for the job the other is doing. He wishes he had more time to spend at home with his kids. She wishes she had more time alone. But they're making it work.

I wondered about the mom's dreams. Which ones kept her up at night after the kids had fallen asleep? What secret aspirations did she nurture, waiting for a time when the kids who need her so much during the day don't need her quite so much anymore?

I wanted to walk over and tell her to enjoy every moment while it lasted, but I knew it was a journey she needed to take on her own. The truth behind the old adage, 'the days are long, but the years are short', doesn't reveal itself until those long days have already slipped through the short years and... *gone.*

Besides, I didn't want to interrupt her reading time. Those moments of peace are few and far between as a mom.

I turned my attention to the dad, still kneeling in the sand. His castle complete, he'd moved on to digging a moat to protect their lopsided labor of love.

I probably looked like an unhinged stalker, but at that point, I was in too deep to give up on their story. I started jotting down questions in my notebook.

Does he want something different for himself or his family? What if he were a secret agent during the week, following the world's bad guys around, trying to bring them down. Going home and playing the role of family man on the weekends. What kind of adven-

tures would he go on? Where would his job take him? Does she know about his secret life? Or is she just as much in the dark as the people he's chasing all over the planet?

Next, to unlock my final stalker badge, I sketched out a picture of the family.

Looking up from my notebook, I saw the mom set her book down on her lap, holding her place with an index finger. She pushed a red curl off her face, and as I studied her profile, I caught a smile that crinkled the corners of her eyes. I followed the direction of her gaze to discover a matching smile sent back her way by her husband. All was right in their world.

I got up, dusted myself off, and walked over to grab an ice cream cone from the vendor on the beach, an older woman with a voice that negated any need for a loudspeaker. She could have been Grace's sister.

My thoughts naturally turned to Grace. I marveled at how she could get the most out of every day. She could easily wallow in grief, having lost the love of her life, but from what I could see, she didn't. The Grace I saw was full of energy and a lust for life that felt like a distant memory to me, but I longed to emulate it.

The beach started to empty and my ice cream cone was long gone. I walked down to the water and rinsed off my hands and thought about how much fuller my life had become in a few weeks' time.

When I pulled into my uncle's driveway less than two months ago, my life had no real direction, and now I had several new possibilities before me. I didn't know which one was best, but a path forward was starting to take shape.

Realizing I needed to be home within the hour to collect the grocery order, I returned to the beach, wiped my saltwater-covered hands on my shorts, and picked up my beach bag. I was headed home to a future that was becoming less uncertain every day.

24

"WITH A LITTLE HELP FROM MY FRIENDS"

JOE COCKER

A fter putting the groceries away, and checking in on Kari, I sat on the couch in the sunroom with a notebook on my lap. I thought about the couple in front of me at the beach, and the hypothetical life they lived, full of adventure and mysteries and secrets. While my typical genre wasn't mysteries and thrillers, it intrigued me to think about the secrets people keep—sometimes from those in their own home.

With that couple in mind, I started to outline an idea for Caleb's assignment—the husband, a covert CIA agent, and the wife, secretly working as a private investigator. I had so much fun putting it together and building character profiles that before I knew it, I had written the outline, the profiles for the husband and the wife, and a few details about the adventures they each had during their week apart.

Five thousand words flowed out of me like honey from a hive on a hot, sticky August afternoon. I read through it, made a few edits, and sent it off to Caleb. The act of clicking the 'Send' button filled me with a kind of nervous excitement I hadn't experienced while writing, and I wished I could bottle it and sprinkle it on the next time I hit a roadblock.

THIRTY MINUTES LATER, my phone rang.

Caleb.

Immediately, I got a knot in my stomach.

I answered the phone with my heart in my throat. "Hello?"

"Hey there, Paige. I just got your short story. I'm waiting for one of my writing mentees to get here, and I thought I would give you a call."

"Hey there, Caleb. Wow, I didn't expect to hear back from you so soon."

"Well, I didn't expect you to get your assignment done so soon. I'm impressed. No writer's block there, huh?"

"I definitely feel like the shorter word count felt a little less intimidating. I took your advice and went to the beach to observe the people around me. I saw a couple playing with their children and invented a whole story in my head about who they were like you had told me to do."

"Sounds like that was an effective exercise judging from what you sent me this morning. The CIA agent and the covert private investigator?"

"We all have dreams, right?"

"Isn't that the truth? I have to say, Paige, I'm impressed with what you've got here. I would make a few edits with some tense changes and word usage, but overall, you have a solid story here. Let me ask you something. Do you think you could take a story like this and expand on it? If you had a story that captured your imagination, do you think an outlining process could help you get to a fifty-thousand-word first draft?"

"Fifty thousand words? Yikes." I felt my stomach clenching up with the thought. "I'm not sure...."

"Okay, why don't we start here? Think about this story. Try to come up with some ways you can possibly expand it, and I will send you some resources you can use to build out characters. Have you done any work with character development?"

"I've done some, but I've mostly been trying to write by the seat of my pants. That doesn't appear to be working as well as I'd hoped."

Caleb's quiet laugh came back over the receiver. "There are some people that can write by the seat of their pants. We call them 'pantsers'. But others prefer to have everything laid out, plotted, and planned in advance, and they write based on those plans. It keeps their thoughts organized and helps pull them through the story as they write. It also helps them remember where the story is headed. You might fall into that camp."

"I haven't had much experience with plotting," I admitted.

"I have a couple tools I used on the last few books I published. I'll send those along to you in an email, but in the meantime, start thinking about what kinds of assignments he could go on. Dig a little deeper into some sticky situations the wife could uncover.

"Perhaps you can come up with some funny or stressful things that happen to her along the way, just to build some intrigue and interest around both their character arcs. Different ways they could grow—separately and together. Think about how you want your story to end. Is there a conflict? Is the conflict the secrets they are keeping from each other? Perhaps it's that he would really like to leave his current role and become a French horn instructor. Have some fun with it. You can always change out details later, but give them each an overarching conflict, then figure out how you would want to resolve those conflicts."

"I can do that," I said, wondering if it were true.

"Wonderful. Can you have it done by next Wednesday?"

"I'll do my best."

"Great. Once I get your notes back, I can show you how to plot out your story using your ideas. I know we have a meeting set for two weeks from now, but I wasn't expecting you to get done with your assignment so quickly. Let's move our next meeting up a bit so I can get you set up for the next step. Can you meet next Wednesday at noon?"

After checking my calendar, we set up the next session and chatted for a few more minutes until Caleb's mentee arrived. When we hung up, I felt a little better about the direction in which I was headed. It felt good to have a plan, even if it was headed into unfamiliar territory. It seemed everything around me was unfamiliar territory, but everywhere I turned, there were people standing next to me, ready to help me find my way forward.

HALFWAY THROUGH THE beef bourguignon I was making 'Paige, party of one' for dinner that night, my phone vibrated on the counter. I picked it up and saw a new text in our group chat, which had been renamed, 'The Sensational Six.'

> Grace: Hey you. The girls and I have been having a little side chat so as not to overwhelm you. We've got some ideas we'd like to run past you.
>
> Elyse: Grace, you make it sound like we're sitting around talking about her behind her back.
>
> Jenna: We have definitely not been doing that.
>
> Grace: Oh stop it. We're just here crafting our master plan for Paige's future. You don't mind, do you Paige?

> Not one bit. Someone needs to have a plan for my future.

Grace: That's where we come in. Are you free tomorrow around one?

My calendar app indicated I was indeed free. Not to mention, my curiosity was piqued.

> Looks like I'm free. What did you have in mind?

Grace: Meet us at Cat's Bites. Bring a notebook.

> Sounds... mysterious... but well-documented. Should I be afraid?

Elyse: With Grace on the case, you should always be afraid. But don't worry, we're keeping her reined in.

Jenna: Barely

Oh. She jokes.

Grace: See you tomorrow

Elyse: See ya

Jenna: Bye

> See you tomorrow

I spent the rest of the time it took to make dinner wondering what on earth they had up their sleeves. I carried my soon-to-be-tattered notebook to the table with me when I sat down to eat. It was time to get serious and start that Pros and Cons list.

Pros:

1. I have friends who are willing to help with the leg work.

2. I'll be surrounded by creative people.

3. It'll give me a sense of purpose.

4. The additional income will help with the utility bills. (Yikes.)

Cons:

   1. ...

I couldn't think of one.

~

I GOT through my work in record time the next morning. None of it was all that difficult. The usual: subject lines, social posts, a blog post, editing a brochure, sending an email to a subject matter expert I needed to interview the next week, a few emails from my boss asking for updates on a few other projects we were working on together, and I was finished in the nick of time.

By twelve-thirty, I had walked Roxy and apologized profusely for needing to leave her behind again, but I didn't think Cat's café was dog-friendly. Golden retrievers loved to leave little bits of themselves everywhere they went, preferably in people's food.

"You and your fur need to stay here, Rox. I'll be back with leftovers." She wagged her tail as if she understood, and I bent to give her a kiss on her snoot before I walked out the door.

After a short trip in the Jeep, I found a parking spot in the back of the lot next to the library. I was walking toward the sidewalk still singing the song that had been playing in the Jeep as Elyse was walking up.

I put my hand up in greeting. "Hey, how'd your morning go?"

"Pretty good. Slow day at the bookstore, so I was able to leave the cashier in charge for a little bit. I couldn't miss this."

She had her backpack with her, as usual, and looked like she was ready to get down to business.

"I'm a little nervous, but... I'll just hear what you all have to say."

"Oh, it's all good. We've all been putting our heads together to try and come up with some ideas to see if we can talk you into this whole endeavor. We know it will be a lot of work, but I just want you to know we will be here to help you with it. We all have a particular set of skills," she said as she winked at me.

"Yeah, but will they make you a nightmare to someone like me?"

Elyse laughed. "Probably, but hear us out first."

We walked in together, welcomed by the smell of greasy bacon and... pie? Directly in front of us was a counter with a register and to the left of it, the baked goods case I'd heard so much about. Cat's head popped up through the opening into the kitchen behind the counter and she smiled when she saw us. "Hey, 'Lyse. You know where they are. Paige, I'm so glad you're here. Welcome to Cat's Bites."

I waved and smiled before she put her head back down, her face a mask of concentration framed by the steam from whatever she was cooking. Elyse pivoted to the left, and when I looked in the direction she was facing, I found Grace and Jenna with their heads together at one of the two U-shaped booths in the back corner.

This smells like trouble.

As Elyse and I walked past a dozen or so booths and a neat row of tables, I took in the eclectic decor of the café. Art of every kind hung on bright orange walls, and it all seemed to be grouped by themes, but I couldn't decipher what they were. I was so engrossed in taking in as much as I could, I nearly slammed into Elyse when she stopped. She turned and saw me staring at a large oil painting of a fully nude dark-skinned woman with one toe dipped into a roaring white-capped river. "Cat does a fair amount of traveling now that her son is grown and she's done paying for his education. Everywhere she goes, she picks up something for the café. These walls are basically an anthology of her travels."

She swung her backpack down and set it on the booth between her and Grace. I sat down next to Jenna and across from Elyse, then looked over at Grace. "Hey there."

"Hey there, yourself."

I wrapped my arm around Jenna and gave her a little squeeze. I had started to feel a little protective of her, like she was the younger, more introverted version of me from thirty years ago. I was hoping I could pull out some of the spirit I knew was in there.

"Alright ladies, I see you all have your pens and notepads in front of you. Is this an official meeting?"

"Indeed it is," said Grace with a huge smile and an unmistakable twinkle in her eye. Yes. An actual twinkle. I was terrified.

"I now call to order the first official meeting of The Sensational Six."

"First things first," Grace said, handing out spiral-bound presentations. I flipped mine open and was met with a Table of Contents.

Grace, Kari, and my mom would get along great. Would the world explode if they stood too close to each other? I chuckled to myself at the thought.

"I'm not sure what's so funny, chucklehead, but the first thing you'll need is zoning approval. Flip to page six. I found this on the website for the village, and it lays out everything you need to do..."

The next hour was a blur of sandwiches, to-do lists, and iced tea. As my cohort began to wind itself down, Elyse spoke up. "I have mentioned my friend Raina is an expert in social media. She's got a huge following that she's grown organically over the years. She doesn't spend a whole lot on advertising; she just creates content. I reached out to her yesterday to run the idea past her. I didn't give her any details, of course, but just a hypothetical situation, and she actually got pretty excited about it and had a few ideas of her own. If you don't mind, I'd love to connect you so she could go over those with you herself."

I was so overwhelmed by that point that, for once, I didn't know what to say. "I don't... you guys... you've put so much thought into this. Sure, I'd love to talk to her. It doesn't do any good to do all this planning and then not have anyone show up. If we're going to put this much work into it, I should probably have someone with local contacts and knowledge doing the marketing for me."

"Exactly," said Elyse. "Okay, so can I give her your number?"

"Absolutely."

"Okay, the next order of business is... Jenna, can you please run and get Cat and let her know she's up to bat?"

I stood so Jenna could scoot out of the booth. She disappeared into the kitchen, returning a moment later with Cat on her heels.

"Paige, good to see you. How was your lunch?"

Jenna slid back into the booth, and I returned to my spot next to her.

"I'll never rue a Rueben."

Elyse scooted over so Cat could settle in across from me.

"Ha. Good one. Anyway, I've been so busy at the café the last few days, but I've had some discussions with the other girls about your retreat. You are thinking of providing breakfast and lunch, correct?"

"Correct."

"I would love the opportunity to earn some of that business. We could work together on an easy menu that fits your budget, and we would deliver the lunches every day. Have you figured out what you'd like to serve for breakfast?"

I felt like I needed a nap at this point, but they had put so much into this that I needed to absorb as much as possible. "I haven't figured out much of anything at this point, but what did you have in mind?"

Elyse cleared her throat, and Jenna looked at her nervously before speaking. "You know how I have been really wanting to... You know I love to bake, and I really wanted to have another way to earn some money and maybe have a little bit of independence. I was thinking, if you're going to be serving breakfast, I would love the opportunity to provide some baked goods during these retreat weekends." Jenna paused and made eye contact with me.

"Okay," I smiled, trying to encourage her to continue. "What did you have in mind?"

"I think it would be a lot of fun, and it would give me some practice planning things out, and I could maybe turn it into a business. Maybe other people would want me to provide baked goods for their events."

"This is a great idea, Jenna, and I would love to talk to you more about that and hear what you had in mind."

She looked down at her hands twisted in front of her, but when she looked up, she was smiling, and it was like the first sunny day after a long, gray Midwest winter. "Okay, I'll put some ideas on paper and start thinking about things I could make. I could even do some different options for people who are gluten-free or have food allergies as well. I think that would be a smart idea for sure."

Grace piped up. "Jenna, I think this is fabulous. I'm really proud of you for speaking up and offering your skills to Paige.

You're very talented, and everything you've ever made has been absolutely delicious. You might make Paige's retreat famous just from your muffins alone."

Jenna beamed, and Cat's eyes shone with pride. "I spoke with Jenna about this opportunity before the meeting today. She can come in early and use my kitchen if you decide to let her bake for you."

"It sounds as if you ladies have this all figured out."

Elyse picked up her backpack and shoved her notebook into it. "I need to head back to the store, but it feels like we got a lot accomplished today. Let me know when the next meeting is." Cat stood to let her out, then Elyse turned to me. "This is going to be fabulous. All of it. I can feel it in my bones." She threw her backpack over her shoulder, placed a twenty-dollar bill on the table, and turned to leave. "See you at league next week. I'll be the one racing Cat to the first tee box." And with a wink, she was gone.

The rest of us followed suit. Cat said goodbye and returned to the kitchen, and Grace, Jenna, and I paid, packed up, and walked outside.

"Productive meeting, I would say," said Grace. "I'll fill Sarah in once she's out of school. She'll be delighted by how much we got done." She reached out and squeezed my upper arm. "Thank you, Paige. This project we've foisted on you is going to change a lot of lives. You wait and see." She took a step back. "Ready, Jenna?"

"I'm ready. Thank you, Paige. Thanks for listening and considering me. I'll put some ideas together for next time we meet." Again, her eyes were on mine, her shoulders back with budding pride.

"I can't wait. I'll see you both soon."

We parted ways, and Jenna and Grace headed for the Range Rover. I had parked in the back of the lot near the library, so I walked the rest of the way, lost in thought.

WHEN I SAW the glass on the ground next to my Jeep, I wondered how I hadn't noticed it before parking there, or, at the very least, when I'd gotten out. I'd never claimed to be overly observant, but broken glass seemed like something I'd notice as I crunched my way through it. I didn't suspect the glass was from my own vehicle until I saw the mess on my front seats. I'd left the windows rolled down when I'd arrived, so my confusion grew until I looked up and saw my windshield. Or what was left of it.

25

"I CAN DO IT WITH A BROKEN HEART"

TAYLOR SWIFT

I immediately looked around, and other than a few people walking into the library and a man sitting on a bench across the street, I was alone. With my heart in my throat, I dialed 911.

The responding officer was there within ten minutes and was thoughtful enough to bring a broom. "Officer Alcott," he said as he removed his hat. Ash-blonde curls sprang from their confinement, and he brushed them out of his face just to have them fall right back down and sit along the top of his sunglasses.

"Paige Rhiann. Thanks for getting here so soon. I was at the café for an hour or so and found this mess when I came back out."

"I don't suppose you saw anyone lurking about at the time?"

"I didn't. I was pretty focused on my Jeep. I saw a few people walking in and out of the library, and that guy on the bench over there—" I looked across the street to point him out, but he was gone. "—but no one seemed to be in a hurry."

"Ok. You're also parked up against bushes that border another parking lot, and someone could have seen an opportunity to smash your windshield and sneak away unseen. Were your other windows smashed, too?" He peered into the back of the Jeep.

"They're rolled down."

"So it wasn't an attempted burglary, and it doesn't feel random, especially considering we haven't had any other vandalism calls lately." He walked to the back of the Jeep. "Hmmmm... Wisconsin plates. Are you new to the area or visiting?"

"A little of both, I guess? I'm visiting indefinitely and considering a move."

"Any chance you've made an enemy since you arrived?"

An enemy? Me? Here?

"I can't imagine how. I've only been here a matter of weeks, and I barely know anyone but my uncle, his partner, and the few friends I've made since I arrived."

"Hmm. Okay." He took his notebook out of the breast pocket of his blue button-up and pulled a pen out of the spiral along the side. "I just have a few questions for you, Miss Rhiann."

After taking my information and a statement, we worked together to clean up as much of the mess as we could while I waited for the tow truck. As it arrived, the Public Works truck was pulling in behind it, presumably to clean up everything that would be left behind when my poor, battered Jeep was dragged from the scene.

Within a few minutes, the tow truck was ready to go, and I easily accepted the driver's offer to drop me off at home. Officer Alcott met me at the passenger door. He was tall enough that his head nearly brushed the top of the doorframe. "Here's my card. Let me know if you think of anything else. I'll reach out if there are any developments or if I need more information. Irony aside, welcome to Dunedin. Hopefully, the rest of your experiences here will be sunny." With that, he shut my door and strode off toward his squad car. I glanced at the card he'd handed me and tucked it into my wallet as the tow truck began to move. The driver looked over at me, sympathy heavy in his gaze. "Buckle up," he gently reminded me.

After asking him to head to Grace's son Bill's body shop, I sat back against the threadbare seat, put my seatbelt on, and closed my eyes. I couldn't yet fully process everything that had happened in the last ninety minutes, but it felt like hope had filled me to the point of bursting. Then life poked a hole in me and watched as I flew around in circles until I was completely deflated.

NOW THAT I had my list of to-do's from the "Sensational Six", it was time to call my uncle again. He answered on the first ring, which he's been doing ever since I first brought up the possibility of doing the retreat. There were times I thought he was more excited about this than any of us.

"Hey there, Paige! What's up?"

I filled him in on the plans the ladies and I had made. Knowing his passion for promoting small businesses, I rounded it all out with the idea of supporting both Cat's business and Jenna's dream of becoming a professional baker.

"I like where this is headed. It's going to take a lot of work to get off the ground, but I can see it being a huge success! Clearwater and Dunedin are full to bursting with creatives, and it sounds like you have a lot of very driven women willing to give you a hand."

"The issue I'm running into is a tough one. I don't know who has to fill out the application with the zoning committee."

"Ah. I see what you're getting at. Okay, well, the good news is when I had the idea to open up a bed and breakfast about ten years ago, I had gotten through some of the zoning application process before I realized the whole thing was going to be too much work. That being said, your idea of having people coming through one weekend a month *and* you being part of that group sounds pretty awesome."

"We also talked about having someone come in and give some writing and publishing tips. I haven't nailed that one down yet, but I have some ideas. Dad put me in contact with one of his old colleagues, Caleb. He's been helping me with my writing, and in one meeting with him, I had completely fleshed out an idea for a story. I'm still unsure if I can make a book out of it, but it felt really good to get some words on a page for once."

"That is such good news! I know that's been weighing heavily on you. Do you think that he would be willing to come to your retreat and host a session?"

"I'm meeting with him at the library next Wednesday, and we're going to go over what I have accomplished based on his direction. I was going to bring it up to him then."

"Well, let me know how that goes, and keep me updated on your book for sure. Now, back to the zoning. Why don't I reach out to my contact at the zoning board and see if my application is still valid? If not, I'll fill out another one, and it can be a temporary fix."

"That would be so awesome. Thank you so much. I have Kari coming this weekend, and I'm going to sit down and talk to her about everything. She's so organized; I'm hoping she can make a spreadsheet or something for me."

"I can't wait to see her! Stop by the store with her some time while she's here. But, I'm surprised your mom doesn't have a pros and cons list ready for you already."

"Oh, she does. They were on that cruise for a couple weeks, but she wasted no time once they were home. She emailed me a nice outline a few days ago. I looked it over and brought it with me when I met with them, but they already had each of her points covered. I have a sneaky suspicion they're biased, so I'm not sure how objective they are, but at least it's a start."

"Either way, I like where all this is headed. I really want to see you stay in that house on a more long-term basis, not just because I want you nearby or anything." He chuckled.

I'd always thought my Uncle Mike would have made an excellent father, and for as long as I could remember, he'd been like a second dad to me, cheering me on from afar. It was going to be nice having him in my corner... from right around the corner.

"I like being near you as well, and staying so close to the water is really helping me. I've been on walks daily with Roxy, so it's been a win-win for me."

"Plus, it sounds like you've made some great friends! How does Kari feel about all of this? It's got to be difficult on her, you being so far away. You haven't really been apart from her for how many years now?"

"Forty-five years we've lived by each other."

"Holy cow. Well, in a few days, you'll be back together for a while. In the meantime, I'm going to see what my guy in zoning has to say."

"I wanted to talk to you about one other thing."

"Shoot."

"When I was coming out of the café today, I found my windshield smashed. The rest of the windows were rolled down, so they weren't trying to get in to steal anything. The officer said it felt personal, but I barely know anyone here."

"I wonder if it was a case of mistaken identity. Yours isn't the only sunshine yellow Jeep around here."

"I hadn't thought of that. I bet you're right. But the body shop owner told me they will drop my Jeep off tomorrow, which is a huge relief."

"Wow! I'm glad they're getting it back to you so fast, especially with Kari coming in this weekend. Ok, Love. I'm getting some major side-eye from Chris. We've got a huge delivery waiting for us in the back room right now. Let me get these jackets on hangers and start steaming, and as soon as he's not looking, I'll make some phone calls to the city." I heard some muffled shuffling and then, "Okay! Okay! I'm coming! Jeez! Paige, I'm sorry for what happened to the Jeep, but I am so proud of you for having the courage to chase this retreat concept down. I love the whole idea, and I'll do everything I can to help you make it happen. I'll let you know what I find out from the city."

We hung up shortly after, and as I grabbed Roxy's leash to head back out into the sunshine, I couldn't stop smiling. What had started out as somebody else's idea was turning into a passion project for everyone involved—especially me. I could see myself surrounded by groups of other writers. I could *feel* the energy and wanted so badly to make that vision a reality. But at the same time, I knew I had to be cautious and make sure it was all built on solid ground. I'd had more than one dream crumble to dust in my hand. I was determined to make sure the retreat wasn't one of them.

I needed to sit down with someone who knew me to figure out if I could do this.

Only two more days until she gets here.

26

"SISTER GOLDEN HAIR"
AMERICA

Before I knew it, Saturday morning had arrived. I had assumed the time would drag on, but between doing research for the retreat, working on the story for Caleb, and my actual job, the time sped by as if Kari was already there.

My Jeep had been delivered the day before with a shiny new windshield, and at noon on the dot, I loaded Roxy into the back, and we took off for the airport. Thirty minutes later, I pulled up in front of arrivals, and as luck would have it, I saw Kari standing there next to her matching luggage and carry-on, dressed in her signature yoga attire with a light hoodie.

I waved as I pulled up to the curb, the goofy grin on my face mirroring the one on hers. Roxy looked out the side window in the back and barked, then tried to climb over the seat.

"Stay, Rox. I know. I get it. She's finally here!" I opened my door, jumped out of the Jeep, and ran around to the sidewalk, pulling my friend into a bear hug. "I've missed you so much. Where have you been?"

"I know, right?" she replied, squeezing me so tight I thought my ribs would shatter. "I've missed you more!"

"Okay," I said, pulling back to get a look at her. It had been nearly two months since we'd last seen each other. "Let's not waste time standing around at the airport. I'll get your bag into the back seat. Go ahead and throw your carry-on back there, and we'll take off. Are you hungry?"

"It's been a long morning. I'd rather just get back to the house and figure out food from there," she replied as she climbed into the passenger seat with ease.

"Perfectly fine with me. I've got all kinds of stuff to make sandwiches. Do you mind if we stop by Dash of Flair to see Uncle Mike and Chris? Be prepared, however. They're both quite insistent that Nick needs a fashion makeover."

"They're not wrong. *Let's go!*"

Kari took off her hoodie, buckled her belt, the latch clicking in unison with mine, and we were off.

We had the windows rolled up to keep the air conditioning in, but as we got closer to the water, Kari asked, "Do you mind if we roll the windows down? I know it's hot and muggy, but I really want to smell the beach as we drive by it."

"Absolutely. I love driving around here with the windows down, but I didn't want to shock you with the humidity."

"It's nothing I'm not used to, and at least here, there's a bit of a breeze."

We drove the rest of the way with the wind in our hair. She caught me up on the boys' first month at college, the progress at her house, and the project that Nick was working on. I caught her up on the progress with the retreat and the story I was developing with Caleb's help.

"Can I read your short story at some point this week?" she asked.

"I want you to. Maybe you have some ideas for some other adventures or fun things I can add."

"If I add something good, will you put me in the acknowledgments?"

"You already know I will. Your name will be first. I might even name a character after you if you're good."

"Aw, darn, that would have been nice." She winked at me, a devilish grin on her face.

"Uh oh. Do I sense a week of *Girls Gone Wild* ahead of us?"

"Only time will tell..." She brushed invisible lint from her yoga pants and looked back at me. "Maybe it's time for this girl to go a little wild."

"Well, alright then!" I knew from experience that Kari's version of "a little wild" was one too many espresso martinis with dinner, but I thought it best to humor her. She *was* on vacation, after all. Finally.

Before heading back to the house, I drove Kari over to Dash of Flair to see Uncle Mike and meet Chris. They were ready for her.

After tucking Roxy into their office with a bone they'd picked up from the butcher that morning, Chris gestured to a mound of dress shirts in a riot of colors and patterns poured across a fifteen-foot-long rough-hewn cherrywood table. "It's been quiet this morning, so I pulled together a few options for you to send home to your paisley prince. Write down his sizes, and I'll pull the ones you like from the back." He slid a leather-bound spiral notebook and black Mont Blanc from his pocket and set them on the table in front of Kari. She neither saw nor heard him, her attention stolen by the sheer opulence of her surroundings.

Uncle Mike looked up from the pyramid of ties he'd been curating for Nick's unsolicited wardrobe makeover. "C'mon, Kari. You should know better than to expect anything less than jaw-dropping when I'm on the case. I'm being humble when I say, this might be my favorite interior design project. It didn't hurt that Chris gave me full control of the design *and* the check-book." He looked over at his partner just in time to see the look of pride Chris was trying in vain to mask with a half-assed scowl.

"Yeah, well, hindsight's twenty-twenty, isn't it?"

"I can always run out to your storage unit and bring back those aluminum racks you had in here previously." Uncle Mike picked up a pair of meticulously folded socks with his free hand and threw them at his partner. "Your choice."

"No, no. The money's already spent."

"...and?"

"You already know it looks great in here. You're just fishing for a compliment."

The smile in Chris' eyes as he purposely goaded my uncle was reminiscent of my dad's when he was poking my mom's last nerve for sport. It made my insides mush to realize someone I loved with my whole heart was so cherished, and in turn, was so completely and utterly enamored. Being around all their sarcasm-soaked happiness was like baking soda and vinegar to my salt-corroded, copper heart.

Kari, who had completed a full, deliberate circle to take it all in, put her hands on either side of the notebook and leaned forward to catch my uncle's attention. "This place is fantastic!"

Uncle Mike broke character and looked down at the ties over his arm, a blush crawling slowly from beneath the collar of his shirt. "Thanks, Kari. That means a lot." His gaze returned to her, and the lip he'd been biting in humility gave way to a smile dripping with pride. "What's your favorite feature?"

Kari repeated her spin, stopping a quarter of the way around facing the back of the store. "I don't know if it's the navy blue velvet and gold foil wallpaper or... the Armani-clad statue of David lounging on the fainting couch in front of the fitting rooms or..." She continued her spin until she was facing a wall-to-wall, floor-to-ceiling shelving grid crafted from the same cherrywood of the table that stretched the length of the store.

"... the vintage top hats and classic hardcover books you have displayed in between each stack of apparel. Or... " another quarter turn "your window display. Is that Madam and Christopher Sly?"

"Good eye," Chris said. "We went to opening night of The Taming of the Shrew at Ruth Eckerd Hall in July, and Mike came straight here after the curtain closed. I barely saw him the rest of the weekend."

"Well it's a show stopper. No pun intended. Is it getting you some foot traffic?"

Uncle Mike, having apparently completed his quest for the perfect tie, slid his selections off his arm and onto the table next to the shirts. "A ton. We've been dressing the show's attendees for weeks now. We've also been able to send some business over to the ladies' boutique next door."

I knew how much supporting local commerce meant to my uncle, and while his face remained passive, his tone was a truer reflection of his pride.

"Uncle Mike! This is huge!"

Kari groaned and muttered under her breath, "Please don't say it. Please don't say it."

"Go on, Paige. You teed it up for yourself, you might as well swing." My uncle chuckled, shaking his head.

"Well, it actually *is* what she said this time. So..."

"On that note, let's get your poor fashion-challenged husband back on track." Chris held up the first shirt on the pile. "Blue with white windowpane or white with blue pinstripes?"

We spent the next hour giving Kari's American Express a workout, but in the end, the general consensus was that Nick's new wardrobe would boost his confidence, resulting in successful sales meetings, and thus... the clothes practically paid for themselves. Anyway, that's how Chris sold it while Kari signed her name to the lengthy credit card receipt.

Once the clothes were all wrapped and boxed up to be shipped to Madison, Uncle Mike and Chris walked us out to the Jeep, doling out kisses and hugs and promises to come by for dinner before Kari returned home. Fifteen minutes later, we were pulling into the driveway. Roxy spun in circles in the back, and her long blonde hairs, having escaped their captor in droves, floated toward the front of the Jeep.

I felt one land in my eyelashes and used the rearview mirror to extract it. "She must have spotted a lizard she needs to chase," I said before hopping down onto the driveway.

"Have you found any in the house?"

"Not yet," I replied, dragging her bulging suitcase out of the backseat. "I don't think you can ever be prepared for something like that, but I know it's going to happen. I'm going to wake up with a lizard running across my face one of these days."

Kari shuddered, then grabbed her carry-on while I let the spinning mass of yellow fur out of the back. Before I could even get the door all the way open, she was off like a lightning bolt in a summer storm.

"There she goes. Go get him, Roxy! Tell that lizard not to dare come into our house."

"At least this week," I heard Kari mutter under her breath.

"Ok. Who's ready to get our suits on and go for a swim?"

"The pool is gorgeous. How do you get anything done with all this right outside your back door?"

"I do spend quite a bit of time floating around thinking about my work projects. It helps boost my creativity. I consider that time 'professional development'," I said, using air quotes.

"Good plan." Kari shifted her carry-on to her other hand as we reached the back door.

"I did find a couple yoga studios around here. I'm sure you're going to want to visit at least one of them over the next week. Maybe you could try out a few while I'm working, and let me know which one you like best. I haven't practiced once since I've been here."

"Oh, thank you so much. I was worried about going a week without moving my body. I hope you're still planning on joining me for a class."

"Of course. Now, let's heave this massive bag upstairs and get suited up. I have our floaties all ready for us."

_____

27

"GIRLS JUST WANNA HAVE FUN"
CYNDI LAUPER

Within twenty minutes, Kari and I were floating around in the pool, our spill-proof Yetis full of piña colada tucked safely into the cupholders in our rafts. I closed my eyes and let the sun warm my body after the shock of jumping into the cold water.

"So... tell me all about this writer's retreat," I heard Kari say from her floatie nearby.

I took a sip of my piña colada and returned it to the cupholder. "As you know, I have five women here who are pushing hard for this."

"Are you pushing as hard as them?" I knew I could depend on her to ask the questions I was afraid to ask myself.

"I am now. I wasn't so much in the beginning because it seemed like a lot of work, but these women are so motivated to make this happen that they've put together to-do lists for each of us. _And_ they have someone lined up to help with marketing."

"Tell me what you are envisioning," prompted Kari as her raft caught a jet and spun toward where I was floating in the center of the pool.

"I'm thinking the women that sign up will arrive on

Thursday night. We would have a quick meet and greet, basically a social hour with some snacks, and everything would kick off the next morning after everyone is settled in. We would get up, and there would be a light breakfast for whoever wants it. There's another member of the unofficial planning committee who's offered to provide breakfast pastries."

"Oh, that's always a good idea. Is she offering free samples?"

I laughed. "I can find out. You'll be meeting them while you're here."

"I'm looking forward to that. I've heard so much about them." She fell silent for a moment, and when I looked over, she was sipping her piña colada with a thoughtful look on her face. She paddled one-handed over to the poolside, refreshed the sunscreen on her face, pulled her floppy brimmed hat down to shade her eyes, and then threw the sunscreen at me.

"I feel like I have a permanent coating of sunscreen on my face." I laughed, "but I can always use more."

"It can't hurt. Anyway, I'll admit it, I was a little jealous hearing about all the new people you're meeting, but I'm really glad you have some women to support you here and keep you company now that I can't." Her voice broke on the last word, and she cleared her throat.

How many times had Kari been the one to pull me from the depths of my despair? As it was, she had been calling or stopping by every night since Anna left for college. My mind drifted back to the summer between eighth grade and Freshman year of high school when my dad's mom had passed very suddenly. I'd never lost anyone important to me, and my grandma and I had been very close. At that point, my parents didn't understand me (or so I thought) the way she did, and I ran to her with everything that was even remotely distressing. Somehow Kari knew exactly what to say to soothe my broken heart; no doubt her long history of forced goodbyes came in handy at that moment. She stayed with me for a week straight, forced me into the shower, washed my sheets, and made countless grilled cheese (her specialty) for the four of us. She unwittingly helped us all by caring for me so my mom could care for my dad's tender, broken heart.

Back in the pool, I felt her anguish and wished I could hug her. "I miss you terribly, Kari. I really do." I paused to give her a moment to collect herself. "I've been blessed to meet these women when I did. They've been great. I don't know that I would have the energy to get this idea off the ground without them."

"I highly doubt that."

"Thanks for the vote of confidence, but let's be real here. Tiny details aren't my specialty."

I heard Kari snort at this, probably remembering one of the many times I'd shown up at her door with a look of panic and a pile of papers that needed to be filled out. "I am thinking about having some kind of writing workshop scheduled after breakfast. When I see Caleb on Wednesday, I'm going to ask him if he'd be interested in teaching a few of those. He's been so great in helping me find my way through my writing process, and I really want to provide some kind of service to the attendees other than 'here's a desk. Good luck'."

I heard a splash and opened my eyes to the sight of Kari making her way toward me with her cup held aloft. "Hold that thought. I'm going in to top us off and run to the bathroom. Can I get you anything else?"

One look at my wilting retriever answered that question. "Looks like Roxy is done hunting lizards. Can you let her in and make sure she's got some water in her bowl?"

"Done. Let's go, Rox. Naptime for you."

A few minutes later, I heard the beep signaling the opening of the back door, the swish of water nearby, and moments later, my cup was in my hand, heavier than it had been when it left.

Kari spent a full minute thrashing around, trying to get

back on the floatie before she finally threw herself across it like a killer whale delivering the final blow to its lunch. She wriggled her way around and found herself with her feet where her head should be while the section under her upper body threatened to deposit her back from whence she came. "Does this thing come with an instruction manual? What am I doing wrong here?"

I was laughing so hard I was unable to give any kind of verbal instruction, so I settled in for the show. After a few more failed attempts at turning herself around, she finally managed to get her head pointed in the right direction and lifted her cup in the air in victory. "Thank God for spill-proof cups." She took a hard-won sip of her piña colada and settled back on the attached pillow (the one that should have signaled which side was for her head in the first place). "Phew! Ok, where were we?"

"I thought you were supposed to be graceful, yogi," I teased. "Next time, give me a little warning beforehand so I can record that process for future entertainment."

"In hindsight, that might have been easier with two hands. I would pay good money to see what you looked like getting onto this thing for the first time after a few cocktails! You can barely walk a straight line stone cold sober. "

"I resemble that remark," I quipped while wiping tears from the corners of my eyes. "And I wasn't about to give out any pro tips that would have ruined my chances of witnessing that impressive display of agility." A snicker bubbled up from the bottom of my belly once again, and before I knew it, I was back to a fit of laughter that threatened instant karma if I didn't get myself under control. When I started to wind down and could open my eyes again, I saw I wasn't alone in my amusement. Kari was silently wheezing with laughter and gripping the sides of her floatie with both hands in an attempt to avoid capsizing again.

"Whoo! Oh my gosh! Ahhhh... I needed that! Deep breaths,

Paige." I breathed slowly in through my nose to regain control. "Ok. Ok. We were discussing having Caleb—or someone like Caleb—come in and teach some writing sessions."

"Oh, yes, yes. Geez, that conversation seems like ages ago. I think it's a great idea," said Kari, her own laughter finally winding down. "Maybe you can have sessions that change over time so he's not saying the same thing month after month. Every session could have a different theme, like editing, idea development, or plotting. That kind of thing. They would know what the session topic will be before they sign up."

I washed down this inspiration with piña colada. "Oooohhh, I like where this is headed. Keep going."

"Maybe over time, if he shares his presentations, you can have those printed out in a binder in each room, or you can put them on your website for people to see what the past presentations were about." She paused and tipped her cup most of the way back. "You could put a newsletter pop-up over them so they'd have to sign up for access. Something like that."

"We should have some paper. We're never going to remember any of this after a few more of these," I said, holding up my piña colada before taking a giant swig. "Down the hatch."

"Someone needs to invent waterproof notebooks." Kari mused, then tipped her cup back again, further this time. "So what else are you planning?"

"After the Friday morning session, I think there'll be time for discussion and brainstorming, and then everyone will find a quiet place to work on their books. Then, we all come together at the end of that time to talk about what we'd accomplished and ask the group questions. Maybe get some feedback or get an idea on something happening in their book, or you know... that kind of stuff. Then everyone goes their separate ways for dinner."

Our rafts had floated close enough together that I was able

to throw my right foot over Kari's so we would remain facing each other. I was getting whiplash, trying to look at her while we talked. She drained her piña colada, slid the lid closed, and tossed the cup into the pool. "What about Saturday?"

"That's where it gets fuzzier than my legs before Memorial Day. I'm trying to come up with an activity for the morning, then the rest of the day would be identical to Friday. Sunday would mostly be socializing, wrapping things up, and packing, then they'll all head out around eleven."

"Listening to this makes me want to write a book! I think we need to eat something," said Kari, her topic quickly signaling the end of our float.

"Let's head in and start thinking about dinner. And Roxy is probably green with envy by now."

Kari, realizing that meant she was going to have to figure out how to move from the floatie to the pool in her current condition, leaned so far to the left to peer into the depths of the pool (possibly to devise some kind of rum-inspired game plan), she dumped herself right over. She found her footing a moment later and popped up from the four-foot depth, threw her arms up in a 'V' for victory, and yelled, "Ta-da!"

"Bravo! Bravo! Encore!" I shouted as I clapped with gusto. That earned me a dose of instant Karma and over I went. When I popped up, Kari was ascending the steps to the pool deck, so I retrieved her discarded cup and splashed over to where mine floated next to my capsized raft. "When did I become the responsible one?"

"The moment I stepped off that plane. I'm on vacation, baby. Now, feed me or I'm leaving a nasty Yelp review! 'Hostess got me drunk, pushed me in the pool, then refused to feed me. Zero out of ten. Do not recommend.'"

"Watch it, you." I laughed as I made it to my lounge chair, where a fluffy, yellow towel awaited me. Kari had wrapped herself in the light blue and white striped one I'd purchased for her as soon as she'd announced she was coming for a visit. Seeing her in it soaking wet, dripping everywhere, made me smile. It was exactly what I'd pictured when I'd added it to my Amazon cart. "Let's go, Princess. Time for you to cook me dinner."

Kari threw one arm up and punched the air above her head. "Pizza it is!"

She was asleep on the couch in the sunroom before I'd even finished placing our order.

WHEN SLEEPING BEAUTY AWOKE, we sat at the island in the kitchen and enjoyed the cold spinach and mushroom pizza that had always been our standby. Avoiding any topics related to her house, the twins, or rum, she turned our attention back to the reigning topic du jour. Me. That is, until the topic of my new story came up again. "I was thinking about your story, and I can really identify with the wife," she reflected. "Sometimes, it seems like there must be more that was meant for my life besides teaching a few yoga classes every week. Actually, wait right there."

Kari spun her stool and strode from the kitchen with purpose. I heard her run up the stairs, and a moment later, she was back with a book in her hand.

Oh no. The gratitude journal.

"You must have accidentally left this behind. I found it in your junk drawer."

"I just—"

She held up her hand in the universal 'stop' gesture. "Save it. But I *do* think you'd get a lot out of this." She set it on the counter in front of me. "Please just try it."

"Okay, okay. I will. Thanks for bringing it. Now, back to what you were saying. I'm shook! You love teaching yoga."

"I do, but I'm teaching yoga at someone else's studio. I, too, have been wondering about what's next for me. I just don't go to such dramatic lengths to find it."

"Don't knock it 'til you try it!" I said, throwing another slice of pizza on each of our plates. An end for me, a middle for her.

"Believe me, my sarcasm is a failing attempt to mask my envy. I've been in the same place for so long, I'm surprised I don't have roots growing from between my toes. Staying in your house for the last few months has been challenging, but at the same time, has shown me I can actually survive in a house other than mine. And you being so far away gave me the motivation I needed to get on a plane and travel further than a city in my home state, for longer than a weekend. Anyway, I'm living vicariously through your new adventures right now, but what keeps popping into my mind is a vision of me leading a class full of sweaty baby crows in my *own* studio."

"Oh my gosh, Kari. You absolutely should! But can we back up for a moment here?" I mimicked the beep of a garbage truck reversing for dramatic effect. "Would you ever consider moving away from Madison? You've been there most of your life at this point."

"I don't know. With the boys gone now and Nick able to work from anywhere with an airport nearby, I guess we're not really stuck there anymore. It's more a matter of wrapping my mind around uprooting my life and moving somewhere else."

"Let me remind you," I said, "you don't have to shovel sunshine!"

I finally got a laugh out of Kari. "No, you certainly don't. But you *do* have to keep up with the sunscreen and piña coladas! Oh, God." I could see her stomach roiling at the mention of what we'd substituted for lunch. "It might be early bedtime tonight."

We ate one more piece each and Kari was ready to sleep through the hangover I could see was approaching like a steam train through a tunnel. The kind you could feel shaking the ground under your feet, but couldn't quite see yet. I sent her off to bed with a giant squeezing hug, put the leftover pizza in the fridge, and wrote out the names of the nearby yoga studios on the notepad on the counter.

Chances were my early bird best friend would be down before dawn and out the door shortly after. In that way, we couldn't be more different. I preferred to keep company with the dark, quiet solitude of night and wake up *after* the birds.

28

"LET IT BE"

THE BEATLES

The next morning, Kari was long gone before I rolled out of bed and made it down to the kitchen. The keys and list were not where I'd left them next to the coffee maker, but she'd drawn a heart on the next sheet of my notepad. The shorthand of best friends. I knew she'd wake up with a burning desire to sweat in a room full of *other* sweaty people, and she knew I didn't like to talk in the morning, even on paper.

I decided to take advantage of the distraction-free alone time around the house. It was time to work on my story; only three more days until I met with Caleb.

I sat at the desk in my room and looked out the window into the backyard. I could see the reflection from the pool on the garage doors beckoning me, but I knew I needed to be disciplined and resist the urge to get in the water just yet. That could wait until Kari got back.

I sat thinking of ways I could expand the story. I did some research on what kind of assignments a CIA agent would go on. I tried to think of some exciting adventures for the wife as she tracked down skips and philanderous spouses. Using Caleb's templates, I built out some character profiles, including the two cute little kids I saw at the beach that day, and gave my secondary characters names.

It was nice having a mental picture of each of them. It made the story seem more real, which I'd gone out on a limb and assumed would make it easier to write.

I had accomplished quite a bit of what I'd planned to and lost all sense of time, so I was shocked to see movement from the direction of my driveway. My Jeep was pulling in.

Roxy's quick, high-pitched bark let me know she was excited Kari was back. She did tend to spoil my dog, which was fine. She was used to being spoiled.

I closed my laptop, satisfied with my progress for the day, and headed downstairs to meet her—and hopefully, my lunch —in the kitchen.

I raced through the hallway and into the kitchen, where Kari was unpacking a paper bag from Cat's Bites. I wondered if she had bumped into Jenna or Cat.

I pulled some of the finest paper plates in town from the cabinet behind me. "Ooh, what did you get?"

"Well, after sweating for ninety minutes, I really didn't want anything heavy, so I got us each a chicken Caesar salad. No anchovies for you."

"My hero. I actually had a taste for a salad. I think living in all this sunshine makes me want to eat something in addition to cheese and things made with cheese."

Kari walked to the table with our salad to-go containers while I got two forks out of the dishwasher.

At some point, I'm going to have to put those away, along with the laundry.

As we sat at the table and took the lids off our bowls, I could see Kari's leg bouncing nervously, not a common sight from her.

"Uh, where are you running to there, girl?"

Her leg stopped for a moment while she finished chewing. I could see her brain working behind eyes that couldn't keep a secret from me. "I was trying to clear my mind at yoga, but all that kept popping up was your writer's retreat. You know how you were talking about needing an activity for Saturday morning?"

"Mm-hmm," I replied, shoving a forkful of salad and chicken into my mouth.

"What about having a yoga session? It wouldn't have to be anything strenuous. But you've got plenty of space here where you can have five or six women on mats practicing mindfulness, which would be a great way to start the day, or following along with some beginner yoga moves."

"That's something I'd need to consider because we would have people of all different ages and levels here. I do think it's a great idea, though. It could be completely optional, and I could have some alternative activities for the women who don't want to participate. Where would I start with this?"

"Here's where I come in. I was thinking I could take the next few days to reach out to some local yoga instructors and without giving them too many details, try to find someone who would want to teach that class for you once a month."

"I love it. Are you sure that's how you want to spend your vacation?"

"You know me. I love having a project, and I prefer to be busy. And I know you've got some work to do this week as well. I don't want to feel like I'm holding you up or getting in your way. If I have a project I can work on, I'll feel productive and helpful."

"Have at it. I love the idea, and I trust your judgment. If you can find a few practitioners who would be interested in helping with that part, I'd be grateful."

"I would be happy to reach out to several and vet the ones

who are interested. By the time you're ready to meet them, I'd have the list down to maybe two or three."

"Music to my ears. Can you get the rest of my list down to two or three?"

Kari threw her head back and gave me one of her trademarked but rare full-body laughs. "What's the best way to eat an elephant? One bite at a time, girl."

AFTER LUNCH, we ran up to the second floor to change into our bathing suits for a day at the beach, then met back downstairs in the kitchen.

Kari grabbed the beach bag, I filled up our travel cups with water, and we hit the road, headed for Clearwater Beach. The windows were down, Stevie Nicks was crooning, and the wind blew our hair everywhere as we crossed the Causeway. Kari leaned forward in her seat, scraped her wild blonde curls together, and pulled it all into an elastic band and through the back of her ponytail hat. She turned toward me in her seat. "You seem like you're really enjoying this, Paige. Do you love it here?" she asked, then covered her ears. "I don't want to hear it if you do!"

A quick glance over to her told me everything I needed to know about how she was feeling. While our friendship had stood the test of time, I worried about how the distance would affect it. Would she pull away to protect her heart? Would I? I hoped she could see how much I'd grown since I arrived in Florida.

I reached over to pull her left hand down and gave it a squeeze. "I really do. I *really* love it here, and I feel like I'm making progress. Not just with my book, but with myself, with my life, the direction I'm going."

"That makes me so happy to hear. I can see it all over you.

You are positively *vibrating* with happiness and I can't pretend it's not beautiful here. I don't blame you one bit. I'm just..." She looked off to her right at the water. She cleared her throat, paused, and cleared her throat a second time, then swiped her free hand under her eyes before beginning again. "I—I know I'm probably going to lose you to this place, and I'm having trouble dealing with it." I could hear the tears in her voice.

Kari wasn't a crier, and that was the second time she'd broken down in two days. I knew at that moment how much my being here was weighing on her.

"Kari, no matter where I live, you will always be my sister. One I got to choose instead of getting stuck with. That will never change."

"I know, I know," she said, sniffing and wiping her eyes with a beach towel she'd pulled out of the bag at her feet. "Can I blow my nose on this?"

I looked over at her in shock, and when I saw the humor shining in her green eyes, I knew she was trying to be ok, at least for me. "I'm happy that you're joking, but I'm not. There is nothing in the world that is going to take my friendship away from you. You're just as much a part of me as my DNA."

"Your DNA gets my boys in a lot of trouble," she quipped, "but, I feel the same way about you. It's just going to be so weird not having you two doors down."

"Life is strange, Kari. Who knows what it has in store for us around the corner. Take mine, for instance. One day, I'm crying lonely tears into my Door Dashed chicken almond ding, and the next I'm lounging around poolside every day in a state I used to visit on vacation."

"The randomness of life does not escape me, I just wish it had the decency to give me a little notice before it shook my snow globe."

I reached over and squeezed her hand again, the only

comfort I could give until we were parked, but it had to do for now. "I miss you, too, Kar Bear."

ON WEDNESDAY, Uncle Mike called on my way to meet Caleb. "Hey Paige, I have some good news! I just got off the phone with my contact at the zoning department, and in order for you to have a short-term residential zoning approval, you need to be the one to fill out the application since I won't be the one in residence. I would hate for something to happen, and insurance refuses to pay because of some loophole we could have easily closed."

"Ok. What do we need to do?"

"First, I want to stop over and see Kari again. It's been so busy at the store... never mind, that's no excuse. When can we come over? We can talk about it all then."

"Why don't you two come over tomorrow night for dinner. I'll cook, and we can chat. Kari is going to be so happy to see you again! Everyone should have an Uncle Mike."

"I'm looking forward to it. I'll see you tomorrow night. Text me the time and what we can bring."

"I can tell you now. Come at seven and bring nothing but yourselves. I've got it all covered. I downloaded a recipe for braised chicken breasts from All Recipes, and I absolutely suck at cooking for two. I always make way too much, so this is perfect."

"Seven it is. See you then, honey."

A few moments later, I was slipping my phone into my purse and making a mental list for the grocery store as I pulled into the library parking lot.

After we hung up, a notification buzzed my phone. Uncle Mike had wasted no time sending me his contact at the zoning department. Frank Rizzo.

With nervous energy building in the pit of my stomach, I clicked the phone number, but my excitement was doused when it went to voicemail. As soon as I disconnected the call, the phone rang in my hand, displaying, "City of Dunedin."

"Hello?"

"Hi, is this Paige?"

"Yes, it is."

"This is Frank from the zoning department. I'm returning your call. I am assuming I know what this is regarding. I spoke to Mike Turner earlier in the week, and I think I understand what it is that you're trying to do. You're looking to host overnight weekend retreats at your place of residence?"

"Correct."

"Would you have some time for me to stop by sometime next week? I can explain some of the information we need on the application, and we can do a preliminary walk-through so I can prepare you for what you'll need."

"That sounds great. I'm not one hundred percent sold on this idea, but that decision relies heavily on what you have to say."

"We do have other residents in the area running bed and breakfasts out of their primary residence, so I think we can make this happen. We can discuss everything in more detail when we meet. How does Tuesday morning at ten thirty sound?"

I checked my calendar quickly, but I already knew what was there. "I should be back by noon. Will that work?"

"Works out great. If you give me your email address, I can add you to the schedule."

After exchanging some basic information, we hung up. It seemed too good to be true that the zoning process would go as smoothly as he had intimated, but I decided to have a positive attitude instead of expecting the worst. Positivity had always been my default, and I didn't know when it had stopped, but I *did* know it was high time I got back to it.

29

"BRAND NEW DAY"

VAN MORRISON

The bespectacled librarian behind the desk closest to the entrance looked up from her computer screen and smiled at me as I walked in. That simple kindness felt like recognition, a heady feeling at a time when nothing seemed familiar to me. I waved back and made note of her chic ensemble and on-trend hairstyle—shoulder-length platinum beach waves I hoped to have the confidence for when I reached her age. "I love your hair," I whispered, digging my library books out of my tote bag and slipping them into the depository on the left side of her desk. I checked her name tag. Peggy.

She put her reading glasses on top of her head, pushing her hair back like a headband. "Thank you. I got tired of coloring it once a month and straightening my hair every day, so I decided to let nature take its course. The humidity here doesn't really lend itself to forcibly straightening our hair, so my life got a lot easier when I stopped fighting that losing battle.

"I've seen you in here before, haven't I? I have to say, I noticed your hair right away, too. Looks like we're in the same club, but yours decided to take the dramatic route."

My skunk stripe never failed to get me noticed—and recognized—wherever I went. I'd long since given up trying to color it to match the rest of my hair; it turned its nose up at any such attempt like a petulant child with a plate full of boiled tripe.

"It's pointless to fight it. I gave up a long time ago. Anyway, it's nice to meet you, Peggy. I'm Paige. I'm headed back to a meeting room to meet with my writing mentor."

Her silver eyebrows shot up under her bangs. "Any chance you're meeting with Caleb?"

"I am..." I replied, my confusion evident in my tone.

"He's mentored quite a few aspiring authors at this library, some of whose books are on our shelves now. I'm in charge of procurement here, so when you publish your book—which you will if Caleb has any say in it—come see me. I like to support our local authors."

Something that felt like electricity coursed through me at the mental image her words painted in my head. My name on a book sitting on a library shelf. A woman's hand reaching for it. Flipping it over to read the back. Adding it to her stack.

"I will be sure to do that. Thank you! Ok, I'd better get moving so I can get settled before he gets here. It was lovely to meet you, Peggy."

"Likewise," she replied as I pulled the handles of my tote bag up to my shoulder. I sent her a quick but sincere smile before heading to the back of the library.

I found an open meeting room and laid out my laptop, notebooks, and pens. I was ready.

CALEB ARRIVED A FEW MINUTES LATER, poking his head around the doorway with a big smile on his face. "It's plotting day, Paige! Are you excited?"

"So excited!" I wasn't sure if I would call it *exciting*, per se, but who was I to throw a wet blanket over his enthusiasm when it was something I so desperately needed in my life.

He started setting his laptop and notebook on the table, then sat down next to me. "Not everybody loves to plot, but it's always been something I've enjoyed doing, and I hope to get you to a place where you enjoy it too."

Caleb opened his laptop and pointed to my notebook. "You're going to want to take notes. This is going to be a lot to try and remember."

As Caleb demonstrated each of the tools he used most for the planning phase of each book, my pen poured everything I heard onto the page in front of me.

"I'm going to email you all the links for these tools, but for the time being, let's go over how I use each of them. Did you have time to finish the general outline of your story?"

"I did! I'm sure there will be more that needs to be added as I go along, but for now, this is what I have." I opened my notebook and flipped through my pages and pages of notes. I sucked in a breath and held it while I kept my eyes on the table to my right. It felt so uncomfortable to have something that felt so personal laid bare in front of someone else. I didn't often share any part of my writing, although, up to this point, I hadn't produced much of anything to share.

"Paige! This is awesome. I'm so proud of you. Look at all this hard work. This looks like the beginnings of a bestseller to me."

I released the breath I'd been holding and dug deep for the courage to make eye contact with him. "This was a lot of work, but I know the real work is still ahead of me."

"Doing the hard work at this stage saves you a lot of grief later on. Trust me. I don't know how people write books without planning them out. I would just sit there and stare at my screen, wondering what was next."

"You just described the last few years of my life."

"It's only up from here, then. What we're going to do is

break apart your outline into chapters and scenes. Are you ready?" And for the next two hours, we sat at that table and plotted out my story using Caleb's tools and expertise and my rough outline. When we had finished entering the last scene, Caleb sat back in his chair and put his hands behind his head, looking as carefree as a high school senior on graduation day.

"Look at what you've done, Paige. You have outlined an entire book. Granted, you're going to have to fill in some holes here and there, and you are probably going to discover some missing scenes, but that's okay. That's a normal part of writing. But you've got the bones, and it's a really good start.

"Why don't you focus on creating some depth to your characters? I'm going to email you some of the templates I use. In the meantime, think of things that would make your characters feel real. Give them some depth. Figure out their dreams and aspirations. What do they like to do in their spare time? What do they like to eat? Do they have any funny quirks? Do they have any fun hobbies? Think in terms of some deeper qualities that you and I might have that somebody would connect with. If you can't think of anything, try to pull some aspects of your characters from people you already know. Maybe a funny catchphrase somebody has, for instance."

"Oh, this part sounds fun."

"It *is* fun. It can be challenging sometimes, but it's worthwhile. You need to develop characters strong enough to carry your reader through the book." Caleb looked at his watch as it began to beep. "We have been here for two hours. That time flew by. I have someone else meeting me here in ten minutes, but let's plan on getting together again in another week."

We both opened up our calendars on our phones and settled on a time for the following Wednesday, after which I packed up everything I'd brought and bid Caleb adieu.

I WALKED BACK in the house and after letting a very antsy Roxy outside, I set my tote bag on the kitchen counter. Not even a moment later, I heard my phone buzz once from somewhere inside of it, and I dug it out while stepping on the heels of my sneakers to take them off. The house was quiet and I assumed Kari had walked to the yoga studio she'd discovered less than a mile away.

My screen showed a notification from the Sensational Six group chat.

> Grace: Hey lady, we missed you at league. It seems like you're keeping that friend all to yourself. We'd love to meet her. Do you have time this week to meet at the café for a late breakfast?

I laughed. I'd been so busy enjoying Kari's company that I'd forgotten I had built her up so much to my new friends, and then hadn't followed through.

> Absolutely. We've been running all over town and floating in the pool. What day works for you?

> Grace: How about tomorrow morning?

> I'll check with Kari, but I'm pretty sure she's free.

> Jenna: Tomorrow works for me. Can we meet after eleven?

> Elyse: After eleven works for me, too. I can't leave the store until the cashier comes in.

> Great! We'll see you all at the café tomorrow at eleven fifteen.

> Grace: Looking forward to it!

THURSDAY MORNING at eleven found me sliding into the large U-shaped booth at Cat's Bites. Kari scooted in next to me and we did the butt-scoot boogie around to the center of the seat to make room for everybody else. In true Kari fashion, we were fifteen minutes early. In true Paige fashion, my hair was soaking wet.

"What do you recommend here?" asked Kari as she perused the menu.

"You can't go wrong with the eggs Benedict. It's their specialty."

Kari set her menu down on top of mine. "Sold!"

Out of the corner of my eye, I saw the flash of color that was Grace, followed by Elyse, Jenna, and Sarah. Grace and Sarah slid into my left while Elyse and Jenna scooted in on Kari's right.

"I wish we weren't all sitting so I could give you a proper hello," said Grace. Instead, she reached across me to pat Kari's hand.

"I think she probably would appreciate a handshake at this point, Mom," laughed Sarah. "She just met you fifteen seconds ago."

Kari patted Grace's hand with the free one. "Oh, no, it's okay. I'm a hugger, too, but that will leave us something to look forward to at the end."

"Oh, I like this one," said Grace as she squeezed Kari's hand, then sat back in the booth.

Sarah set her bag down on the booth and smiled across the table at Kari. "I took the day off for a doctor's appointment later, so this worked out perfectly. It's nice to meet you. I've heard so many great things about you."

Everyone else took turns introducing themselves, including Cat, who was able to slip out of the kitchen for a few minutes.

After placing our orders with the waitress, Grace started with the first of what would end up being many, many questions.

"So, Kari, have you found a yoga studio here that you like?"

"Oh, I'm so glad you brought that up," I said, taking the first chance I could to derail the Thompson Inquisition. "Kari had a great idea for the retreat. Go ahead, Kari. Tell them your idea."

Kari put her hands on the table before her and spread out her fingers; her trademark indication that things were about to get serious. "Okay so Paige was saying she's looking into having a writing expert come and speak on Friday mornings during the retreat, and I thought Saturday morning would be the perfect opportunity for the women who are so inclined to come together and practice yoga."

"I love this idea," said Jenna.

Sarah looked excited as she added, "I think that would be a big hit with the women!"

Grace jumped in next. "I think it's a great idea, too. Where do you think you could set it up?"

"There's a lot of space in the sunroom. I would need to get some balance blocks, yoga mats, spray bottles, and a few other things, but I don't see it being very expensive. We could put some heavier drapes in there to block some of the light.

"Kari has already volunteered to vet a few yogis for me to choose from. I'm going to meet with them tomorrow."

"Oh, I hope that works out. This could be the perfect addition to what you already have planned. And it could be completely optional, right?" asked Elyse.

"Yep! Everything is optional. If somebody wanted to hole up in their room for all three days, they can just as easily do that. Heck, we can even drop off their Uber Eats orders right outside the door of their suite."

A few minutes later, our food arrived, and we dug in. The conversation flowed naturally between the six of us, and as I looked around the table at the friends I had assembled in my life, I couldn't be happier knowing that these women were so invested in my success and happiness. It made my heart warm knowing that they were in my life.

After lunch, we stood outside the door saying our goodbyes.

"Well, how about that hug now, Kari?" Grace stood with her arms already open and waiting.

Kari hugged each of them, starting with Grace, of course. "It was so nice to meet all of you."

When Elyse asked Kari when she was coming back, panic flashed on Kari's face for just a moment. "I've had such a great time, and I'm proud of myself for making this trip. I don't travel often—"

"Or at all," I interjected.

"Or at all. Correct. So, I'm probably going to go home and just bask in the glow of this success for now, but I can't imagine it's going to be very long before I come back again. It's gorgeous here."

"And you can't beat the company," I added.

"I look forward to seeing you next time you're here," said Elyse. "I hate to break up the band, but I need to head back to the store. Kari, great to meet you, and I hope we'll be seeing more of you. Travel safely. I'll see the rest of you next Tuesday."

We all said our goodbyes, and as Kari and I walked back toward my car, she commented, "I can't help but feel a little jealous, but you're so lucky to have found them. I'm so happy for you, Paige."

And for the first time, I could honestly say I was starting to feel happy for me, too.

30

"I'M STILL STANDING"

ELTON JOHN

fter a slightly less pickled afternoon float in the pool, Kari and I sat at the kitchen counter wrapped in our towels. I knew shit was about to get real when she put her hands on the edge of the counter and spun slowly my way. "It's time to do the pro and con list. I don't know if I can do quite as thorough a job as Mama Turner would, but we're going to do our best."

"Okay, I'm ready. A little scared but ready." I ran up to my office to grab the notebook with the list I'd already begun. By the time I got back downstairs, Kari already had the tray of sliced cheese out of the fridge. "You can't do a pros and cons list without cheese."

"Well, no, of course not. My brain doesn't do voluntary work until it's fed with havarti. Okay, I've got a few items on here already." I laid the notebook down with the page open to my list.

Kari read it over. "This is a great start. I think we should add the first thing that comes to mind for the Pro column."

Kari bent toward the notebook and wrote. "How about

'meeting more people in the writing community'? That seems like a big one."

"No kidding. Writing can be such a lonely business sometimes, and in the short time I've been working with Caleb, I've completely turned a corner. I can't even imagine if I were surrounded by writers all the time, and people like Caleb coming in and sharing what they've learned along the way."

"What's next?"

"I can think of a con. Having people I don't know in my house."

"I can see how that wouldn't be comfortable all the time, but I feel like you'll get used to that pretty quickly, and it would be easy enough for you to go up to your room and recharge during quiet times, right? But, for your sake, we'll put it down as a con for now. Now, let's see. What else? How about 'giving back to the writing community'? While you're generating income and meeting other writers, you're also going to be providing a space for them to come together. This will foster a sense of community amongst themselves as well. These retreats are going to be the catalyst for new friendships, and you're probably going to see a lot of the same people coming back time and time again, probably with each other."

"I hadn't even considered that aspect of doing this. Let's definitely add 'Giving back to the writing community' in the 'pro' column."

"Now for some other cons. You are going to have to be thinking about more than just yourself in terms of food on those weekends, so it's a little added responsibility. There are also going to be some initial investments as you get started. You're going to have to pay for marketing, a website, maybe some ads, flyers. Nominal, but still investments."

"I thought of another 'pro'. I won't be alone here all the time. Since I got here, I've met so many people, and the women from the book club pretty much come and go, and it's been nice having some more people around."

I noticed Kari turning a little green after that one and decided to move away from the topic of all the friends I'd made since I'd been there. "I will get more writing done. That's one of the biggest pros of all. Having that structured writing time will force me to sit down and put words on the page, or edit—whatever stage I'm in at that time. I'll also have people around to bounce ideas off of and brainstorm with for a whole weekend."

"Being surrounded by writers will give you inspiration. Yes, that's perfect. Okay, writing it down. Anything else?"

"That's all I can think of for now."

When we looked at the list, we could see that the pros far outweighed the cons, and were more valuable than the cons were negative.

Kari tapped her pen on the counter while she read over the list. "This looks like a win to me. Assuming this all doesn't become too much for you once the sessions get underway. But if you manage this the way you managed running your household with two children and a husband who was never home, this will be a slam dunk."

"It all sounds so great on paper, and when I talk to other people about it, they get excited, which makes me feel like it will work out. But there really is no way to know for sure until I get into it."

"I have a feeling once you get the word out that you're having writer's retreats here once a month, you're going to be booked up for a solid year. You wait and see. You might end up doing more than one retreat per month!"

"We'll have to see how the first few months go before I commit to any more." I laughed as I waved my hands in front of me. "This was all somebody else's idea that's bloomed below my feet, so it'll take a few months of real-life application before I know how big of an undertaking it will actually be. Again, it all looks great on paper, but paper makes a lousy business partner."

"You have plenty of people to help you—if you let them. Speaking of which, I did get the list down to a few instructors who would love to come in and teach yoga once a month. I was thinking of setting up something for one of them to stop by for a quick visit before I leave, if that's okay. I have one I really like, and it doesn't hurt to have backups."

"Okay, that's great news. When did you have in mind? I don't have a ton of work to get done today if that works."

"I can check with her and see if she can come by. That way, I know at least I have a chance to introduce you before I go home."

A giant, tear-filled lump formed in my throat. "Don't even talk about going home yet. I'm not ready."

"I know. I know. I don't want to leave either, but I need to check on the progress at the house, and well, I do live there. I'm going to miss you, of course..." She turned toward the nearby dining room window that faced the bay, but her glazed, three-thousand-mile stare told me she was looking more inward than out. "...but I'm also going to miss being this close to the water, and I'm *really* going to miss being here when I'm shoveling the driveway in a few short months. It's been so hard not having you two doors down, especially with Nick's schedule. He's been traveling so much for work it feels like I'm always there by myself. At this rate, I'll probably be back here sooner than you think."

"I'm sorry to hear you've been lonely, but you know you're welcome here anytime!"

"Be careful what you wish for. I might see if your Uncle Mike has any other houses lying around. I could just go home, pack up our whole house, and text Nick with our new address next door to you," Kari warned me with a staccato laugh.

Realizing we'd been sitting there for a while and I hadn't

gotten any actual work done, I looked at the time on my phone. "Yikes! Why don't you go ahead and reach out to the yoga instructor and see if today works for her. I'm going to run upstairs and check my work email. Come up to my office after you hear from her. I'm not doing anything that requires a lot of concentration today."

"And what are you thinking about for lunch? Grilled cheese? Tomato soup?"

She knew me so well; I was a sucker for her grilled cheese. "Sounds perfect."

"Consider it done; I'll reach out to Estelle and text you with her response. I'll let you know when lunch is ready. Muah!" She blew me a kiss as she floated out of the room on her impossibly long legs.

Once upstairs at the desk in my bedroom, I got to work on the projects due in the next couple of days. Nothing difficult: an email, a blog post, a brochure, and some revisions on previous projects. An easy day, overall. I knew how lucky I was to do something I loved every day—from home—and get paid for it.

About forty-five minutes into working through my list, a quick buzz from my phone announced an incoming text.

> Kari Kari Bo Berry: I heard from Estelle and she is free today around three. Would that work for you? Do you have any meetings?

> No meetings today. Three o'clock works great.

> Kari Kari Bo Berry: I was thinking of going for a walk on the beach. Do you mind if I take Roxy with me?

> OMG she would love that! Please feel free. The keys to the Jeep are in my purse. She's allowed on the dog beach on Honeymoon Island. Just put it in the nav.

Kari Kari Bo Berry: Okay I'll see you in a little bit. I cleaned up a little of the mess from this morning and the dishes are drying on the counter. Your lunch is on the island.

Thanks Kari. I love that you always insist on hand-washing dishes when there's a perfectly good dishwasher right next to you.

Kari Kari Bo Berry: They just feel cleaner to me. I don't know why!

Oh, I almost forgot. Don't let Roxy chase any seagulls. She'll yank your arm right off.

Kari Kari Bo Berry: I will do my best. See you soon.

Not if I see you first.

Two forty-five found me in the kitchen loading the dishes from my lunch into the dishwasher. I was in no way in the hand-washing camp with Kari. Rinse, bend, place, repeat was the name of my dish game.

Kari was still not back. I was glad she was enjoying her walk, but I was a little worried about Roxy's behavior on the beach. I was having visions of Kari returning with one arm longer than the other.

The doorbell rang at three on the dot, just as I was wiping the counters down. I opened the door to find a stunning woman towering over me. Wisps of her straight brown hair had escaped her long ponytail and blew gently in the breeze off the bay. She had high cheekbones, a glowing olive complexion, and her expression could easily be described as tranquil. She looked like a goddess.

Behind her, parked in the driveway was a purple Jeep and I

knew instantly this was going to be a good match. There's just something about Jeep people.

"Estelle, I'm assuming? I'm Paige. Come in."

Without waiting for confirmation, I opened the door wider, sweeping my arm to welcome her into the house.

"Yes, I'm Estelle. Kari warned me about how gorgeous your house is, but I wasn't prepared for *this*." She gestured toward the yard, and the pool sparkled, seemingly in response to the compliment.

"Yeah, my uncle has put a lot of effort into this house, and I feel like I won the lottery every time I pull into the driveway."

She stepped nimbly through the doorway and turned to me with her hand outstretched. "It's great to meet you."

"Nice to meet you as well," I said as I shook her hand. "Let's talk in the kitchen." I closed the door and led her through the foyer while she turned and took in as much as she could in those five steps. "I'll take you for a quick tour in a few minutes," I promised.

We briefly went over my rough plans for the retreat weekends, and I explained my theory that a bit of yoga in the morning might help them get their creative juices flowing.

Estelle glowed. "I love this idea. I really do. When your friend Kari approached me after class yesterday, it sounded so wonderful; I love to be in the midst of creativity. I have a bit of a right-brain mentality myself, so I appreciate what you're doing here, and I would be honored to be a part of it. Could I see the space you had in mind for us to practice?"

"Of course!"

Once in the sunroom, I detailed what I had envisioned. "I was thinking we could pull these shades down and put shelves in the back of the room with some yoga mats, blocks, and anything else you think we might need."

"Maybe a speaker would be good. This looks like a really great space. You have enough room here for about six people and me, which, from what Kari told me, is all we'll need. What about the people that aren't going to do yoga? Will you have an alternative for them?"

"I've been considering that possibility and I was hoping you had a way to work in some kind of mindfulness practice for the non-yoga people. If so, would they come in here? Would they be elsewhere in the house?"

"Let me give that some thought. I would love for them to be included, but not distracted by what we're do—"

There was a commotion at the back door, cutting off the rest of Estelle's sentence. I heard the door fling open and hit the doorstop, then the scrabble of Roxy's claws on the wood floor.

"Oh God. We're back. We're back. This dog is going to be the death of me!"

"Oh no. Let's go see what happened," I said to Estelle, then wasted no time making my way to the foyer. We found a wind-blown disaster where my neat, fastidious friend had once stood. Her hair, which, to be fair, has never been described as orderly, was wrapped around her face and puffed up around her head like a woman who had just been discovered after a lifetime of living with wolves. Her shoes were soaked and coated in sand, which was now all over the floor. And Roxy was desperate to spread the sand she'd brought back far and wide throughout the house.

"Go ahead and let go of her leash, Kari."

As if she hadn't realized she was still holding it, Kari dropped the leash, and her hand remained in a claw in front of her. "Well, you weren't kidding about the seagulls! We were ten feet onto the beach when a seagull landed on the sand about twenty feet in front of us and Roxy took off and dragged me thirty feet through the sand while she chased this poor bird. Luckily, I had the leash wrapped around my wrist, or she'd be in Tampa by now!"

She pulled up her long-sleeve UV shirt to show me the red

marks around her wrist. "All those years of perfecting my balance were no match for an eighty-pound golden retriever on the hunt for a new friend."

"No, I can't say yoga would do a whole lot of good in that instance. I don't think Arnold Schwarzenegger could hold her back from a seagull. I'm going to have to get her some training."

Just then, Kari realized what time it was and noticed the visitor in the hallway with us. "Estelle! I'm so glad you made it. I'm so sorry I wasn't here to greet you when you arrived. As you can see, I had my hands full."

"No worries. We talked through everything, and Paige showed me the space."

"Wonderful, what do you think?"

Estelle turned to face me. "I'm in if you'll have me. I love what you've got planned here, and I want to be a part of it."

"I'd love to have you. I know this is going to be a bit of running behind the kite while trying to get it off the ground. You'll need to bear with me as the plans ebb and flow and change upon the hour. Especially as we get closer to opening weekend."

"Well, one thing you can say about me is that I'm pretty flexible."

Kari covered her face with one sand-covered hand. "Not another one with the puns."

"I can't help myself. Anyway, I'm going to let you both get back to your day." She looked around at the floor, then at Kari, who looked every bit as ragged as she probably felt. "And clean up. I have to run and teach a four o'clock class, but I'm so grateful for the opportunity and I'm really looking forward to seeing where this goes. It's such a neat idea."

Kari stepped forward and started to reach out her hand, then thought better of it when she realized it was still covered in sand. "I'm headed home tomorrow, but it was so great to practice with you. I'm sure I'll be back again soon."

"I enjoyed meeting you as well. It's always nerve-wracking to lead a class with another yoga instructor, but you made me feel so at ease. Paige, it was lovely to meet you. Kari has my information, so reach out any time, and we can get the details worked out."

With that, Estelle swept out the door, carrying a swirling tuft of golden retriever hair in her wake.

Kari and I saw it at the same time and the hilarity we'd held in while Estelle was there bubbled up and over.

"Clean up in aisle one," I said.

"Chaos, party of two," said Kari.

31

"PEACEFUL EASY FEELING"
THE EAGLES

Within thirty minutes, we had all of the hair and
most of the sand cleaned out of the foyer. Kari
emptied the last dustpan into the kitchen garbage
and pushed a blonde curl back into her always-messy bun.
"What time should we expect Uncle Mike and Chris? Should
we start cooking?"

"I told them seven. Chris is always early, and my uncle is
always late, so I'd say right around seven, and both will look
annoyed."

Kari laughed as she bent to dry her freshly scrubbed hands
on the palm-tree-printed towel that hung from the oven
handle. "Sounds a lot like us."

"I pulled the chicken out of the freezer last night and put it
in the fridge, so it should be ready to marinate."

We got to work on dinner preparations, stopping periodi-
cally to check the recipe I'd hung from the fridge or throw Roxy
little bits of carrot and trimmed chicken fat.

"I don't know how this dog isn't four hundred pounds. She
will eat absolutely anything. I fully believe she would have
eaten that seagull if she'd managed to catch it."

"I have a feeling our lizard population has decreased dramatically since we arrived. I had to call a service to clean up after her in the backyard because I'm afraid I'll find a tiny femur sticking out of one of her landmines."

That mental image set off another round of laughter, and before we knew it, dinner was ready and Roxy was spinning in circles in the foyer. I checked the time on the microwave. "They must be here. Seven on the dot!"

Our party of two (three as far as Roxy was concerned) grew to four (five), as did the laughter that filled the entire house through dinner. Kari entertained everyone with tales from the twins' first month at school, and Roxy patrolled the floor around the dining room table, looking for any food that could have possibly escaped someone's plate.

"You've certainly had your hands full with those two," my uncle laughed, wiping his eyes after the last story. "How did they get their hands on that much plastic wrap?"

Kari sat back in her chair and folded her paper napkin, setting it on her empty plate. "I foolishly added them to our Costco account and they used their card to buy two giant rolls of cellophane. The RA called Nick once he finally found out it was the twins who had completely covered every toilet seat in the bathroom. He said they should have come with warning labels."

By then, everyone was roaring with laughter. When I stood to start collecting everyone's empty plates, my uncle cleared his throat. I looked up from the stack in front of me to see him giving Chris 'the eye'.

Immediately picking up his secret message, Chris stood and said, "I'm going to get this all cleaned up. Paige, why don't you and your uncle go for a walk while Kari and I get to know each other a little better? Kari, I hear you're a fan of washing dishes. Do you mind giving me a hand?"

Never one to turn down a cleaning project, and always the

first to pick up on subtext, Kari pushed her chair back and rose from the table. "At your service."

Again, I found myself walking the sprawling grounds with my uncle. It was clear he had something on his mind, and anxiety fought for space in my very full belly.

"So, here's the thing," he began. "No one enjoys these conversations about the inevitable day that someone we love won't be here with us, but sometimes these conversations need to be had whether or not they're comfortable."

The knot in my stomach jerked tighter, and an involuntary gasp escaped.

"Hear me out! The intention has always been for you to inherit my 'estate' when I'm gone. I don't—"

"What? I'm sorry, what?"

"Well, I won't need any of it at that point, so why not? Anyway, this move has accelerated the plan a bit; I figured they would carry me out of this house feet first. Life is funny, isn't it?"

I was stunned. Actually, 'stunned' didn't even come close to adequately describing my mindset.

"Here's what I'm thinking," he continued. "This is actually perfect timing. Honey, it's no secret that you were in limbo in Madison and I think this is going to be so good for you. Here's what I'm proposing. We can go one of two ways here. I can either sell the house and put the proceeds in trust for you, and you can have a little peace of mind knowing it's there should you need it."

"Uncle Mike, I—"

He didn't leave me room to protest. "Option two seems like a lot more fun. For both of us. I am attached to this house and I'd love nothing more than to not have to sell it. You might love this house as much as I do, and you've made short work of building a life for yourself here. A real life, not the one you were pretending so awfully at in Madison. So option two is for me to essentially 'gift' you this house. I'm not sure about the legalities of that scenario, but I'm sure my attorney will know exactly what would need to be done. That being said, the next step would be one hundred percent your choice. I own the house outright, so you would only need to cover the property taxes, maintenance, and utilities. I'll get a list of typical expenses together so you can make an informed decision. I've been looking forward to this moment for weeks! Talk to me. Are you ok? You look stunned."

"Uncle Mike, I—I don't even know what to say. For once, I am speechless."

"Not even one sarcastic jab or joke? Wow! I have silenced Prolix Paige! Don't panic, honey. You've got some time to put all the pieces in front of you and really give it some thought. I'll get the expenses together and give you any updates from the attorney once I have them. Make notes about questions you have. I already know you'll have a lot, so don't hold back on my account. Take a few days, a week, a month. It makes no difference to me. But let me just say, honey, I'd love to have you nearby, and I'd *really,* really love it if you were the one living in this house. No pressure. But think about it. It could be pretty aawesooooome!" he finished in a singsong voice.

"I don't know what to say. I'm beyond stunned. This house is like your baby, and you want to just *give* it to me?"

"This house *was* like my baby, but all the work I put into it was just a distraction from my loneliness. I've got an amazing companion now, and he keeps me plenty busy at the store, so no use hanging onto what's no longer serving me. Like I said, the intention was always for this house to go to you when I was gone, but now I get to be here to witness you enjoying it. Assuming, of course, you decide you want to stay here and hopefully keep the house. Please don't make me pack up all this stuff."

As we completed our circle and rounded the side of the

house, uncle Mike put his hand lightly on my arm to stop me before we reached the back door. "I know I'm pushing hard for you to stay here, but no matter what, the choice is yours." He hugged me as my stunned silence stretched on. "Just know, if you choose not to keep the house, you have to help me pack and unpack," he whispered in my ear, then ended our hug with a hearty pat on the back and his signature breathless laugh.

I didn't know if I had enough space in my head for all I had to unpack as it was, but I knew one thing that always helped me think a little better.

"I think it's time for dessert, although, at the moment, the cheesecake I picked out seems woefully inadequate considering the circumstances."

"Cheesecake sounds perfect. They should be done with the dishes by now, so it's probably safe to go back in. Ready?"

When we walked back into the kitchen, Chris was standing in front of an open cabinet drying the last plate, Roxy was posted by the sink waiting for leftovers, and Kari was wiping off the already gleaming island. She looked up as we entered, and it was clear she could see the shock on my face. She shot me a questioning look, to which I responded by widening my eyes, giving her the universal 'you are not going to believe this' look. When Chris turned around and saw us, he sent a conspiratorial wink my way.

"All set?" he asked, looking at my uncle who stood next to me, the tall, thin Duke of house gifting.

"Yep! Who's ready for cheesecake? Paige has promised this will be the best we've ever had."

"Oh, it'll be memorable, alright," I quipped, and as soon as Chris turned around to reach for dessert plates and my uncle headed toward the fridge, I mouthed to Kari, "Oh my God!"

I hoped my face had come unfrozen enough to convey it was a good "Oh my God" instead of bad, but either way, it was tough to hold the news in until after they left.

By some stroke of luck, the cheesecake managed to loosen up my vocal cords enough that I could carry on a normal conversation through dessert, and within a half hour, we were all standing in the foyer saying our goodbyes.

Chris was the first to step forward. "It was lovely to see you again, Kari," he said, hugging my friend. "Please come back often, and bring more stories about those boys of yours. They must have been so fun growing up."

"Oh, yes, just a regular barrel of monkeys, those two. Depending on how long Paige stays here, I may be back for another visit. Probably over the winter. It was great to meet you too, by the way. The aesthetic in Dash of Flair is other-worldly and I can't wait to hang up everything we picked out for Nick. He could use a little more style in his suitcase."

My uncle was next to hug Kari goodbye. "That man wears way too much paisley. Thank you both for dinner. It was fantastic, as was the company. Paige, honey... when you recover from your shock, call me. In the meantime, I'll get to work." He bent and wrapped his long arms around me. "It's gonna be great. I know it," he said just loud enough for me to hear. "I love you so much, and I'm so happy I got to be here to witness your reaction. I have never seen you this quiet in all the years you've been alive. This is absolutely the best!"

I squeezed him back and whispered, "Thank you," still too disoriented to come up with anything more eloquent, praying I didn't seem ungrateful.

We stepped apart, and his delight was written all over his face, his smile as close to 'ear to ear' as one could get without physical harm.

"See you ladies soon," he said over his shoulder as they made their way toward the driveway.

"What the hell was that all about?" Kari asked as soon as they were out of earshot.

"First, let's grab the rest of that rum. This is a conversation for the pool."

FOR THE NEXT HOUR, Kari and I floated on our rafts, sipping piña coladas and discussing my uncle's offer. I was so glad she was with me as I processed all I had heard that night, because no one could deconstruct and analyze a situation better than her. As usual, she began with the hardest-hitting questions first.

"What do *you* want to do? This is a life-changing offer, Paige. But, at the end of the day, it has to come down to what you want for your own life. Can you see yourself living here?"

I took a moment to answer, knowing she wasn't going to like my response. "I can. I don't know if I can afford to live in this house, but I need to wait until I have all the information to make a decision. But, whether or not I decide to keep this house, it's looking more and more likely I'll end up staying in Florida." I looked over at her just as she pushed off the side of the pool with her foot and spun my way. When she was facing me, I put my foot on her raft to keep it still. "Are you ok?" I knew the answer to my question, but couldn't help but ask it anyway. Her feelings had always mattered to me, and that was never going to stop.

"I mean, I'm going to have to be, right?" Her voice caught and broke on the last word and she swiped at a tear with the back of her free hand. "I kind of knew I was losing you to this place when you drove away. I've been preparing myself for this moment ever since, but hearing you confirm my fears hits differently. That was hypothetical. This is real."

Our straws declared our cups empty at the same time, breaking the silence that stretched between us as we floated through our own thoughts.

"I'm getting cold," she said into the darkness settling around us.

"Let's go in. I'll put on a movie, and we can make popcorn and cuddle up in the den."

"'*Say Anything*'?"

"Of course. What other movie is there?"

Later as we polished off our bowls of popcorn and washed it down with Dr. Pepper, I felt my throat tighten as I wondered how many nights like this we'd have if we were living thirteen hundred miles apart. As usual, Kari was able to read my mind. "This will never change," she declared in a voice so small I barely heard it.

"Pinky promise," I swore. And I meant it.

32

"CLOSER TO FINE"
INDIGO GIRLS

September 7, 2023
When Kari gave me this gratitude journal, I didn't feel as if I had a whole lot to be grateful for, and I threw it in a drawer for another day. Oddly enough, it ended up in my hands again, thirteen hundred miles from where it began, so I guess that day is today. So much has happened in the time she gave this to me, I don't even know where to start, so I'll just make a list of all I'm grateful for today.

1. My kids are healthy and happy
2. I'm healthy and getting happier
3. My parents are healthy
4. I have the best friend in the whole world
5. Roxy hasn't brought a lizard into the house yet
6. I have five new friends
7. I am living in Florida!
8. I have a pool (Finally!)
9. I am making progress on my book
10. I have the perfect job for me
11. I have a new project to work on—the retreat!

This seems like a lot more than I had to be grateful for just a few months ago, so I guess I have <u>that</u> to be grateful for as well! I'll for sure do this on a regular basis because Kari was right (don't tell her!) —I do feel better seeing all the blessings I have in my life.

33

"SHE'S GONE"
HALL & OATES

On the way to the airport the next morning, Kari and I swung by the haberdashery so she could say goodbye to Uncle Mike and Chris. After hugging Kari at least twice each, they packed us into my Jeep and stuck their heads through the open windows.

"It was great to see you again, Kari, and don't be a stranger! The fall collections are coming in soon, and you won't want to miss out on all that revenue potential!" Uncle Mike laughed at his favorite kind of joke—his own.

"You're incorrigible, Mike. It was lovely to meet you, Kari, and I do hope you come back soon, with or without your credit card." Chris shot his partner 'the look'. "I'm glad you already know Mike's sense of humor, otherwise I'd be mortified right now."

"You would not. You cash the checks my humor writes every single day."

"Yeah, after I follow each customer out to their car to apologize."

I put the Jeep in reverse to signal my desire to extract myself from the center of their banter, and uncle Mike reached through the window to scruff my hair. Unable to resist the nickname he'd given me as soon as my skunk stripe grew, he pinched my cheek and said, "See you later, stinker."

As EXPECTED, the ride to the airport was... emotional. After a full week together with very little time spent apart, neither of us relished the thought of saying, "See you soon", and the air surrounding us was thick with the despair that only forced separation from our closest friend can cause. I was afraid to turn on the radio. There was a good chance a song like "Leavin' on a Jet Plane" would pop up on Spotify and there wasn't enough Kleenex in my Jeep for that.

As we reached the Tampa side of the Causeway, Kari's voice finally cut through our silence. It was clear and stable, but barely, and I was ready to hear what she had to say. "This has been one of the best weeks I've had in a very long ti-ime." Her voice cracked at the end.

I slowed as I approached a red light and looked over at her, but gave her a moment to compose herself enough to continue. Kari turned in her seat and faced me, swiping at a few tears that had gone rogue. "I know it's kind of a joke that I don't travel and refuse to move, but this week showed me that it's possible to leave home without needing to be heavily sedated." She kind of chuckled a little. "But in all seriousness, I was thinking I could come back again soon if that would be okay with you."

"Are you *serious*? Any time, Kar! Any. Time. I mean it!"

"Okay, good. Because I didn't realize how much I missed you until we got in the Jeep to leave for the airport after we saw your uncle and Chris. Nick is traveling next week, and I'll be alone again... and you'll be here. I'm starting to feel bad for how much I lectured you about holding your bed down for months after Anna left for school. This shit is so hard."

"Oh, honey..." I reached over and covered her hand with mine. "I understand. And hell, I'm the queen of the castle now, so you can come back whenever you want and stay as long as you want. I mean it."

Kari put her free hand over mine and squeezed. I looked over to see the tears in her eyes that mirrored my own, and when we smiled, they spilled over at the same time and raced to our chins. Unwilling to let go of my hand, she bent her head down and wiped her tears one raised shoulder at a time.

The rest of the drive was filled with stories about our week, and by the time we pulled up in front of departures, our sad tears were replaced with those caused by side-splitting laughter.

I pulled her suitcases out of the back of the Jeep and rolled them up to the curb while she pulled her phone and ID out of her purse. "Travel safe, Kar Bear. Text me when you get home." I wrapped her up in my arms and squeezed.

"Thank you for this week. It's been better than I even imagined. I'm going to miss you... but I'll be back before you know it. Quit your blubbering." We started laughing all over again, and as we separated, a hot wind blew about half of her hair out of her earlier attempt at a ponytail. "I might have to shave my head before I come back. This humidity's got me looking like Monica in Barbados!"

She knew the surefire way to my heart was through *Friends* and *The Office* references, and the mental image she'd gifted me with was exactly what I needed.

"See you soon, Kar Bear."

"See you soon, *stinker.*"

I gave her a playful shove and moments later, she collected her suitcases and rolled through the sliding doors and back to Madison—back to the house that used to be my home.

～

ON THE DRIVE BACK, I realized I hadn't called my parents to fill them in on my conversation with Uncle Mike. Admittedly, I needed the advice only they could give. I dialed my dad's phone, knowing the chances were good that he was reading in his favorite chair.

"Hey there, Tiger! Did you drop her off?"

"Yes..." My voice broke, and I took a few deep breaths to stop myself from crying. Again.

"Let me go get your mom. We've been waiting for your call." A clatter and some shuffling later, my mom's distant speaker-phone voice greeted me.

"Hi, honey. How are you doing?"

I released a shaky breath and swallowed to try to gain control of my vocal cords, but they were hopelessly locked by emotion.

"It's ok, Tiger. Your mom and I understand. You don't have to talk. We can just sit here for a minute."

I was grateful for the way my parents understood me. What had irritated me to no end as a teenager, was now something I relied on as an adult. Wonders never ceased.

My dad's voice came through the speakers, clear, strong, and compassionate. "Even the happiest times of our lives come with sacrifices and sadness. It's okay to embrace that sadness. It doesn't mean you're ungrateful. It means you're human."

I choked out a sob. "I told her, 'See you soon,' but I have no idea how soon it will actually be."

"Then why don't we assume it'll be sooner rather than later? You've got a lot going on there to keep you busy and your mind occupied," my mom pointed out. "But I have a feeling you'll be seeing her before you know it. Maybe she'll come back for another visit once the contractors are finished with their house. They're making some real progress over there. We stopped over on Wednesday to check in on Nick, and he showed us the new kitchen. It's gorgeous! There's a little finishing work left, but I think they'll be wrapping up soon."

"That's good to hear. I'm sure Kari will be so happy to get back to her normal life."

"I expect she doesn't know what normal is going to look like just yet," my dad said. "With Nick traveling so much for work and the boys off at college, we're going to have to gear up for 'operation empty nest' all over again!"

"Does she have an uncle I don't know about handing out houses?"

My Dad chuckled at that. "So I take it my brother talked to you?"

"You guys know already?"

"He called us earlier this week to find out when we are coming for a visit, and he spilled the beans right away. Exciting stuff! Are you in shock?"

"Beyond. Also, what did you tell him? When are you coming for a visit?" I sniffed as I searched my center console for a fast food napkin or stray sock to blow my nose. Anything would do at that point.

"Soon, honey. Really soon," was my mom's reply.

"Let's talk about your gorgeous new house now. Any room for your dear old dad to lounge around and read?"

"And I can help with anything you need around the house," my mom offered.

By this point, my tears had slowed, and I'd located a tiny pack of tissues with one remaining. It would have to do.

"Everything is changing so fast, and watching Kari walk through the airport doors made all of it so real. Up until now, I've been *visiting* and my return felt imminent. I don't mean to sound ungrateful, but this changes everything. Just when I start getting a handle on life, it changes again."

"Change is life's greatest constant. It's kind of like the weather in Chicago. Don't like it? Wait a minute; it'll change.

And the opposite is also true. But your mom and I are excited about your new adventure, and we talk about you all the time. How proud we are of you reclaiming your independence and finding your way forward. We can't wait to come down and meet all your new friends."

"I can't wait for that either, Dad. Ok, I'm about to go over the Causeway, and I want to be able to pay attention. I'm going to let you guys go, but can you do me a favor?"

"Anything, Tiger."

"Yes, anything, Paige."

"Can you check in on Kari every few days? I recognize that look in her eyes. I have seen it in the mirror every day since Anna left for school. Until recently, anyway."

"Consider it done," my mother promised.

"Drive carefully, sweetheart. We will talk to you soon."

I heard another clatter and the muffled voices of my parents, most likely coming through my dad's pocket.

"How about BLTs for lunch?"

"How about a nice chicken salad?"

"Why do you hate me, woman?"

I ended the call, already knowing how the debate would end. Chicken salad.

34

"NEVER GOING BACK AGAIN"
FLEETWOOD MAC

I spent most of Saturday floating in the pool, but I did manage to get Roxy into the Jeep and over to the dog-friendly beach nearby. By the time Sunday rolled around, I was more than ready to FaceTime the kids. They seemed more surprised than I was about Uncle Mike's offer.

"I can't wait for winter break! Which room is mine? What does Roxy think of all this?"

Anna and Roxy had always had the cutest relationship, behaving more like siblings than anything else.

"She's thrilled. But she wants to know when you two are coming for a visit."

"This project is going to be in full swing once the designs get approved, so I'm working with the team to see when the best time would be for me to disappear for a few days," Jason replied.

"And my semester is starting to pick up, so it might be a little bit for me, but I will try really hard to get down there as soon as I can, Mom."

"Okay, okay. I know you both have lives of your own. I just miss you. And I want you to meet everyone here."

"Sounds like quite a cast of characters. Anna and I will make a plan. I promise. We will be there soon, Mom. I actually need to run a little early. I'm going to the Patriots game tonight. They're honoring Patriot's Day tomorrow, so I need to go a little early so I can stop and pick up a new jersey at the stadium. I'll send you some pictures from the ceremony before kickoff."

"I'd love that. I hope you have a blast."

"I'm going to scoot as well, Mom. My roommates planned a game night, and I'm in charge of snacks."

We said goodbye and ended the call, and I couldn't help but laugh that my kids had a more active social life than I did.

But that was quickly changing.

LATER THAT NIGHT, I got the text I'd been dreading from Kari.

Kari Kari Bo Berry: Guess what?

Chicken butt?

Kari Kari Bo Berry: Will you ever grow up?

Not likely. But you love me regardless.

Kari Kari Bo Berry: You know I do. Anyway, I wanted to let you know the contractor gave us the timeline for a potential move-back-in date. They made a lot of progress on the house while I was gone.

That's great news!

Kari Kari Bo Berry: It is. I think. I'm not sure how I feel about it, actually. On one hand, I'm thrilled to go back to some semblance of my normal life, but I know what that means.

Kari Kari Bo Berry: *grimace emoji*

Kari Kari Bo Berry: You're going to be making a decision about this house, and I'm pretty sure what that decision is going to be.

I know this is difficult for you, and I'm so sorry! But you're right. I do have to make a decision about selling that house at some point. It might as well be sooner rather than later.

Kari Kari Bo Berry: Ugh. *single tear emoji* I know. What do you need me to do?

Could you maybe look around and see what I would need to fix up in order to get the house ready to put on the market? Maybe have your contractor go over and get an estimate together on any repairs that would be needed?

Kari Kari Bo Berry: I'd be happy to. I can also see what personal photos and things like that should be taken down and try to hide some of your valuables. You've got a lot going on there right now, and you don't need to be going back and forth handling all this. You've been so kind to let us stay here, especially not knowing what kind of mischief the boys would get into while under your roof. I'm happy to take the lead on some of this and get your house ready to go on the market if that's what you decide.

I appreciate that. It shouldn't be too bad. It's just been me for the last few years, and I don't make much of a mess. So the majority of it should just be maybe some chewing damage from Roxy.

Kari Kari Bo Berry: I think it's only minor touch-ups.

So what is he thinking as far as the timeline?

Kari Kari Bo Berry: He says they're going to be finished within the next week. So he could probably be here working on your house the following week, but let me check with him. Do you have a realtor in mind?

> I haven't moved anywhere in a while, but I can ask around.

Kari Kari Bo Berry: I'll do the same and send you a few phone numbers so you can pick one.

> I know this is a sad time for us both, but hopefully with the boys in school, you'll have more time to visit.

Kari Kari Bo Berry: Trust me, I'm already planning my next trip. Are the kids coming down for a visit soon?

> Yes, I just spoke to them, and it sounds like they are making some plans to come down in the next month or so. I'm sure I'll be seeing them a lot during the cold weather months.

Kari Kari Bo Berry: Now that you'll be living in a vacation destination, you'll probably see them more than ever.

> From your lips to God's ear.

I waited a minute to see if any more texts would come in from her, but I understood her well enough to know she was probably stress-cleaning my house and wouldn't get back to her phone until it was time to call me later.

As I was making myself a quick dinner that night, a text came in from my uncle.

Uncle Mike: Are you busy tomorrow morning?

No meetings, just a few projects to work on.

Uncle Mike: Can you meet me at the attorney's office? The papers are ready.

Papers?

Uncle Mike: For your new house.

...

Uncle Mike: It'll be fine. I'll send you the address. Meet me there at ten. I love you!

I love you too!

While the idea of owning the house I was currently vacationing in had still not quite settled in my mind, the reality was here. Or it would be in less than twenty-four hours.

The next time I made myself dinner in that kitchen, I would officially be a Floridian.

IT WAS SIGNING DAY! I'd gone to bed the night before a jumble of emotions, but when I woke up, the sun was streaming through my windows. When I stepped out onto the balcony to stretch and say good morning to the flowers in the pots I'd set out there, a family was walking out of the birthing center with a brand new baby... and it felt like a sign.

New beginnings were everywhere. Even for me.

I pulled into the parking lot of the attorney's office complex at nine forty-five and decided to sit outside for a few minutes to collect myself.

Just two short months before, I was struggling to visualize

the direction my life was supposed to take. And there I was, hundreds of miles away from the home I had created for my family, in the process of creating a home near a family that had *chosen me.*

What did this mean in terms of my home in Madison? Was I ready to let go of all the past that it contained? And would my new house in Florida ever feel as if it were truly *my* home?

I still had difficulty wrapping my mind around the idea of Uncle Mike's house becoming mine, but I had no trouble grasping just how lucky I was.

I had a general idea of what my responsibilities were moving forward, and the thought of having to come up with the funds for a tax bill that was five times as large as the one for my house in Madison kind of made me sick. But not having a mortgage hanging over my head and the potential for some additional income definitely helped lessen those concerns.

I turned off my Jeep and got out just as Uncle Mike pulled into the parking lot.

"Looking dashing as always, Uncle Mike."

"Hey, kid! It definitely helps to own a clothing store. Well, are *you* ready to own a home in Florida?"

The knot already growing in my stomach twisted just a bit. "I just—"

"I know you're looking to say thank you again, Paige, and you don't need to. Just knowing you will be loving the house, taking care of it, and appreciating it the way I have makes it all worthwhile. Plus, knowing it's going to be such a big part of your fulfillment in this next stage of your life is more than enough thanks for me. It makes me so happy to do this, honey. It honestly does."

As we approached the door to the office, he added, "This was always the intention. The benefit to us doing this now is that I am alive to enjoy it."

"I'm grateful for that as well, Uncle Mike."

Ever the gentleman, he held open the door for me. As I walked past, he shouted, "Let's get this party started!"

"Inside voice, Mike," said the portly pinstripe-suited man standing inside the reception area.

"I'm just sad I forgot the confetti."

"And I can't thank you enough for that." The man turned his attention to me.

"Paige, it's great to meet you. My name is Phil," he said as we shook hands. His brown eyes were kind, and his hands soft, both of which helped put me at ease.

"My Uncle Mike has nothing but good things to say about you."

Phil chuckled. "Your Uncle Mike is a liar, but that's neither here nor there. Shall we get started?"

Phil turned and led us into an office just off the reception area. The window looked out onto downtown Dunedin, and I could see my soon-to-be-new neighbors walking here and there. The thought that I would come to know many of them in the days and years ahead excited me.

"Everyone have a seat," said Phil, holding his arms out to point out the chairs on the other side of the table. "I have three copies here, one for each of you to keep and one for me to file. Let's begin."

As we went through the voluminous stack of papers in front of us, initialing and signing next to bright orange tabs, it seemed there should be more involved in the process of taking over someone's house, something they've put their all into for decades. But alas, a mere few signatures later and Uncle Mike's dreams became mine.

Phil stacked the papers neatly in front of him, then rubbed his freshly shaved dome. "All done, and in record time. Be sure to contact a good accountant. I have a list of those I recommend to all my real estate clients. They can help you plan for next year's tax season. And, Mike, as I'm sure you're already aware, there will be some tax implications involved in this transaction. But if you plan ahead, it will make your life a lot easier next April."

Uncle Mike stood and stretched the long limbs he and my father had hogged every last gene for. "I appreciate the heads-up. Alright, we're gonna get going now. Thank you so much for all your help with this, Phil."

"My pleasure, as always. And if you have any other houses to give away, you know where to find me. Paige, it's been a treat meeting you. If you have any questions about this paperwork, or if your accountant needs any additional information, just have them reach out to me."

As we walked toward the door to leave, my uncle turned around. "Phil, that tie could use a refresh. Stop by the store, would ya? It's right across the street. Let me know if you need me to draw you a map."

Phil laughed and lifted up the end of his tie, inspecting it. "The kids gave me this for Father's Day last year."

"Well, they have impeccable taste." He rolled his eyes. "However, if you're looking for something a little less... horizontal striped, you know where to go."

"That I do. Point taken, Mike. I guess I'll be stopping in soon. Thanks for the heads up on my fashion faux pas."

"That's what I'm here for! Look forward to seeing you."

We shook hands with Phil and walked out of the office together.

Uncle Mike held the door open for me again. "Do you have time for lunch?"

"We've met before, right? I always have time for lunch."

We headed three doors down to Cat's Bites. Betty looked over and smiled when we walked in. "Sit anywhere, and I'll be right over."

As we walked to an open booth, I looked around. The café

was busy, but there were plenty of open tables. "It looks like we beat the rush."

"That's too bad. Definitely not looking forward to going back to the store to fold V-neck sweaters. And socks. Why must we fold socks? I've asked Chris several times if we can throw them into a big basket and let people dig for them. It'll help them feel right at home. He hasn't gone for the idea yet, but I haven't given up."

"Well, I have plenty of clothes to fold at home myself, so feel free to take your time."

Betty stopped by our booth and took our orders. She and Uncle Mike gossiped about some drama that had befallen the store owner next door. I was trying not to eavesdrop, but it sounded like a lease issue, and they would be closing up shop soon. I always hated hearing news like that, even secondhand about someone I didn't even know.

When she walked away to put our orders in, Uncle Mike jumped right in. "What's going on with the retreat? Tell me about your progress."

"Oh, my goodness. So much progress! Kari found a yoga instructor who will come in on Saturday mornings to lead a class. And for those who aren't confident or able to do yoga, she's going to put together a mindfulness session."

His face twisted in an exaggerated grimace. "Oh, that sounds terrible."

"Well, be sure not to stop by for it. But I'm hoping my writers will love it."

"I'm sure they will. I'm just not so keen on all the bending and sweating that's involved."

"You could do with a little more flexibility in your life. You'd be surprised what you can get out of a tree pose. "

"I doubt I *could* get out of a tree pose."

We both had a good laugh at his turn of phrase, but Uncle Mike had always appreciated his own brand of humor best. His loud wheezing laughter, followed by an ear-piercing "HA!" turned a few heads in our direction.

"I can't take you anywhere," I said, shaking my head. "I've met Dad's friend, Caleb, a few times now, and he's been so helpful to me. I plan on asking if he would come and teach a few sessions on Friday mornings."

"Oh, that would be *huge*, Paige. That's definitely a value add you can put on your website and social media to attract more writers."

Betty had returned with ice-cold water, and my uncle took a sip of his while looking at me over the edge of the glass. He set it down and made himself busy using his napkin to wipe up the condensation that had dripped on the table.

"Honey... I... I know how much you were struggling, so to hear the confidence in your voice right now means so much to me. I cannot wait to read your book when you finish."

The small difference between "if" and "when" did not escape my notice. His confidence in me after years of producing nothing but excuses caused an unfamiliar feeling to swell in my chest. *Pride.*

"What about food? I'm assuming you'll be offering food at some point over the weekend. Hopefully, something aside from cheese."

"Haha, so funny. Actually, Cat is going to deliver lunches, and my friend Jenna from book club has offered to provide some of the breakfast items. Mostly baked goods and maybe some desserts to keep around for later. We writers tend to get a sweet tooth right around two a.m."

"Excellent! Cat's a real firecracker and her food is excellent. And Jenna... Jenna... She works here, right? Is her husband's name Craig?"

I got a sick feeling at the mention of his name. "It is. How do you know him?"

He looked down at the table where his hands were fiddling with his napkin.

"A little too well, unfortunately." His tone suggested he was done with the topic, but his expression said otherwise. He looked concerned.

"Your face is telling me there's more to the story. Spill."

"I would like you to be careful around Craig."

The plot thickens.

"How do you know him?" I repeated.

My uncle stretched his long legs out under the table and sat back in the booth, crossing his arms. "He was my groundskeeper for a few years, and he started out great. But several months ago, he became unreliable and a little volatile, and I had to let him go."

"Oh no!" This simple disclosure, mixed with Jenna's odd behavior, had started to paint a picture, and not one I'd hang on the fridge.

"It was just as well because I found that I was able to do most of what he was doing for me on my own. So if you find that you need a little help, I will give you the number of the person I've been using for everything beyond my ability."

"That would be great. There's not a lot of grass, but I'm not one hundred percent confident I can maintain all the tropical foliage. Can't say we had a lot of palm trees in Madison."

"No, that's for sure. It took me a long time before I was familiar with how to care for what was growing on the property when I bought it, but over time, I figured most of it out. You're going to have your hands full, so it might not be a bad idea to have someone around who can help you maintain them. Just not Craig. Promise me."

Our lunch arrived, and the rest of our visit passed without further mention of his former groundskeeper, but he lingered like the smell of burnt hair. We talked about my visit with Kari, the house, the retreat, book club, golf, and the haberdashery, but in the back of my mind, I couldn't stop thinking about the expression on his face when he was talking about Craig.

I was shocked by how my uncle had danced around the subject while still being quite direct. I knew without a doubt my uncle did not want me dealing with Craig. I just had no idea why he was so adamant about it.

I'd find out soon enough.

35

"NORWEGIAN WOOD"

THE BEATLES

I raced home from league on Tuesday with just enough time to meet Mr. Rizzo.

When I met him on the driveway, he was making notes on a clipboard, but he looked up as I approached. He was wearing shorts, a golf polo, and leather driving shoes with no socks and his thick, close-cropped light brown hair had apparently not gotten the same memo as his prominent midsection that he'd reached middle age. And while I could have been bowled over by a feather to learn he had not been a forward on an Olympic rugby team, his light brown eyes were kind, and reflected his easy smile.

"Mr. Rizzo, I'm assuming? I'm Paige."

"Please call me Frank," he said in an accent reminiscent of the 'Da Bears' SNL skit. He thrust his enormous bear paw out toward me for a proper greeting, and I shook it as heartily as I could with my own doll-sized hand. He felt a little like home, and I realized this was probably why my uncle had clicked with him as well. There's something about that accent that takes you right back to the midwest, no matter where you are in the world.

"I was just counting your non-street parking spots. I have six in my notes from when I was here before. I was really hoping your uncle was going to get that B&B off the ground; I have tons of family from Chicago that would have loved to stay here."

"Any chance one of them wants to write a book? They might still have a chance."

"They'd write a phone book to have the chance to stay here. Shall we?"

We made our way to the back door where Roxy was high-pitched barking to be let out so she could meet our guest. "Brace yourself."

"I love dogs. Let 'er rip!"

After Roxy had thoroughly inspected our guest and found him to be woefully underprepared in the tennis ball department, we were able to go in. We walked through the areas of the house that would be open to the retreat guests while he made notes. It went quickly, and we were back on the driveway within thirty minutes.

"It looks as if your uncle made a lot of improvements since the last time I was here. I don't see anything that would cause a problem, so once your application comes through, I should be able to fast-track it. We have a thirty-day period for local residents to file any grievances, but once that period is over, I'm confident you'll have the green light from us."

My shock was probably written all over my face. I had not expected that part of the process to go so smoothly. But I knew I still had a little while to wait before I could start celebrating. "We just signed the papers to transfer the title, so I can get the application filled out today and drop it off for you tomorrow. How often do residents have grievances during this process?"

"Not very often. If we do hear something before the next meeting, I can give you a heads up so you can try to smooth things over ahead of time."

"That would be wonderful. Thank you for handling your inspection so quickly. I expected this part of the process to take months. Now I need to get moving on everything else."

Frank laughed and shook his head. "Luckily, I had been here before, so we already had a file open. And it's my pleasure. I'll be in touch."

Once he left, I realized it was barely twelve-thirty, and I still had the entire day ahead of me. I headed to my office to prepare for my meeting with Caleb the next day.

BY THE NEXT MORNING, I had not only finished plugging my outline into the plotting software, but I had developed my characters, printed them out, highlighted the most important parts of their personalities and characteristics that I wanted to make sure I focused on in my story, and I also had a proposal ready for him to discuss him coming in to teach a few sessions during my retreats.

Peggy was busy with a young reader who had a stack of books so tall in front of her on the counter, she couldn't even see over it. I caught her eye as she was explaining the limit to the budding bibliophile, and I gave her a conspiratorial wink. I was again set up and ready to go in 'our' meeting room when Caleb arrived. I had some butterflies flitting around every time I thought about talking to him about teaching a retreat session. I was wary of asking too much of him when he was already helping me out so much already, but I knew I needed to suck it up and ask anyway. He had been such a great resource to me and I knew he was the perfect choice.

Caleb arrived right on time (as usual), took a sweater out of his backpack, and put it on over his t-shirt. "It's always so chilly here. I don't mind air conditioning, living in a climate like this, but it doesn't have to rival the temperature in my refrigerator."

"No kidding," I said, wishing I were better prepared for the arctic-chilled meeting room.

He took his laptop out of his backpack and set it on the table. "Tell me how the week went."

I was positively beaming. "I got so much done. I feel like I'm ready to start writing, but I wanted you to look it over to make sure. My fingers are itching to get started."

"That's so great to hear! Let's see what you've got."

Caleb was silent and thoughtful as he paged through my binder full of character profiles and my printed outline.

"This is excellent work. How do *you* feel about it?"

"I feel like my story is in a really good place. It feels solid. I'm sure I'm going to have some plot holes and I'll need to add a lot after I get through the first draft. But just feeling as if I can get through a first draft is incredible."

"I completely understand. There's nothing better than getting through all this work and writing 'The. End'."

I could feel the tears welling up behind my eyes. "I can't wait to get started."

We spent about thirty minutes scanning through the outline. He showed me where the obvious chapter breaks were and what each of my three acts would include. After that, we took a look at my characters, and he made some suggestions for additional scenes I might need. I took notes as he spoke, picturing him imparting this wisdom onto my retreaters.

Caleb continued flipping through my binder, nodding and tapping his pen on the table. "This all looks solid, Paige. But remember, as you go along, you're going to find that you need to add or delete scenes, or maybe add a character or two, or change their personality, change what they wear, or give them some kind of funny quirk or nuance that you hadn't thought of at this point. But that's the nature of storytelling. Things are going to change and evolve as you go along. If you consider that part of the adventure, then you will embrace these changes, because they will only make your story better. How much time do you have over the next week?"

"Well, the planning for the writers' retreat is turning into a part-time job. There is actually something that I wanted to talk to you about. I hesitate to even bring this up, because you have already been so helpful, and I don't want to keep asking you for more and more of your time…" I trailed off, hesitant. "One idea that I had was to offer some professional development sessions for the attendees."

"That would be a great idea! And who did you have in mind?" he said with a wink, picking up on the nervous energy that pulsed around me like a Vegas nightclub.

"Grace, one of the women helping me put this together, has published six books and is working on her seventh. She's offered to teach a few sessions, and I'm really hoping that you would be willing to do what you've done for me during a few sessions."

His eyes lit up. "I would love that. Is lunch involved?"

Relief flooded through me. "Absolutely! As much as you want. Take home leftovers. How much would you charge for each session? I want to pay you for your time, and I want to make sure I'm pricing the retreats appropriately."

Caleb laughed. "Does seventy-five dollars and a muffin per session sound fair?"

"More than fair. You could probably even get away with two muffins."

"You've got a deal. If you tell me when and where I will be there. Helping authors find their hidden talents and strengthen their writing is what I'm meant to do right now, and I'd be happy to help you."

"You're amazing. I can see why you and my dad are friends."

"Next time you talk to him, tell him I said hi, and he'd better give me a call when he comes into town." With that, he stood up and packed his laptop into his backpack, followed by his carefully folded sweater. "Shall we say a week? You'll have at least six thousand words by then, I imagine."

"I'll be happy with six thousand words. It's more than I've been able to write so far," I said, feeling hopeful about completing this goal for the first time since I'd given up on the first book.

By the time we walked out of the library, I had a clear direction for my book—and my life. That feeling would last until I reached the back of the parking lot.

36

"BREAKEVEN"

THE SCRIPT

I could see something looked "off" as I approached my Jeep, but it wasn't until I saw how low the door handle was that I realized the issue. My front driver-side tire was flat. When I saw the slash across the top of the tire, I felt like I'd been dumped in cold, electrified water. It didn't feel random anymore. I took pictures and called 911. Again. Luckily, my dad had taught me how to change a flat tire before I was allowed to get my driver's license, so while I waited for the police officer to arrive, I got the tire switched out with the spare on the back. I was parked up against the bushes again, a mistake I wouldn't make a third time.

"You again?" came a voice from behind me as I stowed the jack in its compartment in the back.

I turned to find Officer Alcott standing behind me in street clothes and a baseball cap. "Me again. Apparently, I have a secret admirer."

He pushed his aviator sunglasses up further on his nose. "Apparently. The report came in from dispatch, and I was at the café so I figured I'd walk over. Didn't expect to find a repeat performance. I think you might be right; this doesn't seem to be a random occurrence anymore. Let me get your statement so you can salvage the rest of your day. After we're done here, I'm going to head over to the office building on the other side of those bushes. Maybe they've got some cameras up, but I'm not too hopeful, considering whoever did this felt comfortable enough to do it twice. In broad daylight, no less."

"I'd really love to know who is doing this. I haven't even been here long enough to piss anyone off, so I'm stumped, and if I'm being honest, I'm starting to get a little nervous. Not to mention, this is getting expensive!"

"I wish I had answers for you now, but I will do my best to find some. You didn't happen to take a picture before you changed the tire, did you?"

"I did. I can email it to you."

He handed me another business card and I quickly sent the photo off to him.

His phone dinged from his pocket. "Thank you. I'm sorry this happened again. I can assure you, Clearwater and Dunedin are relatively boring as far as petty crime goes—any crime, really. I've got one of the most cushy jobs in town next to the snow plow driver."

"You've got... oh, I see what you did there."

"Just trying to lighten the mood. I'll let you get on your way, but I'll be in touch as soon as I hear anything."

"I appreciate that. Thank you for coming by so quickly."

"My pleasure. Talk soon."

I climbed into the Jeep after he sauntered off.

"What the hell is going on here?" I muttered as I rolled my windows down to let the hot air escape.

I didn't expect an answer, but it would only take a week for one to materialize.

37

"BLUE SKY"

THE ALLMAN BROTHERS BAND

L ife in Dunedin was definitely taking on structure. Tuesdays were for ladies' league, Wednesdays were for Caleb, and Thursdays were for the Sensational Six. Having made a considerable dent in my to-do list for the week, I felt pretty good about meeting with my friends. I showered and chose a bright yellow sundress from my closet, noting how easy it was to get dressed now that I'd started making it a point to hang and fold my laundry as soon as I brought it upstairs. I slid my feet into my flip flops, slid my notebook into my tote bag, and headed for the Jeep.

We all arrived right about the same time, and after the traditional hugs and 'hellos', a flip-flop, denim-cutoff, and Nirvana-t-shirt-clad Elyse opened the door and held it as Grace, Sarah, Jenna, and I filed into the café one after another. Grace stood next to the hostess stand and smoothed imaginary wrinkles from her white linen capris and bright orange linen t-shirt. I wondered if she held stock in Tommy Bahama. "I'm sad Ethan has an ear infection, Sarah, but I'm glad you were able to get an early appointment so you could join us today."

Sarah removed a headband that perfectly matched her

white and navy floral button-down top, and smoothed her hair back as she slid it back on. "Me, too. Jeff was working from home, so it worked out perfectly."

At that point, the hostess that had been standing behind the counter chatting with the cashier when we walked in strolled over and led us to our usual booth in the back. We all spread out with our notebooks, ready for action. Jenna, seated next to me, tucked her long denim skirt under her thighs, a nervous habit I'd picked up on at our last meeting.

Within a few minutes, Betty stopped by our table. "The usual, ladies?"

"The usual," we all said in unison, then laughed.

"Quite a team you all make. Cat was ready for you and is just finishing up your eggs Benedict. I'll go grab those now. Coffee and water for everyone?"

We all agreed, then got to work opening our notebooks as soon as she walked away.

"Alright, ladies, let's hear it. What did you get done this week?" began Grace, our self-appointed forewoman.

"My meeting with the zoning commissioner went well. I filled out the application and he's going to try to fast-track it since my uncle had already begun the same process about ten years ago."

"Oh, that's awesome!" said Elyse as she fist-bumped me across the table. "It's good to know people who know people, am I right?"

"I also met with my uncle, and ladies... I have some big news. It's been so hard to hold this in, but I wanted to tell you in person."

"What is it?" asked Elyse, bouncing on her seat at the end of the booth to my right, her eyes alight with excitement.

As if on cue for dramatic effect, Betty returned at that moment with an overflowing tray. She set our plates in front of each of us, and I waited as she headed behind the front counter to retrieve our coffee and water carafes. She set them in the center of the table along with extra napkins and bid us a delightful lunch before walking away.

I looked around the table and four sets of eyes wide with curiosity stared back at me. "We have signed the paperwork, and the house is officially mine!"

The ladies all whooped with joy, and everyone high-fived me in excitement.

"We're on our way, girls!" exclaimed Grace.

"And one more thing. Two more, actually. I found a yoga instructor named Estelle to lead practice on Saturday mornings. I'll give her a trial for a few months, just to make sure she's a good fit. But Kari did a great job, and I have a really good feeling about her.

"And..." I took a bite and slowly chewed and swallowed my eggs Benedict for dramatic effect, because I could never resist. "I spoke with Caleb yesterday, and he agreed to teach a few professional development sessions on Friday mornings."

This news was met with even more raucous enthusiasm than the news about the house, and Cat peered around the door from the kitchen. "Everything okay out here? What did I miss?"

Elyse slid out of the booth and walked over to Cat. "Take a few minutes and come over. There have been some big developments this week."

Cat's eyes sought me out as she made her way to our table. She was being led by the arm by Elyse, who didn't take "I'm busy" for an answer.

"What's up, ladies? There must be something in the Hollandaise this morning; you all are a little keyed up—more than usual, anyway." She tucked the egg yolk-streaked towel she'd been holding into the waist of her emerald green apron, and perched on the edge of our booth to the left of Jenna. "Ahh-hhhhh... it feels so good to sit down. El, did you just volunteer to rub my feet? So kind of you!" As Cat leaned back to lift her left foot toward Elyse, who recoiled in mock horror on the other side of the table, she removed the yellow bandana keeping her tight brown curls from taking on a life of their own in the hot, steamy kitchen. She balled it up in her hand and swiped it across her forehead, and the thin layer of sweat left behind only served to accentuate the exquisite perfection of her smooth, mahogany skin.

"Well? What's all the hubbub out here? I heard you from the walk-in cooler."

Sarah, who for the most part, had been quietly enjoying her lunch while everyone around her behaved like fools, sat up straight and slapped the table. "It's all coming together! Cat, Paige hit the trifecta this week." She looked at me. "Can I tell her?" She began again before I'd even finished nodding my bewildered consent, her sudden excitement having stunned me into silence. "She signed the papers to make the house transfer official, she found a yoga instructor for the retreat, and her writing mentor has agreed to come in and teach a few sessions!"

The net sum of my week tumbled out of the mouth of my new friend and swirled around me. I let it be for a moment, until it settled like cooling rain over the hot-poker anxiety that had been building in me for months. Years. The steam that rose threatened the corners of my eyes and burned my eyelids. Where once a road to a gray nowhere stretched endlessly in front of me, a sunlit path had formed, and it was lined with these heaven-sent women. Cheering me on. Investing their time and energy and resources into me. *Me.* I was verklempt.

As the ladies chattered about the latest developments and which step should come next, I felt a light pressure land on my left arm. Jenna's hand. "This is a lot, isn't it?" she whispered, leaning in. "It's coming off you in waves. Is it relief? It must be relief." The last statement sounded more like she was answering her own question. I didn't know how, with all that was going on, she could pick up on the change in my state of mind without my demeanor having changed at all.

"It is relief," I whispered back, mirroring her posture. "Not to take a turn to negative town, but I've grown accustomed to things not going my way, and I was starting to feel the 'me' I used to be slipping away. Does that make any sense? Do you ever feel like that?"

Hesitation stilled her momentarily before she looked at her hand still resting on my arm and answered simply, "Yes."

I wanted so badly to engage her, draw her out of her shell a bit, but no sooner had Jenna returned her hand to the fist waiting in her lap, the peanut gallery seated around us turned their attention to us.

Grace nudged me with her left shoulder. "What are you two conspiring about over there?"

Jenna and I straightened up and found the rest of the group staring at us. "What are you four conspiring about over there?" I volleyed back.

"Before I realized you two were in your own little world, I was starting to tell you I'm going to get a few session ideas together, and I can fill in where you need me to. Between Caleb and me, you should be set for a few months. I'm sure you're going to have other authors volunteering to come in and teach sessions. Maybe you can have local authors come in and do Q&As, too."

"I love it. Thank you, Grace. And if you think of some way I can repay you for all of this, please tell me. I'd be happy to—"

"We'll figure that out later. I'm getting so much out of the planning process, and just the thought alone of a full weekend with fellow writers is like a dream come true. Anything I can do to help, I'm there. Pay it forward someday. That's all I ask."

Turning to face as many of the other women as I could, I felt my emotions threatening to rise again. "I really have no idea what I would do without you ladies," is all I trusted myself to say.

Cat stood and tied the bandana around her hair, tucking the tail under the knot to force it into submission. "This is what friends are f—," A sharp burst of breaking glass from the kitchen interrupted her sentiment. "Okay, party people, that's my 'Cat' signal," she threw over her shoulder as she whisked the towel out of her apron, tucked it into the collar of her shirt like a cape, and cackled with laughter at her own pun.

Her counterpart, Elyse, was doubled over with joy-fueled laughter. We all waited as she got control over herself. Sarah, seated to her left, playfully drummed her fingers on the table, but her smile exposed her amusement.

"Okay, okay. Phew! That towel threw me right over the edge." Elyse took a deep breath and wiped her eyes. "I was in the store this morning wondering what more I can do to support this whole endeavor. Let's have Raina add a one-pager to her marketing strategy and we can start at least getting the word out. Even if you don't have a full website yet, she can put up a 'coming soon' message with basic information and 'stay tuned for details' to start warming people up to the idea."

"I'm actually meeting with Raina tomorrow at noon. She's been very busy, which is a good sign for me, but this was the first chance we've both had in our schedule to get together. I've got a whole list of projects for her. I'll add the one-pager."

"You are going to love her. I contract her services for the store all the time, and she has sold out so many of our events. I call her my marketing maven. She is so good at what she does. You're gonna have to start turning people away at the door."

"No complaints there!"

"When you meet with her, ask what she thinks about putting some flyers up before the website is ready, and if she says it's okay and sends me the file, I will hang it in the store right away."

"And I can start sharing the info on some of my social channels as well," offered Grace. "I have all these followers. They might as well do you some good as well. Ok, you're up, Jenna. Let's see what you've got."

Jenna cleared her throat and stared at her hands folded in her lap. "I've had some trouble finding time to work on these this week. Craig has been so..." she trailed off, then shook her head quickly. "Well, I just haven't had a whole lot of time, but I did put a few things together. I'm sorry I don't have more."

Jenna flipped open her notebook, and we were greeted with the most beautiful sketches of cupcakes, cookies, and pastries.

"These look good enough to eat, Jenna," breathed Sarah. "Who knew you could draw like this?"

Jenna reddened as she absorbed the compliment. "I have always loved doing little pencil sketches. It relaxes me, but I'm not very good at it."

"Who told you *that*? How did we not know you had this kind of talent, Jenna?" Elyse fired back, incredulous.

"It doesn't matter. I just... anyway, here's the list of what I was thinking I could do on a regular basis, and we can switch out any of these for seasonal items."

They were passing the notebook around the table, everyone oohing and aahhing over her sketches, when we caught a disturbance at the front of the café.

Jenna's eyes moved from the scene at the door to the notebook that had just come around to me. She plucked it from my hands and shoved it into the tote bag squeezed between her feet. Her rapid change in behavior stunned me. My eyes followed the notebook until it was secreted away, then up to her face, frozen in the undeniable expression of someone who knew the rabid cat they'd tried so hard to contain had come tearing through the bag.

38

"SLOW DANCING IN A BURNING ROOM"

JOHN MAYER

I peeled my eyes away from her to see what had caused such a visceral reaction. Standing in front of the hostess stand twenty feet away was a disheveled, short-statured man with shoulder-length brown hair I could clearly see—even from that distance—was in need of a wash. His red face oscillated like an overheated desk fan, searching. "*JENNA! Where the hell are you?*" His tightly curled fist came down hard on the hostess stand as his voice boomed through the small café, highlighting how close the unhinged man was to us. To Jenna, who was quaking like a half-frozen chihuahua next to me.

"Oh, good grief. This guy's a real piece of shit. Sorry, Jenna," Elyse said, then slid from the booth, followed by Sarah, who stepped aside to let her mother out. Grace put a hand on the back of the booth and a hand on the end of the table and pulled herself out. She took a step forward and held a hand out to Jenna, whose eyes dashed back and forth between Grace's hand and the door.

At that moment, a flustered Cat peered around the door from the kitchen to investigate the commotion at the front of her café and, in three seconds, stood next to the hostess stand. Hands on hips and chin raised in an unspoken challenge, she formed a human barrier between the dazed hostess and the unhinged man on the hunt for our friend.

Elyse exploded forward, and before I could even process her movement, was standing rigidly at Cat's side. "Do you want me to handle this?"

Grace was next to arrive on the scene, trailed by Jenna who was looking down at the floor in front of her sandals. She stepped between the man at the door and the two women poised for attack. "This isn't the time or the place, Elyse. Cat, let's take a ten-second cool-down. Why don't you and I step outside together?" Grace said as she took a step toward the man with a hand held out toward the door.

From what I could see between the women who blocked his path—and sightline—to our booth, his clothes looked relatively clean, so I didn't think he was homeless, but everything about him seemed unkempt. He was vaguely familiar, but I couldn't zero in on where I'd seen him before.

Sarah's voice broke my concentration as I flipped through my mental Rolodex. "Might as well stay here while my mother and the two hotheads handle that meathead. My mom and I are firmly in the 'cooler heads prevail' camp, which balances out the group and keeps everyone out of the slammer."

"Who *is* that?"

"That would be Craig," said Sarah. "To use Elyse's sentiment, he's a real piece of shit."

"Jenna's *husband*? What's his deal?"

"I would venture to guess he tracked her here. He tracks her everywhere she goes. He's always been a bit of an asshole, but he wasn't always this bad. It's gotten a lot worse over the last year or so and no one really knows why. Jenna has been very patient with him, but things like this are embarrassing for her, as you can imagine."

"I can't believe anyone would treat Jenna like that. She's the sweetest person I've ever met."

A hiss flowed over Sarah's front teeth as she contemplated her next few words. "Despite her upbringing, Jenna used to have a little more fire in her, but you can only have that fire if someone isn't throwing buckets of water on you every time you try to take a step forward."

"Oh my God. I feel terrible for her." My eyes settled on the shrunken figure walking out the door behind Grace. Sarah began to slide out of the booth, her relaxed pace demonstrating her obvious confidence in her mother's ability to diffuse the situation. I scooted out after her, but we continued to stand next to our table. It seemed the bill for today's meal would have to be paid later, as everyone else responsible for procuring it had spilled out onto the sidewalk.

"Is she going to be okay?"

"I think right now she's trying to wrap her mind around the extreme changes in her husband and how they affect her marriage. If things continue like this, I can't see it working out the way she'd hoped, but Jenna isn't a quitter, and she is doing everything she can to smooth things over until, God-willing, Craig goes back to his normal 'asshole-reduced' behavior."

"No one knows what sparked this?"

"No, but I'm sure all the jobs he's lost all over town due to his piss-poor attitude haven't helped matters. Right now, they're living on Jenna's café income, which is why I think she's so excited about this opportunity with you. Not only does it give them a little more income, but it gives her some autonomy and brings her one step closer to where she'd actually like to be, which is owning her own bakery. Assuming Craig ever allows it."

I shifted my weight from one foot to the other. "My uncle mentioned that Craig used to do his groundskeeping at the house, but he had some issues with his reliability."

"Yeah, that's a common refrain amongst anyone who's worked with Craig in the last couple years. I feel terrible for Jenna, but this is something that, while we can put our arms around her, we can't solve for her, so we're just trying to give her as much support as we can."

"I can't believe he just showed up here like that."

Sarah must have come to the same realization as I did about the bill, because she looked down at the abandoned table filled with the detritus of our lunch and placed a few twenties in the center. "He's done it before and he'll do it again." She looked around the restaurant. "I just guessed at the total. Cat will tip Betty with this and let us know later if we owe more. You can just Venmo me. Ready?"

We made our way to the door, but fear tickled my subconscious. "Is she going to be safe?"

"I don't think he's ever been physical with her, but we all worry because the statistics are not good for this situation. These things tend to escalate over time, especially considering the rate at which he escalated to this point without anyone knowing why. So, no, I don't think he'd put his hands on her, but part of that might be his fear of what would happen to him if Cat and Elyse saw a single red mark on her." She opened the door and held it for me.

We stepped out into the harsh sunlight, and a mental image slid into place. Craig cowering in the center of a ring. Elyse crouched on the ropes, waiting for Cat to tag her in. I nodded, satisfied by the knowledge that Sarah was probably right. For now. But even a watched pot eventually boils over.

"Looks like we've timed our exit perfectly," Sarah observed as we reached the sidewalk. The only people left milling around outside the café were Cat and Elyse.

"Grace left with Jenna after a futile attempt to talk some sense into Craig. He sped off in his car, and it sounded like Grace was taking Jenna back to her condo. I'm going back to the bookstore to work off some of this adrenaline with some super strenuous paperwork. I'm going to grab my backpack from the booth and take off. Cat, let me know what I owe for lunch."

"It's covered," said Sarah. "We can settle up later."

"Thank you, Sarah. Paige, it's been delightful. I'm sorry that asshat let the air out of our excitement, but I am so thrilled with where this is headed, and I am *so* happy for you!" And with that, she opened the door and disappeared inside the café.

"I'd better head back in and get everyone calmed down." Cat smoothed the front of her apron. "Ladies, we will pick up where we left off next time. Don't worry about the bill."

"I threw sixty dollars on the table. Let my mom know if it was more than that." Sarah turned back and hugged me. "Paige, Paige, Paige. So much drama since you arrived. Your head must be spinning. I hope the rest of your day goes better than today's meeting." She stepped back, but left her hand on my arm. "Okay, I'm off to the grocery store." As she walked toward her car parked on the street, she called back with a lilt in her voice, "Making a new recipe tonight. Maybe I'll make a 'special' dish for Craig. Toodles."

Sarah wasn't wrong. My head was spinning and continued to do so all the way home. I had learned so much about each of my new friends in the last thirty minutes. They were a force, each of them in their own way. Fiercely loyal to one another. I felt lucky to have found my way into their circle.

39

"DREAMS"
FLEETWOOD MAC

Raina and I had decided on Cat's Bites for our meeting. Thanks to Roxy's quest to finally catch a lizard landing her in the pool five minutes before I planned on leaving, I skidded into a parking spot ten minutes late. I'd texted Jenna to ask if she could please get Raina set up at a quiet table as I dried us both off and chose a new (dry) outfit. Between the residual adrenaline from jumping into the pool to 'save' Roxy, who had clearly never heard the term 'doggy paddle', and the mad dash to the café, I was breathless by the time I arrived.

Jenna stood behind the counter. She gave me a tiny wave and pointed to a booth in the back corner where I could see a mass of brown curls bent over a laptop. I blew Jenna a kiss which she returned and then made the universal 'slow down' signal with her hands. I hated being late, especially for someone I'd never met before and on whom I wanted to make a good first impression. I took Jenna's advice. As I made my way to the booth, I practiced the 4-7-8 breathing Kari had taught me years ago, and I seldom remembered to use.

"Hey there, Raina." I set my tote bag down on the booth

opposite her and held out my hand. "I'm so sorry I'm late. You wouldn't happen to want a golden retriever, would you?"

"It's no trouble. It gave me a few minutes to get caught up on a few emails that came in while I was driving here," she said as she stood and shook my outstretched hand. "It's great to meet you. Elyse has told me so much about you."

She returned to her seat and I slid in opposite her. "So, is that a yes on the golden retriever?"

"Oh no," she said, chuckling. "Your text earlier sealed the deal on me getting any sort of pet until the kids are old enough to help take care of it. And they're enough trouble as it is."

"Well, let me tell you, golden retrievers don't get quite the bad reputation they deserve sometimes."

Renia threw her head back and laughed. "Elyse was right about you. Smart *and* funny. My favorite combination. I can see why everyone's fallen in love with you."

A searing blush spread across my face and warmed my ears. "Aannnyway..."

"Elyse said you'd deflect a compliment. The way things are going for you here, you might want to get used to receiving them. Now," she rose from her side of the booth and moved to mine, "scooch over so I can show you what I've got so far." She sat in the space I'd made warm for her, and reached across the table to slide her laptop around so we could both see the screen. "I know we haven't made anything official, but I like to give potential clients a little taste of what they can expect."

She touched the keyboard to wake up the screen, and the front of my house flashed into view. I had never considered myself a 'gasper', but gasp, I did when I saw what she had prepared. It was a website layout with a gorgeous shot of the house from the street. The color scheme for the rest of the design was exactly what I would have picked myself, and the whole vibe was tropical but airy. It was like my new home was decked out in a vintage Lilly Pulitzer dress.

"Raina! This is... I just... I love it!"

"I'm so glad. This is only a mock-up. I stopped by yesterday and took a few photos from the road in front of the house. I am really hoping you hire me because I am dying to see the inside."

"If the rest of your plans look like this, I will hire you right now." I was blown away by how she'd captured the essence of the house and the aesthetic I envisioned for my branding without us ever having discussed it.

"Why don't I show you some of my ideas for other marketing materials and a few mock-ups I put together for your social media accounts." A few clicks later, she pulled up a PDF with images and graphics that perfectly matched the website design.

Seeing it all brought together like this, where I could physically *see* what the marketing for my own business would look like after being a part of that process for *other* businesses for so many years, made it all feel so real—*and* surreal.

Seeming to read my thoughts, she explained. "It's so much better when you can see it on a screen. I have a potential strategy laid out as well." After reviewing a few of the beautiful design options she'd shown me, we set a date for her to come take pictures of the rooms and other areas of the house they'd be seeing during their stay.

"I'll send you a contract later today. There's a lot to do and decide before everything goes live, but you'll be a part of as much as you'd like. I'm excited to work with you!"

We made some small talk about our mutual friends and she packed up a few minutes later. I slid out of the booth after her and we shook hands again. "It was nice to meet you," she said, "and I'm really excited to be working on this project with you. It's going to be a lot of fun!"

Jenna walked up to the booth as Raina was leaving. "How did it go? I was trying not to be too obvious by staring, but I could see your facial expressions, and it seemed pretty positive overall."

"Oh my gosh, Jenna. I can't wait for you to see." My body was so full of fervent energy that it overflowed into my words, and rushed them out of my mouth. "She made a mock-up of the website and some social media graphics and it's all so gorgeous I can barely stand it." Realizing I was one decibel shy of a charge for disturbing the peace, I looked around, but we were alone, aside from a young couple in a back booth. They were so engrossed in their own conversation that I could have stood there buck-naked reciting the preamble at full volume, and they would never have noticed.

"Cat is going to be so disappointed she wasn't here for that, but I'm glad she didn't come in on her day off. She is *always* here." Something I couldn't identify slid across her face, and her relaxed posture shifted as she clasped her hands in front of her. The international sign of 'shit's about to get real.'

"About yesterday..."

I stepped forward and placed my hand on her forearm and was relieved to see she didn't flinch. That made me feel a little more confident that Craig wasn't getting handsy with her at home. Yet.

"Jenna, we absolutely do not need to talk about yesterd—"

She put her hand up to stop me, then quickly brought it back down. "I feel I need to defend Craig a little bit. He wasn't always like this. I mean, he's never been Prince Charming, but he's..." Her eyes settled on a spot on the ceiling somewhere behind me. "He's struggling with something, and he won't admit it, let alone tell me what it is, but it's manifesting itself as jealousy. He can't bear for me to be away from home any longer than my shift here at the café. He hasn't been able to hold a regular-paying job in a few years, so he's sitting home all day waiting for me and imagining the worst.

"I've tried to stay busy to keep from suffocating at home, but

I end up feeling guilty the whole time I'm gone. What's worse is, I don't drive. I've never really had to because Craig has always driven me wherever I needed to go, but now it makes me feel a little helpless. And isolated. Basically, the more I try to distance myself from the Venus flytrap at home, the more overzealous he becomes. Yesterday was an eye-opener for me, and I wanted to apologize to you for how uncomfortable the whole situation must have made you feel. Some impression I've made."

This was more than I've heard Jenna speak the entire time I've known her. "Thank you for trusting me with all that, Jenna, but you do not need to apologize for someone else's behavior. The impression you've made on me is completely separate from the impression your husband has made on me. I do have to say that I am concerned. I've grown to care about you, and what happened yesterday is worrisome."

"Thank you for understanding. And for caring. I ended up staying at Grace's last night. She was able to find the app he's been using to track me and I deleted it and silenced my notifications. Even though I know he's going to be mad when I get home later, I've actually had a pretty good morning here. I think it was partially to do with how well I slept last night. I fell asleep at eight-thirty and slept until my alarm woke me up at five this morning."

"Five? In the morning? Why on earth did you have to be up in the middle of the night?"

"Cat had someone coming to install some cameras in here, and she asked if I could come in an hour early to let him in. I usually get here at six to start my baking, so it was no trouble."

"Okay, well, I'm glad you got some sleep last night. I'm going to let you get back to work, but you have my number. Any time you want—or need—to get out of the house, please feel free to call me, ok? I mean it. Will you be okay at home tonight?"

She looked down at her feet, her embarrassment seeming

to have returned. "If he's even there, he's just going to yell. Grace is going to drive me home and go in with me to be a buffer and make sure he's calmed down. Anyway, thanks for everything, and for understanding." She looked me square in the eye. "I don't care what Grace says about you. You're pretty great."

My heart seemed to grow three sizes and cut off my airway for a moment. "You don't... What does... I... *Grace?*" I sputtered.

"Kidding! Oh, you should have seen your face." she giggled like a twelve-year-old with a fresh bottle of fart spray and doubled over to clutch her knees for support.

"Jenna! Woo! You scared me there. I didn't know you had it in you. Wow. Sneaky with the jokes. You and I are going to do just fine."

I began to laugh just as she started winding down, which only served to wind her back up again. After a minute or so, we regained our composure, and aside from a few rogue giggles, we managed to say our goodbyes after which Jenna shocked me further by initiating a hug.

I drove all the way home on a cloud of joy.

NEXT THURSDAY NIGHT, Book Club was being hosted at Sarah's, and Roxy was overjoyed to be invited, or so I told our hostess as she was being assailed by the wagging tail of a spinning dog upon our arrival. As usual, she stole the show—and their hearts—and was somehow invited back.

When we got back home a few hours later, we were both exhausted from our outing, but when I opened up the back of the Jeep to let Roxy out, she sniffed the air and went on high alert.

40

"KILLING ME SOFTLY"

LAURYN HILL (THE FUGEES)

As soon as Roxy jumped down onto the driveway, she immediately started sniffing the air with her tail up. She cut a path, left to right, right to left, back to back, across the driveway, and up the walkway to the back door. A low growl rumbled from somewhere that until now had been dormant.

"What is it, Rox? What's gotten into you? Attack lizards this time? Little green ninjas? Terrifying!" I joked in an attempt to quell my growing anxiety.

She continued with the odd body language but stopped sniffing long enough to turn and look at me, then at the back door with the same low growl.

"A cheese emergency, then?"

When she didn't answer with her typical "yes!" bark in response to the magic word, my instincts kicked in.

Roxy wasn't, by *any* stretch of the imagination, a guard dog, but she did have excellent instincts, and I felt compelled to pay attention to them at that moment.

I tried the handle of the door, and it was locked. The

chances of it actually being a cheese emergency were becoming more likely, so I turned my key and opened the door.

What I saw in the foyer took my breath away.

The place was a disaster, to put it mildly. There was glass all over the floor, and I immediately closed the door and got Roxy and myself back into the Jeep and out of the driveway.

I parked around the corner and, with shaking hands, dialed 911.

"911, what's your emergency?"

"I've had a break-in at my house."

"Are you currently at the location? Are you inside your house right now?"

"No, I saw the damage and broken glass on the floor, and I left immediately."

"We'll get someone over there right away. What's the street address?"

I gave them the address and immediately texted the Sensational Six after I hung up.

> Someone broke into my house while I was gone.

Grace: I'm on my way. Are the cops there?

Elyse: I'm turning around now. I'll be right there.

Sarah: Are you kidding me? Let me have my husband put the rest of the food away, and I'll be there in a few minutes. Please be careful.

Cat: I just parked my bike. I'm putting my helmet back on, and I will be there in five. Do NOT go in until the police get there.

Grace: Yes, please don't go in.

> Oh, I definitely won't.

I called, and they are on their way.

I'm parked around the corner.

Jenna: Oh no.

I was relieved to see the squad car pulling down the gravel road. My hands were still shaking as I tried to grip the wheel and pull the Jeep back into the driveway.

A uniformed Officer Alcott was getting out of his squad car as I opened my door. I hopped down and told Roxy to stay. "Is it okay if I let my golden retriever out? She's a little anxious right now."

"Feel free, but please wait out here while I make sure that everything is safe inside. Do you know how they got in?"

"I don't. This door was locked, but I haven't checked the front door. I saw the glass in the foyer and left immediately."

"Okay, I'm going to go in and have a look around. You wait right here."

He went inside through the door I'd left unlocked in my haste to flee, and remained inside for what was probably ten minutes, but felt like a hundred. He returned and opened the back door, then waved me in.

"Come on, Roxy," I said, but I'd wasted my breath. She was already halfway to the open door, her nose down and her tail up.

"The front door was also locked. There is broken glass everywhere," he said. "Do you have somewhere you can safely put your dog so she doesn't cut her paws?"

"Yes, I'll put her in her room off the kitchen."

I walked to the other side of the patio and unlocked the door to Roxy's room, which was at one point a workout room and which would at no point in the future be used for such nonsense.

"Roxy, wait here, and I'll come and get you once everything

is cleaned up. Be a good girl," I said and patted her head before giving her a smooch on her snoot.

I wished I could stay with my arms wrapped around her fluffy neck, but I had some adulting to do instead. I left Roxy's room through the hallway to the kitchen, closing the door behind me, to which Roxy protested with a high-pitched bark.

"I'll be right back, Roxy. Hang in there."

I tiptoed through what had to be dozens of smashed plates and bowls in the kitchen to the equally destroyed foyer and found him waiting there with a notepad. The table that had been holding up a beautiful antique vase filled with an enormous silk floral arrangement was lying on its side, surrounded by shards of blue and white glass and an oxymoronic sea of brightly colored petals violently ripped from their stems. The enormous round mirror that had hung just inside the door was a goner, and I couldn't help but think about the seven years of bad luck that would be following whomever had ripped it from the wall and heaved it onto the hardwood floor. Its mangled frame had been relieved of all but a few pieces of reflective glass at its edges and was face-up in submission inches from the baseboards along the staircase.

"You've got yourself a real fan here, Paige. As you can see, there is broken glass everywhere, particularly in the foyer and kitchen. There's some damage to the walls headed up the stairs, and the room that looks as if it's inhabited—which I'm assuming is yours—has the most extensive damage."

We carefully picked our way through the great expanse of broken glass and went up the stairs to the second floor. I could barely look at the gorgeous murals on the walls. It was obvious they were going to need some extensive repairs.

"The mirror in the bathroom is smashed. The mirror above your dresser is smashed. The pillows have been sliced open, and feathers are everywhere. It looks as if the bedding has been slashed with a knife. Do you have any idea who would do this?"

When I started to reply, I realized my mouth had been hanging open in shock. "I have *no* idea, but if I were a betting woman, I'd put my money on the lunatic who has been vandalizing my Jeep."

Officer Alcott tapped his pen on his notebook. "That'd be a safe bet, I'd say."

My shaking had been replaced with a full-body numbness.

"Hello? Oh my god." Grace's voice traveled up to us.

"Grace, we're up here. Hang on."

"Is it okay if my friend comes upstairs?" I asked Officer Alcott. "I could use a familiar face right about now."

"She can come up, but please warn her to be careful and not to touch anything."

I parroted his instructions and within moments I could hear Grace's footsteps on the treads of the stairs as she made her way up to the second floor. Her eyes were full, blue moons against her tanned, worried face. "What on earth happened here?"

"I wish I knew. The doors were locked, so I have no idea how this could have happened."

"I can't even believe this. So what has been damaged?"

"Right now, it looks as if it's the foyer, the kitchen—"

"Oh, I saw the kitchen on my way to the staircase. I'm nearly speechless. I'm glad to see you here, Ben," Grace said, turning to where Officer Alcott stood in front of my bathroom door to her left.

"Hello, Grace. I'd say it's nice to see you, but..." He looked around the room and back to her.

"Knock, knock," came Elyse's voice up the stairs.

"Is that Elyse Bennett's voice I hear?"

"Yes, we were all together earlier before I came home to find this... disaster."

"Well, I'm going to dust for fingerprints, then I'll be on my way. I'll let you know when I'm done so you can start cleaning up."

A short time later he cleared us to start in the kitchen, and we began sweeping up all the plates and mugs that had been pulled out of the cabinets and thrown to the floor.

"I'm glad none of these beautiful countertops were damaged," said Grace as she placed an empty cardboard box on the floor.

Elyse came around the corner from the dining room with a dustpan full of broken bits of plates and teacups. "If I find out who did this, I—oh, hello there, Ben."

"I would suggest not taking the law into your own hands, Elyse. Miss Rhiann, if you think of anything else, please give me a call. I'll be in touch." He handed me his card. "I'm glad you have a dog here. Keep her loose tonight and listen for her. Do you have an alarm system?"

"I do have an alarm system, but I haven't been turning it on." Out of the corner of my eye, I saw Grace straighten up much faster than I'd seen her move up until then. "I will start doing that today."

"You better," admonished Grace.

As Officer Alcott left, he passed Sarah on the walkway coming in, and I heard the concern in her voice. "Ben. Thank God you were able to get here so fast. How is she? Everything's okay inside?"

"Yes. She's a little shaken, but I'm sure your company will do her a lot of good. You ladies have some cleanup ahead of you. I'd stay and help, but I need to get back to the station to write up the report and run some fingerprints."

"Thank you, Ben. I hope you find who did this before Elyse and Cat do."

"So do I. Take care, and please remind Miss Rhiann to keep that alarm set, even when she's home, and she definitely needs to have these locks changed. I'm going to drive past here a few times tonight."

I heard this last bit as I walked outside to take a breath.

Sarah looked to me with concern clouding her eyes, then back to Officer Alcott. "That makes me feel a lot better. We will set the alarm right now and remind her to set it again after we leave."

As he climbed into his squad car, I could hear the roar of Cat's bike as she turned down my street. We waited for her to park and take her helmet off.

When she and Sarah walked into my destroyed kitchen and stood in the same state of shock we had all experienced, without a word, I walked to the alarm panel and activated it, then hugged Sarah and Cat on my way back into the kitchen.

"Thank you all for coming. I owe you big after tonight."

"Nonsense," replied Grace. "Let's get this cleaned up so you can let that poor dog out of her room. Her howling is tearing my heart in half. I brought some gardening gloves and empty boxes in from the garage and I found an extra broom. This shouldn't take long."

The five of us continued working in the kitchen without saying much, each of us lost in our own thoughts. Once all the glass had been cleaned up and the counters wiped down, Sarah spoke up. "Is this it? The foyer and this mess in the kitchen?"

"No, whoever it was went upstairs and destroyed my bedroom and bathroom as well."

The dustpan Elyse had been using clattered to the ground. "Are you shitting me right now?"

"I wish I were."

Her eyes found Cat's and widened in shock. "You and Sarah come with me. We will get started up there."

We knew precisely when they'd arrived in my room. "What the *hell*?" (Elyse) "Holy shit!" (Cat) Then, "Holy cow." (Sarah)

Grace closed her eyes for a moment, then opened them and

spoke. "You have a lot of flatware and cups you're going to have to replace."

"It sounds like some online shopping is in order. I'm not looking forward to calling my uncle about this. He's put so much of his heart into this house and in one evening someone just trashed it."

"What do you think you're going to do? Will you file an insurance claim?"

"I don't think I want to start off with my new insurance policy by immediately filing a claim, so I think I'm just going to end up eating this one. It looks to be mostly glass and bedding, which can all be replaced pretty easily. The murals are another story, but I'm hoping my uncle can put me in contact with the artist. With any luck, she can touch up the damage without having to completely repaint those sections."

Within a few hours, the ladies had everything cleaned, boxed up, and tucked into the back of Grace's SUV. "I'm going to take this with me and drop it off at waste management." She put my ravaged bedding in her backseat. "I don't know what I'm going to do with this yet. I just don't want you to have to look at it until garbage day."

"You ladies have been incredible, as always. I don't know what I would do without you."

"The good news is," retorted Elyse, "you don't have to do much of anything without us. But what I *would* recommend is getting some cameras set up."

Cat spoke up. "I *just* had some installed at the café after that fiasco with Craig. Is that something that you are open to?"

I shuddered at the mention of his name. "Yeah, I don't think it's a bad idea at this point. I hate having cameras around, but right now, I wish I had them all along."

"I'll call him on the way home and tell him it's an emergency. Are you going to be home tomorrow?"

"Yes, I'll be here all day."

"Great. Expect a call from Adam. He'll get you all set up."

Grace stepped forward and hugged me, which I gratefully returned. "I can't even imagine what this feels like, but please know we're here for you. Would you and Roxy like to just come back home with me?"

"No, we're gonna be okay here. I'll bring my nine-iron upstairs for protection."

Grace, Elyse, Cat, and Sarah barked out a laugh at the same time, then one by one, wrapped me up and squeezed me tightly.

"That's not a bad idea," said Sarah. "And Ben said he'd be driving past tonight. He's a good guy, and he seemed genuinely concerned about you. Promise me you're going to activate the alarm after we leave."

"The second I walk back in, I'll be turning it on."

Elyse opened the door of her car, but stood behind it. "Keep your phone with you and charging all night. We'll probably check in right around bedtime, and we're just a phone call away if you need any of us."

"You ladies are amazing."

I stood in the driveway and waved as the three of them pulled out of the driveway. When I went inside, I headed straight for the alarm panel, swept the floor one more time, then let an anxious Roxy out of her room. A few minutes later, my phone was ringing on the counter. Uncle Mike.

"I fell asleep watching TV and missed a call from Susie next door. She left me a voicemail saying there was a squad car in your driveway when she got home from her Bridge club. Is everything okay?"

"Yes. It is now. I was going to call you as soon as I got upstairs. Someone broke in here while I was at book club and smashed up a bunch of stuff. Other than a few parts of the mural going up the stairs, nothing that can't be replaced. Other than my psyche."

"*Are you serious?*" he shouted into the phone. "Do you need us to come over?"

"No, my friends just left. They helped me clean everything up, and I just turned the alarm on. Cat is sending someone over to install cameras tomorrow."

"That's an excellent idea. You've got some great friends there, Paige. Do they happen to have any old uncles looking for more friends?"

"I'm not sure." It felt good to laugh; it was something I could always count on Uncle Mike to provide. "I can ask."

"I'm happy you're able to laugh a little. You must be so shaken up! Do you have any idea who this might have been?"

"I have no idea. Between this and the vandalism to my Jeep, it feels personal to me, but I can't imagine who would have it in for me already. I just got here."

"Was the door unlocked when you got home?"

"No, both doors were locked, and the police officer couldn't find any broken glass anywhere other than the dishes and mirrors."

"And you're sure you don't want us to come over? Or you and Roxy are welcome here."

"I'm going to stay put for tonight, but thank you. Hopefully, whoever did this has wound themselves down and Officer Alcott will find them quickly. He took a bunch of fingerprints before he left and told Sarah he's going to drive by throughout the night."

He hesitated for a moment, likely debating whether he should drive over and kidnap me. With a long sigh, he released a breath he'd clearly been holding in as he deliberated with himself. "Ok. I met Ben years ago at a fundraiser. He's a good guy and if he said he's going to drive by, that probably means he'll be camped out in front of the house. But, Paige, I'm serious about this. If *anything* seems strange, call the police and then call me. I'll wake up Chris and we'll be right there. I'm so sorry this happened, kiddo."

"Me, too. My heart broke when I saw all your hard work smashed on the floor."

"It's just stuff, honey. Nothing that can't be replaced or fixed. You, on the other hand,..."

"I know, Uncle Mike. I'll be fine, I promise. But, I'm going to go to bed and see if I can get some sleep."

"Okay. Well, again, let me know if you need us there."

I let a very reluctant Uncle Mike go after promising to double-check the alarm, leave Roxy to roam the house overnight, and bring a golf club to bed.

I wasn't sure if I would be able to sleep, but I couldn't talk about what had happened there for one more minute.

41

"FAST CAR"
TRACY CHAPMAN

I nstead of going straight to bed, I found myself wandering the house one last time. I wasn't looking for anything in particular, but I couldn't shake the unsettling feeling that someone had been walking around my house when I wasn't there.

With the retreats getting closer and closer, I was starting to wonder if it was even a good idea to have other people in the house with someone out there so clearly set on disrupting my life.

I pictured what would have happened if I had had guests there, and that had happened in the middle of the night. My retreats would be over before they even got off the ground.

...*and then what?* I wondered.

"Well, Rox, we're going to have to try to get some sleep. Do you want to stay down here or come up with me?"

I let her out one more time. She sniffed around a little bit outside, did her business, and came back in. I headed for the stairs, but she seemed to have some innate sense of what I needed, and she curled up right in front of the back door and set her head down on her paws.

"Come up when you get tired of standing guard," I said, and I knelt down on the floor to wrap my arms around her, breathe in her fuzzy neck, and kiss her cold, black snoot. "I'll see you soon, okay? Thanks for keeping us safe."

With one final scratch behind her right ear, I headed toward the front door to make sure the lights were on outside. A squad car was pulled along the side of the street, and the glow of an open laptop illuminated Officer Alcott who saw me in the side-light and waved. I waved back, headed for the stairs, and went off to bed. Sleep was slow to come, but between the knowledge that help was nearby if I needed it, and the sounds of Roxy's nails intermittently tapping across the floor downstairs, I was able to drift off around two a.m.

I woke up at seven to the sound of my phone buzzing on the nightstand next to me. It was a text from Jenna, but not in the group chat.

> Jenna: Are you awake?

> Yes, I am.

> Jenna: Did you get any sleep last night?

> I got a few hours. Roxy took the night shift. I heard her walking around all night. She's such a good puppy.

> Jenna: Do you mind if I stop over in about an hour?

> Come on over. I'd love to see you.

> Jenna: Okay. I'll see you soon.

I swung my legs over the side of the bed and stood. The soft, plush rug on the side of my bed greeted me, a comforting way to start the day.

I avoided the closed door of my bathroom and instead

headed downstairs to let Roxy out. She was curled up by the front door, still sleeping with her head on her paws, but as my feet hit the floor at the bottom of the stairs, her eyes slid open, and her tail began to wag.

"I'm happy to see you too, Rox. I missed you last night." She stood, put her paws straight out and her tail up in the air, stretched, and walked over to nuzzle between my hand and leg for a morning scratch.

"You're such a good dog. You must be ready to go potty, though."

I deactivated the alarm, unlocked the door, and let her out in the backyard to do her business. She ran in circles for a moment after sniffing the air and surveying the yard. I stood in the open door watching her, wondering what the day had in store for me and, more urgently, what Jenna's impromptu visit was about. I decided she was probably coming to check on me.

When Roxy was done, we went back inside and had a little breakfast. Some kibble with bone broth for Roxy. A bagel with cream cheese for me.

After I called Kari to talk to her about what had happened the night before and repeatedly assure her that I was safe and taking every precaution, I sat in the sunroom sipping my coffee and making a list of things I needed to get done throughout the day. As I contemplated whether I had enough time to take a shower, my phone buzzed with a text.

> Unknown: Hi Paige, this is Adam from A&I Security. I hope it's okay that I text; I'm waiting for a client who's still in a meeting, but our friend Elyse mentioned that you needed some cameras installed pretty quickly. Are you around this morning?

I quickly saved him as a contact.

> Thank you for reaching out so quickly. I will be around all day today.

> I have some work to get done, but just knock on the back door when you get here.

Adam: Will do. I have everything I will need with me, so I'll come in and look around to see how many cameras you're going to need. Once they're installed, I'll need a little bit of your time to walk you through everything, and how to pull up recordings if needed.

> That sounds great. I'll see you when you get here.

Adam: See you in about an hour.

I needed to take a shower and brush my teeth before Jenna arrived, but decided to use the spare bathroom. I wasn't ready to face the damage in mine.

I HAD JUST enough time to get showered, brush my teeth, and get downstairs before Jenna knocked on the back door. I deactivated the alarm and let her in.

As she stepped over the threshold, the first thing I noticed were her red-rimmed, puffy eyes. I took an educated guess that Craig was the cause of her tears, but I decided to be there for her and just listen. Jenna had never come to my house without any of the other women being around, so there was a definite reason why she was there that morning, and I knew I was going to have to be patient and wait for her to get comfortable enough to share what it was.

I wouldn't have to wait long.

"Paige... I– I don't know where to begin. I..." she trailed off.

"It's ok, Jenna. Take your time. Let's sit in the sunroom. Do you want a cup of coffee?" I led the way as Jenna slinked along behind me.

"No thank you. Coffee would be a bad idea right now."

Once in the sunroom, I lowered myself onto the plush velvet cushions of the rattan couch and mentally thanked Uncle Mike for his knack for aesthetic *and* comfort. Patting the cushion next to me, I invited Jenna to take a load off. She looked like a flight risk.

She sat on the edge of the cushion to my right, smoothed her skirt over her legs, took a deep breath, and let it out, slow and stuttering between semi-pursed lips. She closed her eyes, and when they opened, focused somewhere around the space past my left ear, and began to speak. "Last night... I'm so sorry about what happened last night, Paige. I didn't know what to say when you texted, but I knew I had to come here first thing this morning."

"Jenna, you don't need to be sorry," I exclaimed, reaching across the space between us to put my hand on her shoulder. She flinched nearly imperceptibly under the weight of my hand, so I removed it and set it back on my own lap.

"I'm not like the rest of you. Being so open isn't easy for me, but I'm going to try and get through this." She looked back down to her hands, took another deep breath, and her exhale carried words that entered my ears and bounced off my brain but couldn't take hold. "Paige, I met Craig at a time in my life when I was desperate for guidance and direction. I'd lost both my parents in quick succession, and while they weren't the best parents, they had directed my life up to that point. I felt like I was a sailboat without a mast, following the whims of the water around me. I was doing some volunteer work at my church and Craig was hired to do some maintenance work there. At the time, I thought he saw something in me that no one else had ever seen before. For the first time, I felt seen. Understood."

She paused, shifted on the soft cushions, re-clasped her

hands, and continued. "What he saw in me then was someone whose direction he could control on a whim. And I let him."

I felt a primal urge to reach out to her, pull her to me, wrap her in my arms, and protect her from anything and everything that could do her harm. In one instant, I knew what the other women knew. Understood why they were all so protective of Jenna and included her in everything we did. I wanted to reach out and put a reassuring hand on her again, but instinctively knew that she needed space to continue. Some buffer between us to fill with the words that were to follow.

"Being a part of this group with Grace, Elyse, Sarah, Cat—and now you—has been such a blessing to me. I've gotten to experience love, acceptance, and support in a way I never have before. Without conditions. Without guilt. Without expectations. These friendships have shone a spotlight on what is broken in my marriage. In me. A few months ago, Grace overheard something Craig said to me. I was so embarrassed at the time. Mortified. But the next day, Grace stopped by the café right around the time I usually take my break, and she sat at a table with a book. As I pulled my apron over my head, she stood and approached me."

My throat tight and shoulders tense, I stopped the words that threatened to escape. I wasn't going to interrupt now.

"She asked me to take a walk with her. I can't tell you how terrified I was. I could hear my heart pounding in my ears, but I guess I nodded, because a few minutes later, we were walking down the path through the park. She was calm and kind, but you know Grace by now. She didn't hold back. She told me it wasn't right how Craig treated me, and she wasn't going to tell me what to do, that enough people had done that throughout my life. But she said I was smart and intuitive and I already knew in my head that how Craig treated me wasn't ok, but I needed to give my heart permission to agree.

"She said that she'd been watching quietly since we'd met

and could no longer justify her silence, having a daughter of her own. She told me she had confidence in my ability to take control of my life and break free of Craig's control, but it might take some professional help. We sat on a park bench and she hauled that huge bag she walks around with onto her lap and after digging around for a moment, pressed a piece of paper into my palm. What happened next shocked me more than anything else; she leaned over and gave me a huge hug, stood, and walked away without another word."

"What was on the paper?"

"It was the number for a therapist who specializes in treating victims of domestic abuse, which months later, I finally realize... I am." Another deep breath. "I have been meeting with her every week, and every week, I uncover a part of me I didn't know was there. I've been growing stronger with every session, and I'm seeing things at home for what they are. He's been telling me for so long that I'd never be anything without him, and I would never be able to survive on my own. After last night, I realize that I'm going to have to start my own journey and have faith that the next right step will be in front of me."

I felt a white-hot rage creeping up the back of my neck. "Jenna, did he put his hands on you last night?"

Her eyes found mine again, and I saw genuine fear in them. "No," she continued, her voice shaking once more. "When I got home from book club last night, he wasn't waiting for me like he usually is. He was nowhere to be found. But what I did find was even more terrifying than his anger on his worst days. I decided to get ready for bed and do a little reading before he got back home from wherever he was. When I threw my makeup remover cloth into the bathroom garbage, I saw a small towel in there I didn't recognize. When I reached down and pulled it out, I felt sick to my stomach. It was covered in blood. And it was a towel I knew for a fact didn't come from our kitchen."

Jenna turned and thrust her hand into the tote bag next to her and pulled out a towel. There was no mistaking where it had come from. It was from my kitchen. What was left of my kitchen, anyway.

"Jenna! That's–"

"I know, Paige." Tears were starting to stream down her cheeks. "I know this is your towel. I'm so sorry. I'm so so sorry."

I was dumbstruck. Mute, as I stared at the towel that had just yesterday hung on my range.

How...? Who...? Oh.

"I'm so confused. We didn't find *any* blood in the house."

"Well, apparently he was clear-headed enough to clean up after himself. I could say that I don't know what's gotten into him, but that would be a lie. He's started showing up randomly wherever I am. Sometimes he comes in and convinces me to leave, but other times he sits outside in his car and waits for me to come out. I would have no idea how long he'd been out there, but he insists on driving me home, even when I've planned to walk or already have a ride."

"Honey, this is not ok. I hope you know that. You're a grown woman!"

"I do know. Therapy has been really helpful to me, and I'm seeing things a lot more clearly. But, finding this..." she raised the bloody towel and then opened her hand and let it drop to the floor at her feet as if it contained a sac of spider eggs about to burst. "That towel wiped away the last of my reservations, the last of my hope that Craig could change. *Would* change. I know now that I've been deluding myself, thinking if I loved him enough, gave him everything he wanted, made him dinner every night, supported us financially, and kept our home tidy, he would love me the way I love him. I know now that none of it makes a bit of difference. He's never going to loosen his hold on me no matter what I do—or don't do."

I sat still and silent to give her space to finish.

"As I've gotten more and more involved in our Sensational Six group, he's gotten more and more angry and short with me. The more excited I've gotten, the more vicious he's become with his words, telling me that you're lying about hiring me for your retreats. Trying to make me doubt my friendships with all of you. It's always been him and me, and now my life is full of things he's not a part of, and I guess something inside of him just snapped. I'm so sorry about all the damage to your beautiful home, Paige. I truly am so, so sorry, and I will do everything in my power to help you get it back to what it was."

By this point, Jenna was sobbing, and when she stopped speaking, she folded over her legs, her hands covering her face, her shoulders heaving with each strangled exhale.

I pulled several Kleenex from the box on the table in front of us.

"Jenna...," I began, unsure my words would land where they needed to. I rubbed her back and coaxed the tissues into her lap. "Jenna, I am so sorry for what you've been through. You're right. None of what you've told me is ok. You deserve to be treated like a queen, and it makes me so terribly sad that you've gotten this far in life without having felt the thrill of independence. I am so *angry* that Craig felt it was appropriate to intimidate you into doing what he wanted you to do. You should be so proud of yourself for listening to your inner voice and getting the help you need. I'm glad Grace felt comfortable enough to approach you. Do you think you'll tell your therapist about this?" I was suddenly struck by the realization that while Jenna insisted Craig had never been physically violent with her, his behavior had suddenly escalated in a very public way. I no longer trusted that he'd be able to control that violence around —and toward—her in private.

Jenna unfolded herself, peeled a Kleenex out of the heap on her lap, and blew her nose. "I think so. No, I definitely am. I don't know what the next few months, heck, the next few hours look like for me, but I know my faith—and my friends," her eyes found mine, "will get me through."

I felt the resolve in her words and knew at that moment they were true.

Another realization struck me. "Jenna. I have to report this." I looked down at the towel at her feet. "This isn't just a place of business for me." I took a deep breath, filled with the weight of the words I would speak next. "This is my home."

"I know. I know what you need to do, and I came here this morning to lay it all out for you and tell you I understand what needs to happen next. I couldn't keep Craig's behavior to myself anymore, now that it was affecting someone else. One of my friends. I will be here when you call the police, and I will be here when they arrive. I will tell them everything."

"Jenna..." I trailed off, unsure of my next words, but knowing they needed to be said. "I am so proud of you. This had to have been one of the hardest things you've ever done, and I don't envy you for what's around the corner, but please know we are all here for you. I know I'm new to the group, but I think of you like a little sister, and I will be here to help you find your next steps. I think I can speak for the rest of us when I say, we all will."

With that, Jenna scooted closer to me on the couch, and threw her arms around me.

"Thank you for being so understanding. Thank you for not blaming me for this. I feel so responsible and helpless."

"You are in no way helpless, Jenna. And you are certainly not to blame. We are going to figure this out together. But, we need to make a difficult phone call. Are you ready for what's next?"

"I can't say I'm ready, but I will get ready. Thank you, Paige."

I squeezed her shoulder and wrapped my arms around her. "Thank you for being brave. Let's get this over with."

42

"RESCUE"

LAUREN DAIGLE

W e walked together to the kitchen, where my phone waited on the counter. I scrolled to the number I'd programmed into it last night and clicked the icon to connect.

"Officer Alcott."

"Officer Alcott, this is Paige Rhiann. I've got some information on the break-in last night. I don't know how long you were here last night—thank you for that, by the way—but do you have some time to stop over? I'm sure you're not even on duty anymore after your long night. Should I just call the station?"

"I'll be there in fifteen minutes."

After ending the call and setting my phone down, I turned back to Jenna and put my hand on her forearm. "I'm so proud of your bravery, Jenna. I can't say it enough. Whatever comes next, please know we all have your back. It's going to be okay in the end. And if it's not ok, it's not the end."

Jenna sniffed and balled her collection of tissues tighter in her left hand. I could feel her muscles tighten under my hand. With her right, she pushed back the curtain of hair that had fallen forward as she stared silently into her lap. She looked me in the eye and said, "Whatever comes next has got to be better than this." We sat there in a comfortable silence, both of us lost in our own thoughts, but connected by my hand on her arm.

Fifteen minutes flowed past unseen, and there was a knock on the back door. Roxy, overtired and loopy, decided this was her time to shine and launched herself into a lackluster display of guard dog on duty.

"Your bark is just as fluffy as your ears, Rox. Don't hurt yourself," I grumbled. "Ready?" I asked Jenna, giving her arm one last squeeze in an effort to imbibe some of my strength into her.

I pushed off from the couch and, knees protesting, unfolded myself from the position I'd held since we sat down.

Reaching my hand out, I stood waiting to help Jenna to her feet. "I am," she replied, the slightest tremor returning to her voice. She placed her hand in mine and lifted herself gracefully to a standing position without my assistance.

Ah, the cartilage of the young.

I kept hold of her hand as we went to open the door together.

OFFICER ALCOTT STOOD on the other side of the glass, shoulder to shoulder with a man I'd never seen before, but with whom he was clearly familiar. The stranger's face was partially covered by the brim of a white baseball cap as he scrawled something on a metal contractor's clipboard laid across his right forearm.

I released Jenna's hand and swung the door open to allow them in as he slid the pen behind his ear. The events of the last hour had not done my short-term memory any favors, but my obvious confusion prompted the tall stranger in my foyer to take off his hat and step forward with his hand outstretched. "Paige? Adam. It's a pleasure to meet you."

"Adam! Of course. It's been quite a morning. It's nice to meet you as well. Officer Alcott, I'd like to say it's a pleasure to see you again, but..."

"Please call me Benjamin. Ben. Call me Ben. We've been seeing so much of each other in the last couple of weeks, people are going to start to talk." He winked at me light-heartedly.

I could feel a blush creeping up my neck.

"Should we sit down? I had a long night standing guard over a certain damsel in distress," he quipped, and not so subtly jerked his head toward the kitchen.

There was no doubt in my mind that this guy got along swimmingly with Grace. I could imagine an entire conversation between them, blunt and direct, no words wasted on softening the edges.

"Do you both know Jenna? I never know when I need to do introductions around here. Everyone seems to know each other."

Jenna put up her right hand in a halfhearted wave. "Hi, Ben. Nice to see you again, Adam."

After a few moments of small talk between them, Ben made a move to break from the group and head further down the hallway, probably hoping to pied-piper us into something more comfortable. Like chairs.

"The kitchen is still a bit of a disaster." I felt Jenna stiffen beside me. "But, the sunroom might be our best option right now." I turned to Jenna and saw her resolve slipping away, her shoulders beginning to curve in on themselves. "Jenna, do you feel comfortable showing Ben to the sunroom while I chat with Adam super quick? He's installing cameras today and I just want to make sure he's got everything he needs. I'll be there in five minutes, tops." I gave her my best 'I believe in you' smile, the one I'd perfected over decades of dance recitals, school plays, and football games. I hoped it wasn't too rusty.

"Of course. Right this way, Ben," she said, and a moment later, I was standing in the foyer with Adam, who was patiently waiting, hat still in his hand, clipboard propped on his hip.

"You've got a lot going on here today," he said. He put the clipboard under his arm, folded his hat, and stuffed it into his back pocket. "My mom has spent the last twenty-eight years reminding me to take my hat off in the house," he said, a sheepish laugh chasing his proclamation. He ran a quick hand over his close-cropped brown hair, plucked the pen from behind his ear, and retrieved the clipboard. "Is Jenna ok?" he asked, hazel eyes searching mine, unable to mask his concern. It occurred to me that he probably knew the cause of Jenna's tissue-battered nose and tear-stained face. Most of it, anyway.

"She will be," I replied. "She's getting there."

"She's a strong girl. She doesn't realize it because anyone who's ever held a position of power in her life has lied to her and convinced her she'd be nothing without them. Her parents might be gone now, but they left behind a hell of a lot of collateral damage." He sucked in a quick breath. "Listen to me going on about something that's none of my business. My mom would be appalled. Forgive me, Paige. I swear I'm not much of a gossip. I just hate to see someone try to throw a shade over a light as bright as Jenna's... I– I'll shut up now." Adam's mouth snapped shut, but the muscles flexing in his jaw told me he had a lot more to say on the subject.

I decided to let it go for now, but filed this conversation away in the 'to be continued' drawer.

"Well, Jenna's going to need as much as we have to give for the next few months. You and I can chat about this later, but I feel like I should get in there with her soon. Do you need a tour, or can you find your way around?"

"Oh, no, I'm fine on my own. I've been here for a few of your uncle's legendary New Year's Eve parties. I'm going to take some notes and get straight to work. I will try not to get in your way, but let me know if you think of anything or have any questions."

"Thank you, Adam," I replied. "I appreciate this more than you know."

"Don't mention it. I may be young, but I've seen enough of people's nonsense to lead me to the field of security. Your peace of mind is my number one priority today." With that, he gave me a nod, spun on the heel of his work boot, and headed into my ruined kitchen.

I HEARD Jenna's voice before I even made it into the sunroom. It sounded as if she'd wasted no time diving into the story of what had happened the night before. What she had discovered in her home. I hung back to avoid breaking her flow.

"He texted me while I was at book club asking how much longer I'd be and telling me to get a ride home from one of my 'silly book friends'. I didn't think much of it because he tends to check up on me a few times while I'm out. If he's been drinking, he'll tell me to find a ride home. I figured I'd be walking into the lion's den, but when I got back, our apartment was empty.

"I checked the parking lot, and his car was gone. While I was getting ready for bed, I found this in the bathroom garbage can."

After a pause, I heard Ben ask, "Is this blood? Whose towel is this?"

I took this as my cue and stepped into the room. "It's my kitchen towel. I hung it on the handle of my oven right before I left for Sarah's last night. I noticed it was missing when I went to dry my hands after we finished cleaning up the kitchen." My eyes slid to Jenna, perched on the edge of the couch, taught as a harp string that is one pluck from snapping. Her head drooped under my gaze. Her eyes focused on hands once again folded together on her lap, hanging on for dear life to the only person she felt she could fully trust in this world. Herself. I hoped our little group could begin to change that over time.

"Jenna," I whispered. "None of this is your fault. You're doing the right thing. But not just right for me. It's right for *you*, and it's necessary to get where you're going. This is the next right step, and I'm standing here next to you as you take it."

She looked up at me with eyes that should be ruined from the hours spent dispensing tears, yet somehow, they seemed to sparkle with something foreign that was just now bubbling to the surface. Resolve.

Her mouth opened and closed as if priming itself for words she knew would never come.

"We will all be here for you, Jenna," I continued. "All of us will. Even Ben. Right, Ben? If I *promise* there will be chairs?" I chided, hoping to coax some levity into the room.

"Ah, she jokes." He turned to Jenna. "You've done the brave thing today. I know this wasn't easy for you, but your conscience will never let you down, will it? I will be here to protect and serve as my badge indicates, but I will also be here as one of the innumerable members of this community who care about you."

He reached over and rubbed Jenna's shoulder as her head swiveled back and forth to look at both of us. "I don't know what I did to deserve friends like you guys," she said. "I know I'm going to be ok, but the next few weeks are a little scary. Luckily, I have a lot to keep me busy... assuming..." Her eyes fixed on mine. "...assuming you still want my help with the retreat?"

"Jenna. Of course I do. Your scones are going to put us on the map. The rest of this is just *stuff*. I can replace all of it. It's your friendship that is irreplaceable."

She rose from the couch, dashed forward, and wrapped her arms around me. "Thank you. For... just thank you. For all of this."

Ben was next to stand. "As much as I love a tearjerker moment, if I don't find a restroom quick, this couch is going to be at the top of the list of stuff that needs to be replaced. I must have guzzled a gallon of coffee last night. Paige, I'm going to find my way to the little boy's room, then see myself out. I'm going to head back to the station to type everything up and get this," he raised the dish towel, "into evidence."

Jenna and I stepped apart and stood side-by-side, facing Ben as he continued, "We are likely going to put out an APB on Craig to get him in for a chat. Jenna, do you have somewhere you can stay today, possibly tonight? Just until we can figure out the situation with Craig? I'd feel a lot better if you weren't at home until—"

"She'll be here with me," I answered before he'd even finished. "And it's not up for discussion," I said in my best *Mom means business* voice, throwing Jenna a pointed look. She remained silent, which was for the best.

With that settled, Ben took his leave for the powder room, and a few minutes later, I heard the back door beep as it opened and his voice crooning to Roxy, "You keep them safe, pooch. Jeez, we need to work on your bark." A moment later, the back door clicked shut, and the automatic lock slid back into place.

"Well, what should we do today?" I asked.

"If I'm being honest, I need a nap. Badly. Is there somewhere I could lie down for a little bit? The last several hours have been murder on my nerves, and I rode my bike here this morning."

"Oh my goodness, Jenna! Absolutely. Follow me."

I got her tucked into bed in the room directly across from mine. It was a mirror image of my own and still stocked to the gills with toiletries and snacks after Kari's visit. Dragging the heavy drapes across their track, I flashed back to my days of tucking my daughter into bed during a particularly painful breakup. I never realized how much I would miss those days until after the last one passed without the courtesy of a warning.

I rubbed the arm that pressed the linen duvet to her side. "Sleep as long as you want. When you're ready, come on downstairs. I'm not going anywhere."

"Thank you, Paige," she whispered to the wall in front of her.

"It's my pleasure, sweetheart. Get some rest."

One hand on the doorknob and one hand on the frame, I rested my head just above it and took a moment to absorb the events of the last—*how long has it been?*—fifteen hours. Unbelievable.

I pulled the door shut and turned around to face whatever came next. A nap? No. It was time for an adventure. An escape. I headed to my office on the third floor, the details of Caleb's latest assignment pouring into the space where, at one time, my desperation had lived alone.

43

"RUNNIN' DOWN A DREAM"
TOM PETTY

The next month flew by, and while the final days before the ribbon cutting were a mix of two steps forward, one step back, the evening of the big event arrived with all the fanfare one would expect from a group whose moniker began with 'Fabulous'. Sarah had outdone herself on the kitchen counter- turned-charcuterie-board. It had been transformed into an overflowing city of appetizers, tiered-tray skyscrapers held finger sandwiches aloft, towering over streets paved with cheddar, lined with broccoli trees, cracker-stack houses, and swimming pools of ranch. Brand new flatware waited in the wings, next to shining rows of forks, and neat piles of crisp, white linen napkins.

A loud sound reverberating from the direction of the back door broke me from my reverie. A kick? I glanced at the tablet on the counter. The top left square framed the sight of a smiling Jenna, arms laden with square white boxes filled to bursting with all things sugar, flour, and butter.

I swung the door open, unlocked more often than not since Craig had spent his first night in jail. He'd been unable to cajole anyone into bailing him out.

JESS AMES

With any luck, he'll sit there until his trial, lamenting the pathetic man he's become.

"Head on in, sweetie. Set up wherever you can find space. I think the table in the breakfast nook would work great. Do you need help?"

Setting the last of the bakery boxes on the glass table, Jenna turned around to face me. "Once I made it down the stairs and got everything into my car, I was home free. The setup is the fun part. I've had nightmares about dropping these boxes and sliding down the stairs on a river of frosting."

"Well, that would definitely throw a wrench in the evening, wouldn't it? Are you all settled in now?"

In a town like ours, if there was news to tell, there were plenty willing to tell it. Word of Craig's involvement in the break-in and vandalism of my Jeep spread through the phone lines like Norovirus through a first-grade classroom. Cat had immediately insisted Jenna move into the recently vacated apartment above the café, and Jenna, partially convinced by the lack of commute to work, gave her an answer on the spot. Grace had found an inexpensive used vehicle and worked out a very slow payment plan with Jenna.

Now to make sure that cretin stays in jail while she heals—or forever. Hey, a girl can dream, right?

Speaking of dreams, much of that day and every day that had led up to it since I pulled into town had felt very much like a dream. Not the ones that wake you in the middle of the night, crouched in the corner, waiting to rejoin you when you fall back to sleep. This dream felt like home and looked like a calm day at the beach and smelled like... frosting!

I shook my head to clear it. On the kitchen display, I could see headlights guiding cars into the driveway, and I rushed back to the door to greet my guests.

It was no surprise that Grace was the next to arrive after

Jenna. As I opened the door, I was greeted by the sight of the remaining members of the Sensational Six.

"I can't believe you pulled this off!" exclaimed Elyse, putting up one ring-bedazzled hand for a high five. Mirroring her motion, I managed to make contact.

"Sarah, I can't believe you got all that ranch out of your hair." I laughed, turning to hug Sarah, who had gone home to shower and change after a particularly harrowing experience opening a bottle of dressing. "Yeah, that was my fastest shower ever," she replied.

"Looks like your timing was perfect," said Grace, sending a wink Sarah's way as she and Elyse turned to face the driveway.

Odd.

"Yes, it was *perfect* timing. Well, come on in. Oh, whose car is this pulling in now?" A sleek black SUV I didn't recognize parked right behind Grace's Range Rover. The driver's door opened, and when I saw who stepped out from behind it, I was grateful Grace was still standing next to me and had the fore-thought to set her bags down. I reached out to the side and grabbed Grace's arm to steady myself. I felt a scream bubble up...

44

"SWEET DREAMS"

THE EURYTHMICS

"**D**ad?!"
I ran up the walkway, but skidded to a stop as the back passenger door opened and revealed another passenger. "Jason! Oh my God! I can't believe this!"

"Believe it, sis," said a familiar voice from the other side of the car. I saw a quick flash of blonde, and from around the front of the SUV came the fireball of my oldest friend.

"Kari!" I cried, running forward, unsure of who to hug first. While I stood there shaking with shock and indecision, the sound of the fourth door opening signaled the continuation of the clown car of surprises. "We wouldn't miss this for the world, honey," said my mom's voice before I could see her, my daughter on her heels. "Mom! Anna!"

The decision of whom to hug first was made by my family as they all crashed in on me from all sides. "*Group hug!*" yelled my dad, and I heard my friends' footsteps thundering toward me. From the center of the growing circle, I heard another car pull in, then the voice of the man who'd set all this in motion. "Make room for Uncle Mike and Chris," he called, and moments later, the group hug grew tighter around me.

I was a mess. I needed a Kleenex. "Okay, you guys, I've got every manner of liquid running down my face right now. None of you are safe!" The threat of tears and snots and mascara did the trick, and the group hug quickly dissipated, revealing all the layers of my life—old and new. Uncle Mike, always at the ready with a polka-dotted handkerchief, slipped one into my hand with the discretion of a federal judge.

"Thank you," I choked out. "Every single one of you. There are no words I can offer you that would adequately express my gratitude. All I can think to say right now is thank you. To my family at home that saw me drowning and gave me the gentle push I needed, and to the family that was waiting on the other side to catch me." I searched for Kari's face in the crowd. "Someone very very wise once said, 'There is a beautiful adventure waiting for you on the other side of everything you've ever known'.

"At the time, I questioned this person's wisdom, fool that I am. I questioned it for the full twenty-four hours between the uttering of those words and the homemade drive thru that would propel me down the path toward this so-called adventure."

Kari chuckled, prompting a rash of laughter to spread through the loose circle around me.

I stepped through the family still gathered around me and across the lawn to the walkway. When I reached the front door, I turned and faced them all.

"But here I stand, on the other side of everything I'd ever known, and I've survived. I've thrived. I've grown—and flown—and landed in a life I never could have imagined for myself. Not in my wildest dreams."

"I've given the name of my home, and the home of this next phase of my life, a lot of thought. Life was passing me by, and I let it pass, preferring to remain entombed in the safety of the life I knew. I was asleep..."

I looked at each of them. My family, some by birth and some by choice, and I felt the lightness of their love lift me once more.

"But one by one, you sat with me and coaxed me awake. You believed in me when I felt like everything I did *well* was over and gone. You saw a spark of something in me, and you all tended to it until the flame grew big enough that I could no longer sleep through it... and then you stepped back and gave me space to grow.

"And so, without further ado and before I cry all the mascara off my face, I am so thrilled to be able to share the name of my new home and *our* writing retreat,"

I pulled the cloth from the twelve by fifteen sandblasted plaque I'd hung and covered earlier.

"Sweet Dreams."

In an instant, they were around me again, their voices mixing. I have no idea what anyone was saying, but the sentiment shone through nonetheless.

"Let's get this party started!" I cried, and with one resounding "Whoop!" We all crashed through the doorway. We partied into the night, cut a ribbon, and ate the cheese, and all the while, my friends and neighbors continued to stream through the door.

Laci was one of the first, followed by Raina (who hung out with us until dawn) then Betty. Peggy from the library walked in with Caleb. They both congratulated me, then made a beeline for my parents who were standing just off to my left all night. I heard Caleb introduce them to Peggy and I couldn't fight a smile. That was a good match from what I could tell. Estelle, then Frank Rizzo walked in shortly before the actual cutting of the red ribbon. At some point my favorite home security entrepreneur, Adam, must have snuck in, because I found him chatting with Jenna while she, for the third time, refilled a tiered tray with more variations of cookies, brownies, and muffins than I had ever seen in one place.

When Ben Alcott walked in, I did a horrifyingly obvious double take. He was wearing crisp, tan linen chinos and a baby blue linen button-down shirt with the sleeves rolled up. He caught me red handed when my head spun back around in his direction and he did a little shuffle step, his brown boat shoes sliding across the floor like they were coated in butter. We briefly made eye contact before Grace stepped between us to tell me that Roxy was swimming in the pool and Elyse was nearby but declaring innocence.

The interruption came at the perfect time.

Who needs butterflies? Who wants heartache? Not me.

But it had been years since I'd felt that quivery electric current low in my belly, and as I knelt by the side of the pool to coax Roxy out onto the patio, I let myself enjoy it. Afterall, I was only human, and I was done setting limitations and expectations for myself. I'd already come this far in exploring the next phase of my life, who's to say what it had in store for me, and who was I to close myself off to it?

At ten o'clock, I succumbed to the escalating protests of my feet and flopped down in a chair at the kitchen table. It was just a lucky coincidence that it was the site of so much sugar. Jenna was floating around, straightening a hopeless pile of God knows what. "Do you think it's true for everybody?" she asked, keeping her eyes on the mess in front of her.

"Do I think *what* is true for everybody?"

"Do you think everyone has a beautiful adventure waiting on the other side of everything they've ever known?" She stopped her nervous cleaning and stood with her hands clasped in front of her, her eyes filled with hope.

I took in a slow, even breath through my nose. I wanted to get my reply just right.

"Jenna, I have come to believe the bounty that awaits us in the next season of our life is what we plant in *this* season."

Jenna unclasped her hands and brought them to her face. I thought for a moment she was overcome by sadness. Or fear. Or anything but radiating joy greeted me when she lowered her hands.

"I can't wait to see what's around the corner for me!" she exclaimed, throwing her hands in the air.

"Just keep taking the next right step, Jenna. One step at a time until you get there."

"How will I know when I'm there?"

"I'll be here to let you know."

45

"IN MY LIFE"
THE BEATLES

October 27, 2023

Who knew I'd have so much to write in a Gratitude Journal after all? The last four months have given me so much to be grateful for, and as much as I'd hate to admit it to Kari, the more I focus on the positive things happening in my life, the more positivity I seem to attract.

It has been positively magical to see Jenna's transformation of late. She still has moments when we have to draw her out of her shell, and she still jumps at loud noises, but her confidence has really blossomed and we've all enjoyed meeting this new, self-sufficient Jenna. Last week, she talked to Grace about signing up for a few business classes now that she's been expanding into catering her baked goods at some local events.

Cat's been incredibly supportive, and Sarah even offered to share a few of her own recipes with her. We'd all love to see her realize her dream of opening up her own shop. Hopefully she'll have enough time with her new therapist before Craig gets out of jail next spring.

I can't wait to see what she does next.

～

Keep cheering for Paige and her friends!

1. Read the bonus chapters: "How Soon is Now?" and "You've Got a Friend"
2. Sign up for Jess Ames' newsletter and get updates when new books and exclusive bonus chapters are released at JessAmesAuthor.com!
3. Follow Jenna's story and find out what Cat's got up her sleeve in book two of Clearwater Dreams: Everything You've Ever Wanted! Visit https://amzn.to/3V46z7h or scan the QR code below.

ABOUT THE AUTHOR

 Jess Ames is "Mama" to nine, "Mimi" to four, "friend" to all, and an adequate wife. When she's not writing or editing a book, you can find her hanging out with her husband and kids in "Farmburbia", cooking, golfing, traveling, and of course... reading.

She's knocking on the door of fifty, but has the sense of humor of a twelve year old and the body of a fifty-four-year-old (according to her fitness app). Jess is living the dream of the little girl who wanted to be a writer when she grew up. They are both still waiting for that moment, so she's writing in the meantime.

ACKNOWLEDGMENTS

You. If you're reading this book, you made a difference, and I appreciate you.

To my kids, every single one of you, I love you more than tiny, itty bitty baby bunnies (Not the naked ones, though. Those are gross.) You are my eighty-two degrees and sunny day at the beach. No matter where I am, or how many miles stretch between us, I carry you with me. You are my heart.

George, my ride or bye, you believed in me so hard, you gave me the courage to believe in myself. Thank you for taking care of everyone (including me) and everything so I could make this dream of mine a reality. Of all the stories I've collected, ours will always be my favorite. Thank you for clicking the button. #iuselinkedinliketinder #twiceinalifetime

To my parents who not only knew I could, but knew I would. Your feedback and encouragement kept me going through this entire process. Thank you for unshakable love, your inspiring tenacity, and your solid work ethic. They're the greatest gifts I've ever received.

Years ago, I attended a meeting with the rest of my remote team. At the end of our time together, we had a little fun with a "Most Likely To" activity. Every card I got back that night predicted this day, and they've been percolating in me since.

Shortly after coming home, I reached out to a well-known local author and asked her for recommendations on writing groups. She led me to the Women's Fiction Writers Association (WFWA), and I know this book wouldn't be in your hands right now without me having made the pivotal decision to join their organization.

The copious amounts of practical, usable information that was so clearly presented at the 2023 10th Anniversary Conference in Chicago established a solid foundation for me to build this story on, and the support of that community, and the writing community as a whole, is unlike any I've ever experienced.

One member of that community, author Deonna Kay, came to me as an ad hoc critique partner through some twist of divine intervention. We were both looking for someone whose genre and writing we could relate to, and what we found is a true friendship. Deonna, I am so grateful for you. It's never easy sending our darlings off to be judged, but you've made it as painless as possible while still being constructive. I am looking forward to cheering for one another along this journey.

To Kerry Chaput, author and WFWA mentor: Thank you for taking so much of your invaluable time helping me get each platform set up, answering my countless questions, and encouraging me every step of the way. Without your help, I'd still be stumbling around on BookFunnel. I promise to pay it all forward someday soon!

To my critique partners, Alyssa, Jen, Renda, and Renee, thank you for your candor and discerning eye. Much of your advice was applied to these pages as soon as we ended our calls. I have enjoyed your partnership and appreciate you all!

Amy Scott (Amy Scott Editorial), your feedback has been invaluable, and I appreciate your unique insights. I learned so much through this process and I credit much of that to you. I hope you've recovered from your 576 pieces of exclamation point chocolate(!)

And last but certainly not least, my designer, Ashley Santoro, you took the ramblings of an over-worked, scattered author and turned them into works of art. My cover and characters are better than I ever imagined and I've thoroughly enjoyed working with you.

Made in United States
Cleveland, OH
27 May 2025

17285804R00184